A LESSON IN LOVE AND DEATH

A LESSON IN LOVE AND DEATH

ENDYMION COLLEGE
BOOK ONE

W. H. LOCKWOOD

CASTLEFIELD PRESS

Please note, this book is written in Australian English.

For a list of potentially sensitive content and for more information about the series, please visit the website at www.whlockwood.com.

To Matthew, Alex, Ada and Mary.

I love you.

Thanks for putting up with me.

And to all the girls who grew up on scary stories: this is for you.

CONTENTS

CHAPTER I
AN OMINOUS BEGINNING

Anna had often reflected that receiving the letter from Endymion College three months prior was the one and only thing in this life that could have stayed her slow descent into madness. Exactly how long it could hold her, she did not know. It was a reprieve she had never truly expected, and she grabbed hold of the opportunity with both hands, with her heart and with her soul.

Endymion College was life.

Endymion College was everything.

A light mist of rain was just starting to pearl on her brown, woollen coat as she passed through the forbidding entranceway. She ran her hand along the old, cold, smooth oak of the doors, flung open to weather and students, and she entered into a large atrium, pausing to take it all in.

Opulent, dark wood surrounded her—the walls, the stairs rising high in front of her, the vaulted ceiling, the long hallways to her left and right. She smelled deeply of the wood, the varnish, the dust, and that evocative smell of old books that ancient universities seem to have absorbed within their very walls.

Stained-glass windows set high overhead cast a magical, dusty light onto the granite floors below, which gave off their own particular sharp chill, much colder than that of the stormy atmosphere outside.

Her stomach tightened with delight as she vowed to remember every one of these precious new sensations so long as she should live.

Turning to her left, she took in the view through the seemingly endless row of arched windows which lined the corridor she walked along. Perfectly trimmed green grass and the scattered leaves of autumnal trees framed in ancient Ancaster stone. The leaves of those trees which had thus-far managed to hold on to their foliage were all aflame as a bolt of sunshine cut through the slate-grey sky to illuminate them in brilliant contrast.

She took a right into the belly of the building and found the office crammed into a poorly lit corner that would perhaps have been more fitting as a storage room. Faded, yellow fluorescent lights, the corpses of various bugs in their casings a testament to their long-term neglect, glimmered dimly on the dull browns of the worn shelves, walls and floor.

"Name?"

"Anna James."

"Anna… Ah, I see your roommate has already been and got her key. One moment."

The handsome yet bored-looking man disappeared into a dimmer and smaller room, only to return seconds later with a faded envelope. "So, we have a small problem, Anna. Your key is missing. Whoever had it last year didn't bring it back. But it's all right. We found this one. Except it comes with a warning."

The man, clearly amused, leaned close in a conspiratorial manner, and raised one expectant eyebrow at Anna as she took the faded envelope from him. The words 'Do Not Open' were written across the front in beautiful cursive. Anna's big eyes and delicate fingers traced over the words.

"Don't worry, it's not as sinister as it sounds," he continued. "In here is, or should be, a skeleton key. It will open all the doors in your apartment. Which is fine, because there are only two, but one of those is the old hanging door."

"Hanging door?"

"Hanging door. You'll see when you get there. You're on the second floor. There used to be a staircase leading up the exterior of the building to the door. That staircase has long since rotted away, and now only the door remains. A hanging door. A door to nowhere." He smiled a dashing smile and Anna couldn't decide if he had gone insane with boredom or if he was flirting. Or both.

"Oh, I see."

His tone and face changed in an instant. "Do not open that door. I don't care what happens. Don't let the air through, don't look at the view, don't touch the thing. Health and safety, you know? It's rotting in its hinges and it could fall out at any moment. I shouldn't even be giving you this, but, well, I know how it is. You can't always rely on your roommate." He tapped on an old, laminated map that was stuck to the counter with brown, peeling sticky tape. "You're in the old building, here."

"Older than this building?"

"Oh yes. A good two hundred years older. Go back the way you came and straight across the courtyard. Your building is opposite this one. You will be in the east wing, so turn right when you go inside. You're on the top floor at the very end of the building. You have the corner view."

Anna was absolutely delighted. She signed for her key, thanked the man, and made to leave.

"Ms James?"

"Yes?" As Anna looked at him, she noted a strange intensity in his manner, in his stormy, blue eyes.

"That key—that's our little secret. Really, I probably shouldn't have given it to you. Don't tell anyone and don't let anyone else borrow it. Not even your roommate. And whatever you do, don't bring it back here. Not until you graduate, anyway."

"Uh. Are you sure I should be taking it? I can just wait a few days to get a new one cut."

"I'm sure. Take it."

"Okay then… Thank you..." Anna turned to leave again.

"Anna?"

Something in his tone of voice. Anna looked back at him. His face was still serious, but softer now. His eyes seemed to want to say something he would not say, though she, having never met him before, did not trust her own impression enough to push for an answer.

"Be careful." Her stomach tightened ever so slightly as she awaited the explanation, which, when it came, was less than satisfactory for the weight of the warning. "Maintain a high standard of work, do not draw attention to yourself, and never let your scholarship be called into question. And make sure to keep one hand on the handrail when you go up and down the stairs. It's not safe."

"The interior stairs? All right. I guess that's old buildings for you."

"Yes. Old buildings. They should knock the thing down before anyone else gets hurt." And the man disappeared abruptly into the back room, presumably to go on with his work. Anna stood still, unsure for a moment whether he was coming back, then eventually she shrugged to herself, turned again, and walked back to the corridor.

Seconds later, she heard the quick tap-tapping of a pair of expensive brogues on the granite floor behind her. "Anna!" The office man ran up and paused, slightly out of breath. "Ms James, I need you to do something for me."

She tried to hide her increasing irritation with a tight smile. "Yes?"

"Can you just come here? Come to the window." She walked over as directed, a little disconcerted by his sudden, warm, breathless proximity. She stood close enough to smell his undoubtedly expensive cologne, and he leaned over even closer, his chest touching her shoulder, his face almost brushing hers, his lovely, dark hair tickling her cheek as he pointed through the window. Even if he was a little annoying, he was also appallingly handsome, and her heart quickened slightly. "See that building over there?"

She nodded. "Yes."

"That is your building. Top window on the right. That's your apartment."

"Okay..." She blushed to think that was all he wanted. "Thank you, then. I'll just go... there..."

"No, no, wait. Look at the bottom floor. Under your window. What do you see?"

"Another floor?"

He sighed heavily. "Well obviously, Anna, but what do you *see*? Describe it for me."

Taken aback by his sarcastic tone, she would have left immediately if not for his being employed at Endymion College. Instead, she scowled up at him and pushed forward. "I see two bricked-up windows on a grey stone wall. Is that enough?"

He clapped his hands twice delightedly. "Thank you for your time." Then he walked away, never looking back as he called out, "And remember, that key is our little secret!"

Happily, the interaction with the odd and particularly attractive man in the office did nothing to dampen Anna's enthusiasm for her new life on campus. If anything, the mystery of it all only added to her excitement.

Back outside, Anna stopped in the middle of the green space to take it all in—her new home for the next few years. Maybe longer. Her eyes ran across the "old building" in front of her, admiring the ornate wooden doors framed in their thick stone archway. Not a reassuring and regal Ancaster stone like the building she had just visited; her new home was built from cold-looking but beautiful bluestone. The building was two levels, and she followed the line of arched windows to the very end, to the apartment where her new life would take place. And there, looking back at her, she saw her new roommate. She could only make out a little of her features due to the distance. She looked pale, with dark hair. Anna hoped she was just as bookish as she considered herself to be. She smiled and waved, but the face in the window made no sign of having seen her. Hoping they were not already off to a bad start, Anna made her way into the building.

It was dark inside, with no lighting in the hallway, save the occasional ornate sconce. As she approached the end of the corridor, she encountered the staircase she had been warned about. Indeed, the edges of the stone steps had been worn down to a smooth curve, the handrail polished by millions of hands until it was as slippery as glass. She wrapped her hand around it and held tight, obediently never letting go until, after three turns, she stepped onto the wooden landing.

The hallway was, to her eye, an endless, windowless, black line of doors on both sides. The dim sconces here appeared as little more than small orbs of fire floating in almost complete darkness as the rows of doors all but disappeared at the far end of the hall. She turned back to the door that was to be her own.

Room 235.

The key, a delightfully old-fashioned barrel key, turned easily in the lock and she opened the door. A flood of light met her eyes as she discovered a handsome living area, lit by two huge gothic windows sitting above an antique-looking couch with enormous armchairs on either side. A small, round coffee table, a square dining table set against the wall with three chairs, and a bookshelf, already replete with old books, completed the furnishings in the room.

To Anna's left, set deep in the exposed stone, was the hanging door. Its pale-blue paint, flecked and peeling, gave the room an eerie yet cosy charm. To her right, Anna saw the bedroom, from which her roommate must have been looking down at her earlier.

"Hello?" she called. "I'm your new roommate, Anna."

"Anna?" she heard her roommate reply. She locked the door behind her and went through to the bedroom.

She saw no one.

She turned. She looked over the two beds, the two desks, the two small dressers at the foot of either bed. There was no one else in the room.

"Hello?" she called.

"Anna."

Anna jumped and felt her skin crawl. The voice seemed to come from right next to her, as though a person stood with their mouth at her elbow and spoke up to her. She could have sworn she felt someone's breath hot on her arm, yet still, as far as she could tell, she was alone.

A key turned in the lock.

Anna stood frozen to the spot as an extraordinarily beautiful woman came into the room. The woman stared back at her. "Hello?"

"Did you just say my name when you were outside?" asked Anna.

"Out there? In the hall? No."

"Are you sure? I thought I heard my name, but it was in here. And there was someone in here just before. But not you."

"I, uh, I don't know your name. Or... Are you staying in this room?"

"Yes... I'm... someone's... roommate... I think..." Anna's heart was beating fast, her hands shaking a little. Her frightened eyes appeared particularly large and wild in her pale face, which showed an unsettling twitch on the left side.

"Oh..."

There followed an awkward silence in which the woman's tightly drawn lips and raised eyebrows spoke volumes.

CHAPTER 2
NEW ACQUAINTANCES

Anna forced herself to brighten, determined to make the relationship work. "My name is Anna! Anna James. Sorry, I just got here a few seconds ago and... It doesn't matter. It's so good to meet you."

The woman brightened accordingly. "Candi Lenoir. Sorry, I wasn't expecting anyone to be here. And you're my roommate? They actually gave you a key?"

"Yes."

"Huh. Okay then..."

Anna thought her reaction odd, but considered it no stranger than her own, given the false start they had already had. "What do you think of the place?"

"Oh, wow." Candi looked around for the first time. "It's beautiful."

"Isn't it?"

"Yes! It's not at all what I was expecting. I had heard it was nice, but... Wow. This is how the other half live."

It was only now, as the young women took a few moments to look over their new home together, they realised how luxuriously appointed it was. The couch was a deep green velvet, an ornate, rich, wooden frame running along the back and down each arm. The huge arm-chairs were just as spectacular as the couch.

Overlooking this opulent setting was an even more opulent chandelier. It hung from a dusty chain set into the high ceiling. The chandelier itself was all twisting and curling brass, made in a Spanish style that instantly made one think of the inquisition. It unsettled Anna in a primal way, as one reacts with revulsion deep in their stomach when a spider crawls over their hand. She loved it.

All these beautiful things sat above thick, dark, wooden floorboards, presided over by two gigantic gothic windows.

Anna, having grown up with little money, had spent all the hours she could in richly furnished environments—museums, hotels, all manner of galleries, art books—and had consequently developed a refined taste. She could never have imagined living in the same space as these beautiful things.

Her keen eyes focused on the coffee table. It was probably, upon closer inspection, the most valuable item in the room. It made a perfect circle, a raised trellis of brass forming a barrier all the way around. The top was inlaid with pale teak fleur-de-lis pointing in six different directions. It was so smooth and highly polished it appeared almost to be made of glass. The four legs were mahogany like the top, circular and smooth, disappearing at the bottom into brass lions' paws.

"That shouldn't be here," Anna said, as it was her gut reaction.

Candi raised an eyebrow. "Why not?"

"Isn't it odd how nice everything is? I mean, I know this is Endymion College, but seriously, that must be worth a small fortune. Do we even own coasters?"

"Oh, I see what you mean. Yeah, this is very unusual. The other students don't get this."

"Really? How do you know? Why do we get this?"

Candi appeared caught off guard by the direct questions. "Uh, just luck, I think. What I heard was, one of the professors was living here, and it was all refurbished for him only a couple of years ago."

"And he left all this stuff?"

"I guess so…"

"That's some serious professor money he's earning. I can't imagine walking out and leaving all this."

"Maybe it wasn't to his taste? Not everyone likes things to be so… done."

Anna looked at her suspiciously. "But then, why would he buy it all?"

"I don't know…"

"And then just leave it here?"

"I don't know."

"That just makes no sense at all."

"Honestly, I have no idea," Candi snapped. "Can't we just be happy we have it?"

"Sorry." Anna murmured. "You should know I always say the wrong thing. I don't mean to."

Candi softened in an instant. "Oh, no, it's not you. I'm sorry. You're absolutely right. It is odd. It's all very odd to tell you the truth. Shall we go look in the kitchen?"

Anna followed Candi to the comparatively rundown kitchen. It had perhaps been refurbished in the 80s and the corners of the off-white cupboards were starting to peel. Copper pipes ran along white tiles above the double sink, which sat beneath another gloriously beautiful, arched window.

Anna opened the refrigerator. "It's stocked!" she said in disbelief.

"I'll bet it is," said Candi.

"You didn't do this?"

"No. It's been put here for us." Candi's voice was a combination of boredom and irritation. "Almost as though *someone* didn't think we could take care of ourselves."

"I'm glad it's here," Anna said, as noncommittally as possible.

"I bet there's no wine, though." Candi looked through the cupboards, confirming her suspicion. "Typical." She rolled her eyes, and for the first time in a while, Anna felt like the less strange person in the room.

"I brought some with me," Anna ventured. "I thought maybe we could celebrate?" It seemed to work.

"Anna! I knew we'd get along. I brought some too."

"Okay, great… And which bed do you want?"

Walking back through the apartment, Candi paused at the ancient-looking door set in the wall at the end of the living area. "Where do you think that goes?"

"It's a door to nowhere," said Anna brightly. "A hanging door."

"A hanging door?"

"A hanging door."

"I love it!"

Candi set about inspecting the door while Anna walked to the bookshelf. The books were old, almost all classics. Many she had never heard of before. "Hah, they have a copy of the Necronomicon here."

"The-what-now?" Candi asked, standing back from the noisy kick she had just given the door.

"Um, I don't think we're supposed to do that."

"But it won't budge! I'll see what I can do about a key." Anna chose not to reveal the secret of her own key, given what the handsome office-man had told her.

Defeated, Candi went through to the bedroom. She said, if it was okay with Anna, she preferred to sleep by the interior wall, as it would be warmer than the bed by the window. Anna preferred the view from the window anyway, looking down over the hill and green fields beyond, to a quaint village sitting some distance from the university. She imagined she would feel perfectly at home sitting, lying, drinking coffee for hours in that bed, reading Earth-shattering novels and looking out at the spire of what was most likely the village church. It was such a romantic idea that she looked at Candi wistfully, wondering if she would be able to share in any of her pleasure.

Candi was very pretty, very blonde. She was thin and lightly muscular, with a perfectly feminine shape. Probably a cheerleader, thought Anna. Probably got in on a sports scholarship. Or just rich. Anna felt terrible about judging Candi like she was, but she also felt disappointed that she was not going to get the bookish roommate she had hoped for. A kindred spirit to spend the next few years with; a best friend she might keep for life, maybe write novels with... But at least they wouldn't move in the same circles which could only be a good thing, considering how any attention, male or female, would instantly fall on Candi rather than her own, less conventionally attractive self.

"Did you leave your suitcase in the car?" Candi asked.

Anna became aware she had been staring at Candi while lost in thought. She blushed a deep red. "I did, yeah."

"Let's go over and get them together. Do you want to get a coffee too?"

It was clear Candi was making an effort, which softened Anna's disappointment considerably. It could be three years or more they would be living together. It was vital she pull herself together and make this woman comfortable in what was, after all, her new home, too. "Let's do that."

Anna removed all books but one from her satchel, placing them on the desk next to her bed, checked the skeleton key was still safely with her and left the apartment.

"Hold the handrail," said Anna.

"They told you too?" Candi laughed.

"Yes! It was all very ominous."

Down the stairs and back out in the central courtyard, Anna saw him for the first time:

He was walking across the bright-green expanse towards her. At that moment, in the golden glow of a brilliant autumn sunset, Anna thought he was the most beautiful man she had ever seen. His fair skin was smooth and radiant, his eyes bright and grey, his cheekbones delicate behind the pale pink hue of his cheeks. His hair curled about his face in dusky tendrils, the sunlight picking out golden strands. His eyes and lips were unmistakably masculine, yet softly and elegantly drawn. She looked at his hands, long and exquisitely shaped, holding an armful of books, which her eyes quickly sought the titles of. Keats, Byron, Shelley… Her heart beat a little faster, and she felt a warm flush rise to her cheeks.

His sweater was a tawny orange, and it sat beautifully over his arms and chest and down to his hips, where it met his well-tailored trousers. His worn, brown boots made a delightful sound as they crushed the many-hued leaves underfoot, and too much in awe to feel self-conscious, she did not know where best to place her eyes to take in his many glorious features. He was absolute perfection to Anna. Then, as he approached, he smiled at Candi, looked straight through Anna, and went on his way.

Anna wasn't so much crushed as deflated, but she felt his obliviousness in the pit of her stomach. She had fairly forgotten Candi's presence until his reaction brought into sharp focus the physical differences between them both. His look had been familiar, intimate, as though there were something between them, but Candi's apparent ignorance of him suggested otherwise.

No men, Anna considered, would notice her in the company of this cheerleader. She would have to branch out on her own, find a book club full of handsome and passionate literature students. Something that would bore this Venus and pave the way for Anna's new life at Endymion College.

Even so, she wondered what that handsome boy was studying, and how she might find out and run into him again. She looked behind her at his back, his shoulders, his brown satchel and his easy stride, and she thought she felt a small piece of herself go away with him.

"Subtle."

"What was?"

Candi laughed. "Don't worry. He's used to it."

CHAPTER 3

A GHOSTLY AGREEMENT

Anna was still reeling with embarrassment as they found their way to a table. The cafe had been decorated in a stereotypical "French" style, vulgar in its lack of subtlety, but the fact it had been done some thirty or forty years prior gave it a sense of faded glamour. The walls were decorated predictably enough with paintings by Toulouse-Lautrec, damp and ageing under glass. Dark wood all around the central circular bar was set off with decorative bronze, tarnished through years of misuse. The cafe was large but had enough cosy corners to feel intimate. The coffee was good, and more importantly, it was cheap. Anna thought it would be a nice place to spend her afternoons and evenings studying. Of course, she had not, at that time, seen the library.

Candi and Anna spent the next hour switching between awkward silence and anxious spurts of conversation. As it transpired, this was not Candi's first year of university. She had spent the previous year living off-campus, but for "personal reasons" had not been able to complete her work on time. She had almost lost her scholarship. This year, she would be taking extra courses to make up for it.

"So, no more frat parties?" Anna joked. She knew it was barbed as soon as she said it, though she was not sure she intended it to be that way when she sent it out.

"Heh, no. Not really." Candi's open smile faded slightly and Anna was not proud of herself. As a rule, she wanted to be the kind of woman who appreciated other women for who they were, regardless of the way they looked. She knew it was wrong to be uncomfortable with Candi (though what kind of name was Candi anyway?) just because she was tall, and lean, and clearly knew about hair-care products and all that sort of thing. Just because that lovely man out in the courtyard was so obviously drawn to those cute freckles and green eyes. Candi seemed to be a very nice person, and even within the short time they had spent together, Anna felt herself warming to Candi, feeling increasingly comfortable in her presence, surprised she was slowly feeling able to be herself around someone so apparently different to her. She sensed a camaraderie, and it soon became apparent Candi was feeling the same way.

"Listen," said Candi, "I know we just met, but as we're going to be living together for a few years, I want you to know something about me—about the last year. You'll hear it from someone else before long and I would prefer you had my version. Please don't judge me too harshly."

"I won't," Anna said reassuringly, and leaned in.

"Okay. I'll just come out with it." She didn't, though. She paused, took a sip of coffee, looked around the cafe, tapped her fingers anxiously on her saucer, sighed, then looked seriously into Anna's eyes. "I was seeing someone last year. A member of staff here."

"Really!"

"Yes. You know, universities and sexy professors pretty much go hand in hand."

"I never thought about it, I suppose." Anna was completely enthralled, having spent hours daydreaming about young, beautiful literature students, though to be fair her mind hadn't gone far down the path of fusty old men coming on to their wide-eyed, first-year students. Still, this man must have been very good looking to attract someone of Candi's calibre.

"Do not recommend. Anyway, it turns out I was not the only student, or person, seeing that person. It turns out, lots and lots of other people were seeing that person too."

"Oh, okay. And you thought it was exclusive?"

"That's what they told me. That's what I wanted. I had some problems in the past, and I told them I can't cope with any sort of open relationship or cheating or mixed messages or lies… Well, you know how it is with relationships between students and lecturers. It's always a big secret. No one says anything, so I guess they thought they could get away with it."

"Awful," Anna breathed in quiet awe, her own mind playing out all manner of romantic dramas in the background.

"It was. It was an awful time, and it crushed me and I did not react well. I was already dealing with some things going into the relationship, if you can call it that, and it was the last thing I needed. It's a fairly open 'secret' now, so you're bound to hear something. It's been implied my marks were better than they might have been because I knew the right person, or people, as has also been implied, but that's not true at all. I worked really hard to get here. I don't want you to think I, uh, slept my way into Endymion College or whatever."

"I believe you, Candi. I'm so sorry that happened to you. What a jerk."

"'Jerk' barely covers it. It's over now though. More or less. I still see them around campus a lot. You'll hear all about it eventually, but I just wanted you to hear my side of things."

"Thank you for trusting me," Anna said, genuinely touched by Candi's early confidence.

"I just feel like I can. Already. Isn't that odd?" Candi laughed awkwardly to break the increasingly intense atmosphere. "Anyway, you haven't told me what you're studying."

"Oh, sorry. I'm taking literature."

"Oh, how exciting! What's coming up first?"

"Romanticism. 5pm tomorrow."

"You don't say," Candi smiled. "I took it last year."

"You did?"

"Yes, but only as an elective. It was my first subject, too."

"I'm so excited. I'm slightly obsessed with Keats, so this is kind of a big deal to me."

"Obsessed with Keats? The guy who teaches that course is obsessed with Keats. Obsessed! You are going to love it."

"Then I will be front and centre."

"Then you will be very pleasantly surprised."

"Candi, this is such a relief. I wasn't sure how we would get along when we met. It was a weird start."

"It was odd. I wasn't expecting to have a roommate at all."

"Oh no. You thought it was all yours? I can see why you would be disappointed."

"No, not disappointed. It was just a surprise. A nice one, though. I think it would be spooky in there all alone all the time. I don't know why anyone would think *that* was a good idea." Candi looked mildly irritated and spoke again as though she were referring to something Anna knew nothing about, so Anna changed the conversation.

"I haven't asked what you're studying either."

"Ancient history."

"Ancient history?" Anna's eyes lit up with surprise and excitement.

"Yep. Specialising in lost languages."

"That sounds so hard. But so interesting."

"It is actually really hard," laughed Candi. "That's why I had to move onto campus, so I could get some peace and quiet for studying. Share-houses are the worst. Especially if you live with frat-boy types. You're not going to keep me up all night with parties, are you?"

"Hah, no, I'm not that type at all."

"But you thought I was," said Candi.

"Maybe a little."

Candi laughed gently. "That's all right. I do give off that vibe sometimes. I guess I used to be that way. For a while." Then, as much as they would both have liked to continue the discussion, they were told the cafe was closing early as it was a Sunday.

Walking back across the courtyard from the carpark, Anna wanted to explain her weirdness from earlier but she was worried she would seem even weirder by bringing it up. How do you explain having possibly seen and heard a ghost without seeming incredibly odd?

"Do you know," said Candi, as though picking up on her thoughts, "they say our building is haunted?"

Anna stopped. "And who do they say haunts it?"

"I don't know. The stories vary. Anything from an ancient demonic presence to a lost little girl. They never explain how a dead little girl would turn up on a university campus."

"Dead?"

"Well, she wouldn't be haunting it if she were alive, would she?"

"No, I suppose not. It's just so grim."

"The world never was a safe place for little girls, despite what they would have you think. Study ancient history and you would know that. Or modern history. Or any history."

"Oh my God, Candi, look, that's her!" Anna grabbed Candi's arm and pointed up at their window where the face was staring out again, clearly, watching them.

Candi blanched slightly at the sight, but her colour soon returned. "How do you know that's a ghost?"

"I don't, I guess, but I saw her before."

"Earlier today?"

"Mmhmm. Then when I got in there, she was gone."

"And that's why you got a shock when you saw me?"

"Yes!"

"Okay, makes sense." The two stood still, leaning close against one another. They were silent, thinking for a time. "Well, what are we going to do? We can complain about the room, but I don't think they will have another one for us."

"Mmm, arts scholarship students don't exactly get the pick of the bunch at this university, I imagine. You know, I wondered why our room was so beautiful. They must know it's haunted! But surely they don't just stick young women in haunted rooms. Do they? What are we going to do?"

Candi thought for a second, then turned to Anna with a voice firm, resolved and confident. "Anna, how badly do you want to stay here?"

"Our apartment?"

"Stay here, at Endymion College. Study literature. If there's no other option but to live with her or go home, do you want to go home now?"

"I want to stay. Of course I want to stay!"

"Then we're going to be living with a ghost."

"What? You're totally fine with this?"

"Well, why not? We can sort it out. Oh! We'll help her 'move on'. That's what they do on television."

"We can't watch television or anything with a ghost haunting the place. She'll make the screen go all fuzzy, and the lights go on and off. That's what they do."

"We don't know that."

"You're the one using television as a guide."

"We're gonna need some salt."

"Do we need salt?"

"So much salt. We're going to deal with this. We'll be fine."

"Is she still looking?"

"I don't know—I can't look."

"I don't want to look either!"

"I'm going to look."

"Do it. Look!"

"She's still there!"

"Oh my God, she's still there!"

"Do you think she can hear us?"

"No! Maybe? Ghost stuff."

"Ghost stuff. Shit."

"Anna, here's the plan: we are going to walk in there and tell her it's fine, we mean her no harm, we just want to share the room for a little while, but we respect that it was her place first."

"That sounds great."

"And if that doesn't work, we'll exorcise her."

"Candi!"

"That scholarship was hard work! I'm not giving it up for some ghost."

"Let's just go in there and be nice and see what happens."

"Okay. Oh look, she's gone!"

The two women exchanged worried glances. "I liked knowing where she was," Anna said.

After a few more moments of hesitation, they continued pulling their suitcases across the lawn and to the base of the interior staircase.

"Hold the handrail."

"You don't think she's the reason why?" asked Anna.

"It's possible she's angry about something," said Candi.

"That's reassuring."

At the top of the stairs, they paused outside Room 235.

"Are you ready?" asked Candi.

"I'm not sure we should even be going in there. Isn't this that stupid thing people do in movies and the audience are screaming at them to leave because they just know it's going to turn out bad?"

"Anna, this isn't fiction. This is real life. If only it were as simple as 'don't get killed by a ghost'. There's a lot at stake here."

"I suppose you're right. Let's do it then."

Candi inserted her key in the lock and turned it. They pulled the handle down and the door swung open slowly.

"I could swear that didn't creak last time," whispered Candi. Suddenly, she pushed Anna back outside and pulled the door closed. "Wait, maybe we should just pretend like she isn't even there?"

"You mean so we don't give her power over us by acknowledging her presence? Okay, yes, let's do that. We'll just pretend everything is normal."

Candi turned the handle and pushed the door open again. It creaked. "Candi, stop," Anna whispered.

Candi pulled the door closed again.

"Is it the whole building that's haunted or just our room?" said Anna.

"Ooh, good question. There's the stairs situation to think about. Is that even the same ghost?"

"What!"

"Oh, no, never mind about that now. But maybe she already heard everything. And she did see us looking at her outside, didn't she?"

"Maybe she will think it's rude if we ignore her, so we should just go in and be nice about it."

"Yes! Unless that encourages her to communicate with us."

"Yes. We don't want that."

They stood still on the landing for a while, considering.

Eventually, Anna said, "I think we should acknowledge her. We will go in, say what we have to say, and then it will be done and we will see how she acts. I mean, maybe it's not even haunted."

"Maybe. Unlikely."

"Maybe it was some weird reflection. We have only seen her at that window, after all."

"Maybe…"

"You do the talking."

Candi opened the door a third time, and they went in, the door creaking behind them.

They looked around the apartment quietly, then Anna met Candi's eye. "Okay," she whispered.

"Okay!" said Candi, loudly. "Hello. If there is anyone else in this apartment with us, I just want to say… hello. We saw you at the window. Um. We would like to be friends with you."

"No!" whispered Anna.

"I mean… we would like to live here with you. And all get along. So please just know we mean well. We're really nice. We just want to stay for a while, read some books. So please, um, do not move stuff around. Or materialise. You know, like appear in front of us, because that would be really scary for us."

"Candi, seriously."

"She needs to know," Candi whispered back, then continued, "And please no loud bangs or breaking things or any of that stuff. Because we will have to pay for that. And we're broke. Or I am anyway. But you can totally make as much noise as you want when we're not here, and we will be out a lot. So… is all that okay?"

There was a resounding silence.

"Seems okay?" said Candi.

"Okay then," said Anna. "That's done." Anna dropped her satchel on the floor and threw herself down on the lounge. "You know, I think we're going to be very happy here."

Candi sat down next to her. "Me too. Let's get settled in and have that glass of wine."

"Sounds wonderful. Hey, where can I shower, by the way?"

"Oh… You are not going to like this."

CHAPTER 4
AN UNWONTED OCCURRENCE

"I t's definitely haunted."

"It has to be, right?"

The bathroom was inconveniently positioned at the far end of the hall. The very end, lost in darkness from Anna and Candi's apartment. It had been refurbished some time in the 1960s but had, for unaccountable reasons, been decorated in a cold, if stylish, Edwardian fashion. The bathroom was freezing all the time, even in the heat of summer, which was still several months away. The cisterns hung high over the porcelain toilets with a copper chain-flush. The shiny glazed tiles were mounted floor to ceiling and someone at some time in the past had unaccountably ordained they be a combination of white and disquieting hospital-green.

The row of showers closed with only a white, plastic curtain hanging limply by each opening, every one giving off the faint scent of bleach. No effort having been made to save them from corrosion, the wide, copper shower heads, exposed pipes and taps all took on a sickly greenish hue. Anna shivered at the thought of winter evenings in this space. "Let's get ready for bed and get out of here."

They did so, both glad to have the presence of another that first day, but knowing they would soon have to learn to spend time alone in what they both believed to be a thoroughly haunted building.

Back in their room, the two made a meal to share, opened a bottle of wine, and sat at the coffee table together to eat. They felt comfortable and calm in their new space, as though their talk with the ghost really had worked. Had there been a ghost at all? They weren't entirely sure now they had a hot meal and the kindling of what promised to be a warm friendship.

Candi was the first to remark on the twisted, vaguely terrifying branches of the nearby tree that occasionally tapped a spooky reminder of itself on Anna's window. "Does that tree bother you?"

"No, I rather like it. It seems to suit the atmosphere around here."

Candi lowered her voice and leaned a little closer to Anna. "What kind of tree do you think that is?"

Anna caught Candi's excited eyes and rose to the occasion. "I think it's an ash tree."

A beautiful curve of Candi's beautiful mouth. "So long as it's not full of spiders." Anna would never have dared to say the words. She would never have dreamed Candi would say them. Thus, their mutual love of classic ghost stories was thrust out into the open and their friendship was cemented.

They talked for hours, and Anna found Candi to be bright, well-educated and authentic. Anna, habitually ashamed of her own humble start to life, was as yet unwilling to share the details of her past, but she was intrigued to find Candi also seemed reluctant to be drawn on these subjects. As such, conversation was based on interests, a great many of which they shared. They told one another their hopes and dreams and reflected on the bizarre nature of that first day. By the time they tidied up the living room and put what was left of the wine away, there was a genuine and abiding affection between Candi and Anna.

Each settled into her bed and while Candi fell asleep almost instantly, Anna quietly got a head-start on her coursework, reading Mary Wollstonecraft Shelley's masterpiece, *Frankenstein*. It felt wonderful to lie back in her new bed and see that almost-naked ash tree blowing gently in the moonlight through a gothic, arched, stone window. Anna was warm and tired from the first day of her own adult life and she only made it through a few pages before she too fell into a deep sleep.

When she awoke, Candi was already out of bed and the apartment was quiet. Grey light flooded the room and Anna, still lying in her bed with the blankets pulled up to her chin, turned her head languidly towards the entrance of their room.

There it was. The ghost girl. Or boy. Now, Anna could see it was a boy, no older than ten years of age. She could see him clearly and completely. He had brown hair, but it looked wet and filthy and hung limp around sallow cheeks. His skin was pale, like—like a dead person. His eyes were sunken and dark and held a viscous green aspect to them. His lips were purple and Anna could not help but recall later he seemed as though he were in the early stages of decomposition. The white dress he wore was old-fashioned and looked like something one would bury a child in. Its base was filthy, damp and ragged, as though it had been dragged through mud and sticks. The boy's hands too were muddy, the fingernails were cracked and bleeding, some peeling off, as though the boy, corpse, had dug himself out of the ground and made his way through some kind of marsh or swamp to be where he was now standing, here, in front of Anna. The boy had no expression, which was somehow even more terrifying. He just stared.

Anna tried to sit up in bed. She could not move.

Anna tried to scream. She could not move.

The boy stood and stared. And stared. Anna struggled internally and wondered how long this could possibly go on.

Finally, the boy took a step towards her, or rather, lurched. It was as though he could not walk properly, could not support his fragile self with that emaciated frame. He lurched again. She felt the tears hot on her cheeks, yet she could do nothing but cry silently in fear. He lurched again and she closed her eyes tight, bracing for the sensation of that putrid skin on her own, for whatever it was going to do to her.

The boy was gone. Anna breathed deeply, gasped for air, now she was able to move again. It was morning, the light was grey and Candi was out of bed. Everything was just the same as it had been moments ago, but suddenly she slipped back into reality from a horrible waking dream. Her heart was beating fast, her body shaking all over. She searched the room several more times. Nothing —no sign of the thing. The floor was dry, no trace of footprints from those wet, black, rotting feet. She did not want to get out of her bed, yet she did not want to be alone. She wrapped her blanket tight around her, and tentatively touching her toes to the cold floor, she made her way into the living room where Candi sat quietly reading. She curled up on the lounge, her eyes still puffy, her hands still shaking. Candi looked at her, worried, but allowed her the opportunity to start the conversation.

Anna forced herself to get control of her voice, which was still shaky despite her best effort. "I saw him. But I think I dreamed him. I don't know. It was horrible." Candi came and sat by her.

"Saw who?"

"Our ghost. I think it's a little boy. But he's so... Oh, it's so horrible." She closed her eyes tight as if to push out the memory.

"The ghost from the window? Just now?"

"It was in the room with me. I don't know if I dreamed it or not... It felt very real..." She let out a small sob then forced her emotion back down, uncomfortable crying in front of Candi, despite her kindness.

Candi put her arm around Anna, sat quietly for a moment thinking, then said, "I don't know if it will help, but I didn't see anything. Or hear anything. I've been here the whole time and I can see straight into the room. I think you're right, and it was just a dream. But listen, if it happens again—if anything happens again, we'll get some help."

"Do you think we can?"

"Of course we can. And we will."

Anna stared blankly in front of her, trying to reconcile common sense to fact. She had never had a dream like that before. She could easily have described every detail of the way the dead child looked, moved, behaved. Still, it had all the hallmarks of a typical hypna-gogic hallucination, the inability to move as sleep still clings tight to the limbs, eyes open, yet all the horrors of the night visible before them. But then it was the very thing she had seen in the window. Could she really have imagined such detail when seeing it in close quarters?

Candi rubbed her arm. "Let's get some breakfast. Want to come to the kitchen with me?"

Anna did. After breakfast, Candi went with her to the shower room. The care Candi showed Anna all morning made her comfortable and confident enough to be able to believe perhaps it really was a dream, and several coffees later, she was ready to attempt her first real day at Endymion College. Candi had afternoon lectures and Anna planned to familiarise herself with the university while searching for an atmospheric place, outside the apartment, to take up *Frankenstein* again. They parted ways for the rest of the day.

CHAPTER 5
DISCOVERING ENDYMION

E ndymion College was, for Anna, all about the arts, for which it had an incomparable reputation, so she was surprised to find that the world outside her corner of the university was vibrant and thriving. Ancient buildings surrounded her courtyard on three sides, with the fourth side being the grassy hill leading down to the field and village far beyond. Opposite this hill ran a long sandstone structure, perpendicular to both the office building and the bluestone hall which housed her apartment. If one were to pass through the grand archways of this sandstone building, in which was the cafe she and Candi had visited the day before, one would find themselves in a new and fresh courtyard. The trees there were evergreens, unlike the deciduous trees growing in her own courtyard. The buildings there were again sandstone, though these were well-kept, clean and sparkled merrily in the afternoon sunshine. The lawn was spotted with tables and chairs, and several cafes and eateries lined the ground level. On the upper levels of the long buildings, students attended the bright lectures and tutorials that brought fresh money into the university. Anna did not know it yet, but she would have very few classes in this part of the campus.

Looking for somewhere more inspiring, she made her way back into the grand Ancaster-stone building and went straight up the beautiful staircase in search of the library. She was not disappointed.

Through the small doorway, she discovered what appeared to be some kind of impossible architecture. The ceiling looked to be at least three stories high, though the exterior of the building gave no hint of anything beyond two floors, other than the gothic towers that graced the corners.

The walls of the library were of a pale, varnished oak and seamlessly transitioned from wall to arch, bending a flexing, art nouveau style, into subtle branches that adorned the entranceway. The windows, monolithic and stained-glass, illuminated only the upper level, making the lower level dark and cosy. One giant balcony curved around a central void featuring a long, vaulted ceiling high above. That balcony, ornately carved in the manner of the beams holding it in place, supported row upon row of books, each row disappearing quietly out of view, with its own private ladder allowing access to every volume on the towering shelves. On the ground floor too, row upon row of dark, dusty volumes—untold treasures, every one.

She walked past the vacant and fabulously ornate reception desk to her left, and stood in the centre of the room, surrounded by couches and a smattering of dim, green bankers lamps upon small mahogany desks. Along the interior wall was a huge gothic fireplace, a fierce fire roaring within.

She felt the warmth, she saw the beauty, then she felt a flush of anger rise to her cheek. These breathtaking walls, these untold riches, these beautiful, beautiful, endless volumes of books—all of this locked away from the world, for only the rich and the incredibly clever, or lucky, as she mostly suspected herself to have been in obtaining that highly coveted scholarship. Here she was, allowed to sit by this fire and pull any precious volume from any shelf, but only last year—only two weeks ago—she would have been escorted from the premises, one of those whose eyes were not deemed special enough to so much as glance at these lovely things.

Even so, she resentfully threw her satchel down on the oversized leather lounge, took up prime position in front of the fire, and soon was too distracted by the beauty of the room she was in to read very much. She did love every single detail and tried to push down her guilt at being one of the chosen few. After all, she had worked damn hard. Damn hard.

She sat that way for hours, the heavy tick-ticking of a gigantic clock hidden somewhere deep within the library having an almost hypnotic effect on her, making time itself seem to disappear as she stared into the fire, back at her book, into the fire. Then reality finally broke through. It was almost 5pm. Her first lecture.

She ran out of the library, back down the stairs, and at the end of a long corridor, found herself in the lecture theatre with five minutes to spare. The yellows, the browns, the heavily varnished wood all spoke of a refurbishment sometime in the 1960s. Nothing much seemed to have changed since then except the polyester stuffing in the chairs, which were surprisingly plump.

She looked around at the people already in the theatre. They were off to the back and sides, some in the middle, but no one at the very front. Anna wondered briefly if she should sit with them and meet some other students who might share her interests, but ultimately decided she wasn't here to make friends. Not right now, anyway. This was a special moment she should keep all to herself. This was her very first class at Endymion College.

Anna sat in the centre of the second row of the lecture theatre all alone. She pulled *Frankenstein*, the 1931 edition, out of her bag and rested it on her desk. She got out her very nice paper and brought her ornate fountain pen forth from its special case. She sat, and she waited. And waited. And waited.

Fifteen minutes after five, she couldn't help but feel every other student in the lecture theatre was well-acquainted, and she felt increasingly small and lonely. She wondered if she should leave.

At that very moment, the door swung open and that beautiful, beautiful, exquisite man she had seen wearing the tawny orange jumper the day before entered the room. He must have only been a few years older than her. Surely, he could not be…

CHAPTER 6

A REVELATION

"Sorry I'm late," the incredibly beautiful man said, projecting his voice confidently. "First day, too. It won't happen again."

He walked to the central podium. Anna's heart beat a little faster, and she found herself searching for the scent of his cologne as he came close; leather, tobacco, amber, woods, brandy. He smelled delicious.

He set up while everyone else was chatting and Anna watched him, as subtly as she could manage, as he threw his heavy bag onto the podium and started to unbutton his navy-blue coat. She quietly twirled her fountain pen between her fingers, enraptured as he revealed a yellow sweater and taupe trousers underneath. He dropped his coat carelessly over a desk in the front row and started rolling up his sleeves. He paused, the tips of his lovely fingers resting for a second on his shirt-cuffs, and then thought better of it, instead deciding to remove his sweater entirely.

He must have been quite hot.

As he stretched his arms overhead, his shirt pulled up a little at the front to reveal a line of hair running down, down, blotted out by the worn, brown leather belt.

Anna dropped her pen. It stuck upright in the floorboards like a nail in a coffin. She was glad of the diversion to hide her blush, but she kept her eyes on the professor as she sank down and yanked the pen out of the floor. She inspected the tip. Still sharp. It took her six months to save up for that pen.

He started to roll the sleeves of his crisp, white linen shirt to reveal pale, elegant wrists, the left one adorned with the faded leather band of an old watch. He undid his top button, and though she wished he would unbutton just one more, it was only a small glimpse of the well-built torso and graceful neck she was able to discover that day.

His swift, beautiful hands removed various texts from his satchel, pens, papers, spilling a little of the tea he had brought into the theatre with him, then shaking it off one of his books. He paused and looked straight at Anna, alone, lit by the theatre lights, directly in front of him.

"Hi," he said to her, disarmed by the sudden consciousness of both her gaze and proximity.

"Hi," she whispered, blushing a shade darker.

He smiled at her, then he commenced his lecture.

He introduced himself as Evelyn Worthing and wrote it in quick and elegant letters on the blackboard. "That's Eve as in just for the evening, not as in ever after." Anna was aware of some giggles and sighs. Clearly, Evelyn Worthing knew his effect well enough to lightly flirt with a whole theatre of students in his opening class. A small sigh slipped from Anna, too.

"Welcome to what may be your first ever class at Endymion College. Let me congratulate you on making it this far.

"If you are one of the very, very few who got into Endymion College on a scholarship, you already have my respect." He glanced around as if waiting for an answer. Anna didn't move a muscle. "If you are one of the many who have had a seat in this room held for you from birth, you have an ethical responsibility to yourself and to the world at large to show you deserve that place.

"This term we will be studying the Romantic era. This is a world of incredible creativity, shot through with love, sadness, beauty, hope, desperation and death. I cannot think of a book that better encapsulates all those ideas than," he reached for the novel and held it up, "Frankenstein, by Mary Wollstonecraft Shelley."

He spoke in a smooth, fluid manner. His words were eloquent, well-chosen, unpretentious, unguarded. He spoke with an interest and a passion that was genuine and infectious. In a short time, there was an atmosphere in the room, every student hanging on his every word. A room full of complete strangers were all subconsciously aware they were sharing a special moment, the beginning of a kindred passion, because any first year literature student who hears an educated and enraptured lecturer speak from their heart about the wonders of Romanticism cannot help but be lost to the world of great literature for eternity. Anna sank a little deeper into her chair, slightly flushed and very thankful indeed she had put in all the work necessary to earn that place.

Anna learned that day Mary Wollstonecraft Shelley should be called just that—not Mary Shelley. She was the daughter of one of the bravest, strongest women who ever lived: Mary Wollstonecraft. The daughter kept her mother's surname as a badge of honour even after her marriage to the infamous and brilliant poet, Percy Bysshe Shelley.

Mary Wollstonecraft Shelley lived a tragic life that started with the death of her own mother only days after her birth. She would be plagued by death throughout her life, losing almost all those dearest to her.

Anna learned that the daughter of the woman who wrote *A Vindication of the Rights of Woman* also wrote a deeply feminist book, denouncing the treatment of women in society, and she called it *Frankenstein*. A book that was deeply autobiographical, about a creature born of death, deemed a monster by society much as the author was herself when she was seduced by a handsome, married poet as a teenager.

Frankenstein is a story, Anna learned, that was called too good for a woman to have written, too grotesque for a girl's mind. It must have been written by her husband, they said. Even today people say it cannot have a feminist subtext because Mary Wollstonecraft Shelley could not have been thinking of such things at that time. The daughter of Mary Wollstonecraft, the mother of feminism, was not a feminist, they said. Evelyn Worthing said her legacy has been twisted and treated as nothing more than a little monster story because what she was really saying was too dangerous to be heard, therefore it must be denied for hundreds of years. And now it was time to bring her creation back to life in all its powerful and shocking glory.

A whole new world started to open to Anna that day, and it started with Mary Wollstonecraft Shelley. At the end of the lecture, Anna sat, completely overwhelmed, thrilled at her new life, her new experience. No little part of this rapture was due to the orator who delivered his opening lecture with an intensity that kept every person in the theatre entranced, hanging on his every word.

Anna felt all at once she had found the one man she could ever truly love. What other man could speak this way of such things? Yet, even as she collected her thoughts and her books, Anna was aware of the crowd of people increasing around the young man who had so captured everyone's attention. She watched him field their questions as he placed his old books absentmindedly back into the soft, worn leather satchel, never noticing how his hands were distantly admired as he did so.

Anna sighed. At least she could continue to enjoy his lectures for the next few years, if nothing else.

What Anna did not see was the way Evelyn Worthing's eyes rested on her as she passed out of the lecture theatre without stopping to talk to him, to walk back across the darkening courtyard to her haunted apartment.

CHAPTER 7

A FRIGHTFUL NIGHT

E veryone else must have gone out the other side of the building or, she considered, they might still be with Evelyn Worthing, because Anna found herself quite alone. It was a clear night and the moon was almost full, made artificially large due to its proximity to the horizon. The first few stars were just appearing in the dusk.

As she passed the central tree, Anna looked nervously up at her bedroom window. There was no face looking back at her, but then the apartment was dark. Perhaps it was there and she couldn't see it? Not wanting to go in alone, she slowed her pace, wondering what time Candi would be home, hoping someone would be along soon. Anyone. Should she wait on the stairs? Were the stairs haunted? Was the whole building haunted? The doorway to the building looked pitch black, though she knew there would be some tenuous lighting inside to guide the way.

She went through the old stone doorway and approached the ill-lit, looming stairs. Looking up, she was unable to see around the first bend of the staircase in the gloom. She wondered what might be waiting there. Letting out a small sigh, Anna put her hand on the handrail and reluctantly mounted the stairs.

Suddenly, there was a noise behind her. As she turned, she felt something cold touch her hand. Cold, clammy, wet. She felt the broken fingernails, the fingernails of the thing, bending back as it moved along her skin. It was as though a gruesome hand reached out, slid over her arm, clasped her wrist just for a moment, then slid away again. She shrieked and wrenched herself away in fear and disgust at the feeling of it. She stepped back fast and tripped, falling over in the least graceful fashion possible.

"I'm so sorry. Are you okay?"

Her frightened eyes searched the lovely face. Professor Evelyn Worthing! It took her what felt like centuries to be able to respond. "I'm okay," she managed.

He reached for her hand and she grasped it. Even in that brief moment, she could not help but sense the strength in his effortlessly muscular arms as he pulled her to her feet. She was terrified, mortified, and lightly hurt from the fall; her head was spinning, and she found herself unable to find any words. He came to her rescue.

"I'm really sorry, that was stupid of me. I should have let you know I was there. Can I walk you to your apartment?"

Not wanting to play the damsel in distress, Anna said no, she was fine, yet she desperately wanted him to take her upstairs, and preferably stay with her for a while, if only to keep the ghost at bay.

"Are you sure? I live at 244. It's no trouble at all."

"Uh, okay then," she mumbled, flushed. "Thank you."

"Make sure you hold the handrail."

While Anna would ordinarily have found his advice amusing, she could still feel the icy touch on her own hand and withdrew inwardly at the thought of inviting contact again. Still, lest she be considered an idiot by a man she respected and wanted to impress, she pulled herself together, reached out and forced herself to grasp the handrail.

They made their way upstairs quietly and awkwardly, as though they both felt inclined to make some kind of small talk but were undecided whether it was appropriate.. The journey seemed to take hours. As they reached the top of the stairs, Anna felt she may explode from a combination of embarrassment, longing and fore-boding. She knew the apartment would still be empty and even darker now, but she would deal with that situation once she got out of this one.

"I'm just here," she said.

His eyes widened. "You're in 235?"

"Yes. Just moved in yesterday. Okay, gotta go now." She put the key in the lock and prayed it turned easily and she wasn't further embar-rassed by a stuck door.

"Let me know if you need anything," he said.

"Night! Thank you!" She slammed the door shut halfway through her words, and with a shaking hand, reached for the light switch.

The apartment was fine. The apartment was normal. Evelyn Worthing had smelled so good. Was it just his perfume? Whatever he washed his clothes with? His hair? Such lovely hair.

She turned on every light in the apartment, wrapped herself in a blanket, and sat down on the couch.

She got up and walked to the kitchen and boiled the kettle.

She walked back to the living room and looked at the bookshelf.

She went back to the kitchen and poured the water on some ramen and went back to the living room to wait.

She felt like she was being watched.

She ate at the coffee table, wrapped in her blanket, trying to read *Frankenstein* at the same time, but found herself unable to concentrate.

She brushed her teeth and washed her face at the kitchen sink, not willing to venture to the shower room at the other end of the hall by herself this evening, if she could avoid it. Through the entire process, she refused to so much as glance at the windows in front of her, lest she should see the reflection of something terrifying crouching behind her.

She changed into her softest tights and cosiest oversized sweater and got into her bed, propped her pillow back against the wall and sat up, determined to get through a good portion of her book before going to sleep—yet not willing to go to sleep until Candi returned.

As she read, she relaxed, and bit by bit, she felt more comfortable. She thought about Mary Wollstonecraft Shelley and wondered at what Evelyn Worthing had said about her upbringing, about the sadness and loss she faced, over and over. Anna felt a deep tenderness wash over her, hoping she would never have to understand the pain of losing a beloved mother, a child, a lover.

That young woman lived so many lives in so few years. It was no wonder, to Anna, that she could bring a story like *Frankenstein* to life. Only one who has truly lived a life of passion and loss could have such a skill to create. There could be no other person, no other living being in history, who could have had access to all those ideas through her own life experience. That her work, her experience, should be denied, attributed to her husband over and over! Anna grew sick at the thought of how many great works of art and science must have suffered the same or a worse fate. How many great works even today must still be attributed to men who stepped over talented women to steal their accolades?

As she reflected, she stared into the distance, through the well-lit living room, not really seeing the hanging-door her eyes rested on, just thinking. Then she noticed a shape that should not be there. Automatically her eye traced down the line of the doorway, to the foot of Candi's bed. There, just peeking over the edge of the bed, watching her intently, was the boy.

As Anna saw him, he did not move, but a smile came over his face. Not, as it appeared to Anna, a friendly smile. The smile was malicious. The smile was pure evil.

For the first time Anna felt sure there was no way this thing was going to be friendly or leave her alone and she wanted out, but she would have to go past the thing, grinning, watching.

Anna drew herself up against the back of the bed in horror, then without another thought, she ran across her bed, jumped through the bedroom doorway, and ran out the front door of her apartment.

Blindly, she bolted down the dark hall, instinctively avoiding the haunted stairs. She saw a sliver of light and ran towards it. A shadow moved between her and the safety of the light and she felt something reach for her out of the darkness.

CHAPTER 8

A STEEP LEARNING CURVE

A nna pulled herself close and tight into the warmth of what she sensed to be a living human. Snuggling her head down, shaking and breathing hard, she understood the strong arms around her as nothing more than a sense of safety, wanting only to be away from the thing which she felt certainly meant her harm of some sort.

Slowly, her awareness of her surroundings came back, and placing her hands firmly on two strong biceps, she pushed herself up tall. She gasped. Professor Evelyn Worthing!

"What happened?" He could have been talking for some time. Only now were her senses allowing her to fully comprehend the situation.

"There is something—something in my apartment."

He didn't say anything at first. He only looked down the hall towards her door, clearly worried, but with a look of recognition—understanding—on his lovely face. Anna freed herself from his arms, which were now just steadying her, and leaned against the doorframe.

"Do you want me to go take a look?" he asked.

"No, no, don't go in there… Is it okay if I sit down for a minute?" She felt a few tears drop, despite not wanting to cry, here, now, in front of her teacher. Her mind raced at how she would explain this to him. There was no way he would be able to respect her intellectually when she told him she had a ghost in her apartment. Yet she couldn't go back there either.

As she thought these various thoughts, she walked absentmindedly into his apartment and sat down on his couch. He remained awkwardly at the door.

"Oh, sorry." She got up again. "I'm sorry, you probably need to sleep or something. I'm sorry."

"No, no, it's fine. Just, um, just leave the door open, okay? I'll get you some tea."

He busied himself in the kitchenette while Anna sat staring at the door. The hall was impossibly dark outside. It looked completely black, surrounded by the light of the room. She wondered if the thing was trapped in her apartment or if she might see it peek around the corner at her at any moment. She wondered if it might even follow her in here.

"Can we… Can we close the door?"

"I can't. It… It wouldn't be appropriate. Here's tea."

Anna was at first confused, then painfully reminded that this man was not her friend and he had a professional relationship to maintain with her, even given her situation. But then he could have had no understanding of her true predicament.

She took the tea from him and he sat down in an armchair near her, waiting for her to speak.

Anna jumped as she heard a knock on the doorframe. Rather a pretty woman. Anna turned her head to hide her tear-stained face, pulling her knees up in front of her.

"Kate, hey. How can I help?" Evelyn walked over to her.

"Hey, Eve. I just wanted to bring you my essay."

"Oh, okay. It was due last term. Friday would have been fine. In class."

"I know. I just didn't want to keep you waiting. First day back and all."

"Okay, thanks." He took the paper. "I'll see you Friday then."

Kate stood at the door, hesitating, and Anna hated her with every fibre of her being, whoever the hell this Kate was. She wiped her tears away with her sleeves as inconspicuously as possible and peered over her knees. Evelyn had moved his body between them, protectively blocking Kate's view of Anna.

"Is there anything else?" he asked.

"I just... I wanted to ask you a few questions about..." Anna cringed as she heard Kate lower her voice sexily. "Dangerous Liaisons."

At this point, Anna attempted and failed to stifle a laugh, and set into a coughing fit to hide it.

"We'll talk on Friday in class, okay? I have a tutoring session right now, as you can see."

"Oh... Okay..." Kate took a last look over his shoulder at Anna. "See you Friday then, Eve." And Kate made her way reluctantly out of the building.

Eve sat back down near Anna. "Could you stop laughing, please?"

Anna, her nerves a jumble from the thousands of conflicting emotions assailing her that night, was unable to attempt to control herself anymore and burst out laughing even louder. "I'm sorry, that was just so good. You know she rehearsed that all the way over here, right?" Anna grabbed the paper out of his hand. "Oh my God, is that perfumed?" She sniffed the essay.

He smiled, becomingly embarrassed, and snatched it back. "You're not supposed to see that."

"I'm sorry," said Anna, still giggling. "She's not your girlfriend, is she?"

"God, no. She's just taking Erotic Literature."

"I bet she is."

Eve burst out laughing this time. "Who invited you over here, anyway?"

"No, seriously, I'll stop laughing now. That was just *really* funny. Do you get that a lot?"

He made brief eye contact, then looked away again, still smiling. "Only occasionally."

"I'm so sorry, that's none of my business."

"It's fine. There's really nothing to tell," he said.

"I find that hard to believe." She hated herself the second she said it and bit her lip, as though that would somehow erase the words. Her eyes, wide with embarrassment at herself, caught his, surprised and smiling.

"I don't even know your name," he said.

"Oh." She hid her face in her sleeves for a moment, then bravely forced herself to peep out at him. "I'm Anna. Anna James."

Eve's eyes lit up. "You're Anna James? That means you're my scholarship student."

"Oh… surprise," she said, weakly.

"It's nice to meet you." He looked away and sipped his tea, so she looked away and sipped hers.

An awkward silence followed as he sat, increasingly pensive, thoughtful for a short time. His beautiful hands held his brown earthenware mug, tapping his finger on the side as he thought, but he did not drink from it now. She silently, though still blushing, stored away the knowledge that he kept his tea bag in his tea rather than discarding it before drinking. He liked strong tea. That was a very attractive trait. He put the cup down.

"Anna, this is going to sound weird…"

"Not weirder than what I was going to say."

"Do you want to go first?"

"Probably not."

"Because it's the first day we met, the first day of class, the first day we just discovered we are going to be living a few doors apart…" He looked up at her and half smiled, his own cheeks lightly flushed. "Hopefully."

Anna was on the verge of forgetting all about ghosts and starting to realise she was in the apartment of her no-doubt, soon-to-be, hardest crush of her life, and he was saying nice things to her and his cheeks were flushed and she wanted to throw up with how badly she adored him. Then came the blow.

"I want to support you however I can, professionally, and I am aware of how easy it would be to overstep boundaries in a situation like this."

As he talked, Anna's face fell and her body stiffened. He was giving her "the talk". She was brutally embarrassed she had accidentally flirted with him and now he was setting boundaries. He was probably going to tell her he had a girlfriend after all, and that she should go away and leave him alone. He probably thought she was exactly like that Kate woman, throwing herself shamelessly at him. Anna felt herself grow angry with the ill-perceived injustice at the comparison with Kate she had just imagined him making.

"So, having said all that," he continued, "how do I put this?" Anna's face now showed only irritation, and he frowned as he looked at her, clearly disconcerted by her annoyance. "You want to go first?"

"No. You may as well just say it," she spat out, unable to put up with the embarrassment and tension any longer.

He looked confused. "Um, okay. So, I used to live in your apartment."

"Oh... Ohhhhhhh!"

"So, I think I get it," he said meaningfully.

"So, you know?"

"I think so."

"I didn't want to have to say anything!"

"I know," he laughed. "How do you say something like that?"

Anna laughed too, with relief.

He looked at her more seriously. "I saw you looking up at the window earlier and I thought you might be looking for him. He can't hurt you, you know?"

"He can't?"

"No. I know it's really creepy, but you won't see much of him. And you do get used to it. Eventually."

"I can't imagine ever getting used to that."

"I lived with him for two years. He was at the window a few times. I caught him inside the apartment on occasion. Just flashes. Really, he's harmless."

"You just saw him around?"

"Mostly, yes. Nothing awful. I mean, it's still creepy and weird, but he won't intrude any more than that."

"Evelyn... Sorry, can I call you that?"

"Of course. Or Eve if you like."

Her heart fluttered, and she steeled her stomach to attempt to be serious. "Eve, he's not like that with me. He has been very... intrusive."

"How do you mean?"

"He talked to me the day I got there. He said my name."

"Seriously?"

"Yes! And he touched me on the stairs."

"On the stairs?" A look of recognition crossed his face. "Tonight?"

"Yes! That's why I was... like that."

"I thought you just didn't want to go home to him."

"That too." She trailed off, remembering again that she would have to go back to the apartment at some point tonight. She sank a little deeper into Eve's lounge.

"Anna, that all happened today? This doesn't seem right."

"What do you mean? Don't you believe me?"

"Of course I believe you, but that's just not like him. He never did any of that with me."

"Maybe it's just women he doesn't like."

"He never had a problem with women before." Anna felt an ugly pang of jealousy and tried to suppress it. Eve didn't appear to notice. "It's so strange he should speak to you. He never did anything like that in two years."

"And last night," Anna continued, "I thought I had a dream about him, but now I don't know if it was a dream at all. It was like he had control of me and I couldn't move. And he was just watching me." She looked at the open door again and he followed her look.

"He can't come out here. At least I don't think he can. I had heard of something on the stairs. An accident. Last year. Now we all just hold the handrail and it's been fine. I don't know, I just didn't think it was him doing it."

"Oh, it's him all right."

"How do you know?"

"I felt him! His hand was wet. He's all sodden and dirty and cold and his hands are covered in filth and blood, like he dug his way out of his own grave and crawled back home. He's not good, or misunderstood, like ghosts are supposed to be. Eve, he's malicious. I can tell. And I just know he hates me."

Eve stared at her in horrified silence.

"I'm so sorry. I just don't know who to tell or how to deal with this. I can't go home and I can't stay here. What am I going to do?" Her eyes welled up and a tear fell, not from fear or sadness, but from frustration, anger that this was happening after all the work she had put in to get there.

Eve moved over and sat on the coffee table, right in front of her. She could smell his cologne again and she suddenly realised his sweater was a mottled charcoal grey. It looked incredibly soft. She wished he would come closer, if only for comfort, although she knew deep down it was more than comfort she wanted, and she was annoyed at her mind for repeatedly going somewhere other than ghosts because despite her very great attraction to this beautiful man, she really was quite terrified of the ghost.

"We're going to sort this out, okay? We'll do it together."

"Really?"

"Yes. I don't know what to do yet, but we'll think of something. We're going to make a plan. Does your family live nearby?"

"No, I'm from the other side of the country."

"Friends nearby?"

"No, no one. This was supposed to be my fresh start."

"It is, Anna. We'll make sure of that… You know, there's something weird going on here."

Anna laughed in spite of herself. "Yes. Yes, there is definitely something weird going on."

He laughed gently. "No, that's not what I mean." He considered for a moment, then sighed and said, "I really didn't want you involved in this. Or anyone. It's complicated."

"More complicated than an evil ghost-child haunting a university?"

"I'm afraid so. I may as well just tell you. You're already in this. But then I don't think you should be."

"Isn't that my decision to make?"

"Well, it is, and it isn't. You don't know what I'm trying to not tell you."

"But I want to know."

"You don't know if you want to or not if you don't know what it is."

"I'm being stalked by a ghost. A literal ghost. Don't you think I have a right to any information involving being stalked by ghosts?"

"Yes, but we don't know that's what's happening."

"What!"

"What I mean is, there is more than meets the eye here."

"Wow, you're surprisingly patronising."

"Patronising!"

"Yes! Don't treat me like a frightened girl who can't handle the truth. I'm being haunted!"

"I'm not treating you like that! I'm trying to help."

"I don't need your protection. I can look after myself. I just need you to tell me what you know."

"Okay, fine, if you're sure. Are you really sure? Because once you're involved in this, you can't back out. And you're right. It is up to you. I'm not going to try to make that decision for you. But it's big, and if you prefer, we can try to find some kind of alternate accommodation and you could, uh, defer your enrolment, for a year or two, until I have this figured out, and everything will be fixed by then, okay?"

"I want to know. Right now!"

"Are you sure?"

"Ugh! I'm sure!"

"Okay, so…"

"Shhhhhh!"

At that moment, they heard a scratching sound outside the door, like someone running their fingernails along the hallway wall. Anna involuntarily reached for the closest thing her hand could find, which happened to be Eve's knee. He instinctively placed his hand on hers. Neither he nor she seemed to notice their intimacy as the sound became louder on approach.

They exchanged a worried glance and a moment later Candi stood draped across the doorframe.

"Doing a bit of overtime, Professor Sexy?"

CHAPTER 9
AN UNWELCOME VISITOR

Anna was all relief and jealousy. Candi stood tall and beautiful and confident in the doorway, a painful contrast to Anna's tearful, messy neediness. Candi had clearly been home and changed earlier in the day and looked incredible in a tight turtleneck, showing every glorious curve on the way down, past her perfectly fitted skirt, over her shapely legs and her well-coordinated tights and boots. Her hair was long and hung either side of her perfect breasts. Her expertly done make-up made her eyes and lips seem more pronounced, maybe more beautiful, if that was even possible.

Anna was crushingly aware of the speed with which Evelyn removed his hand from hers and stood up, putting the coffee table between them in an instant.

"I saw you," Candi laughed in a sing-song voice.

"Candide, shhh!"

"Oh yes, we mustn't be seen having girls in our room."

"Just, please Candide, go home."

"Nope!"

Candi came in and Anna noticed this time Evelyn did close the door, quickly and quietly. Candi flung herself down on the couch, looked Anna in the eye and whispered, "Didn't take you long, did it?"

"Candi, you're drunk," said Evelyn. "Go home and sleep it off."

"Can't go home. Don't have a key."

"So go wake your roommate. Out!"

"She's already awake." She fixed accusatory eyes on Anna. Candi appeared to Anna like a totally different person. She seemed angry, predatory, mean.

"It's not what it looks like, Candi," she said quietly.

"It never is," said Candi. "It never is, is it Evie?"

"Wait, you know each other?" said Eve. "She put you in Room 235?"

"Oh, you already know her room number?"

"Candide, stop being obnoxious."

"Obnoxious!" Candi cried.

"You said you were going to stop drinking this year."

"I said a lot of things, Evie, but that's not one of them."

"I'm going to go," said Anna.

"Anna, wait, you can't go."

"'You can't go!'" Candi mocked.

"Shut up, Candide! Anna, you don't have anywhere to go."

Anna knew he was right, but she couldn't stay there and awkwardly watch them fight. She stood to leave and her heart sank at the thought of stepping out into the hallway alone.

"No, no," said Candi. "I will leave you two lovers alone. You're boring anyway. I'm taking the bed. I'm sure you will make do."

Evelyn raised his hand to his temple in frustration but did nothing to stop her as she wandered, with no hesitation whatsoever, into what was presumably his bedroom.

Evelyn sighed. "I'm sorry, Anna. This is a really complicated situation—" A pillow hit him. Candi threw another and slammed the door.

"Candide!" He disappeared into the bedroom with her. Anna could hear their muffled conversation, but was unable to make out any distinct words. She thought she could hear Candi crying, and Evelyn saying something or other.

She walked to the front door, opened it, and looked down the long hall. It was so very dark. She looked back into Evelyn's apartment and realised for the first time how cosy it was. The walls were deep green, the lounge brown. The furniture was all wooden and natural, lamps softly illuminating every dark corner. It was all books, and throws, and she saw his record player, and in a second she imagined his whole life in that space and felt a gut-wrenching disappointment that she would never be a part of that.

She looked back down the hall. The light was still on in her apartment, and she could see a sliver of it escaping from under the door. Then, just for a second, she saw a shadow move and break the light.

She shuddered and closed his front door. The bedroom was quiet. She picked up a pillow, one of the throws, and lay down on the couch.

It was at this moment Anna had the sinking realisation that Evelyn Worthing must be the member of staff Candi had been seeing the previous year. She sat upright, a sick knot in her stomach. Evelyn must be the lecherous serial cheater who took advantage of Candi. No wonder she was upset at finding Anna here. It must seem an even bigger betrayal when she had revealed her secret only the day before.

Anna thought over every action, every reaction she had witnessed from Evelyn, and found herself unable to reconcile the little she knew of him with Candi's description of his behaviour. He had been so kind to her all night. He had not led her on in any way. Or maybe he had. Or maybe he just wasn't interested in her and it would be a different story if she looked like Candi. That made the most sense. How many professors could Candi be involved with? It must be Evelyn.

Anna sighed and lay back down on his pillow. He had been so caring when she needed him and he was so beautiful and he must be a creep. Candi also wasn't who Anna thought she was, and Anna felt more alone than ever. How could so many small disasters all take place at the same time, seemingly conspiring to ruin her only chance of freedom, success, happiness? Maybe she should just forget Endymion College. Go home and give up. How could she find her way here if she didn't even have a safe apartment to live in? Let alone anyone to share her new life with.

These thoughts and more filled her mind, and so preoccupied was she that she didn't notice when her eyes closed and sleep overtook her. She dreamed of ghosts, libraries, angry arguments, disappointments and of Evelyn Worthing.

Anna had barely slept for several days in her excitement to move, her long drive to get to the college, and then her haunted sleep in the new apartment. Now, given the opportunity, she slept long and deep, and when she awoke, the room was bathed in golden autumn sunshine. The blanket was warm, and she snuggled deeper, enjoying the scent of the pillow. Slowly, a dark realisation came upon her and she remembered where she was and why. She sat up, a feeling of desolation washing over her anew.

Then she looked over at the armchair and saw Evelyn sleeping there. She studied his features in silence. He had fallen asleep with his black-rimmed glasses on, a book about to slip from his hand, no doubt having intended to stay awake through the night. His eyelashes were long, and his lips were parted slightly. His soft grey sweater rose and fell again with every deep breath.

He must not be seeing Candi anymore. Why else would he be here and not sharing her bed? Was that better or worse? How could she ever date him with that kind of history with her roommate and the closest thing she had to a friend? How could she ever trust him knowing his history with women and what he had done to Candi?

She hadn't known he wore glasses. He was even more attractive with them on.

She deliberately shifted her gaze to look at the still-full teacups sitting on the table. What made her think he would ever be interested, anyway? You don't follow up a woman like Candi with a woman like Anna. What could all Anna's smarts matter to him when a beautiful girl turns up at his door at midnight? But then, Candi was smart too. She must be one of those perfect women who are smart and beautiful and to whom Anna could not compare.

Anna, sensing a change in the atmosphere, gazed across to see Evelyn looking back at her. Her eyes met his, and still half asleep, he didn't turn away. The moment was quiet, close, and peaceful. Anna found herself, for the first time, completely at ease in his presence, and he in hers, as though it were the most natural thing in the world for the two of them to wake up together, to share unspoken, all-consuming intimacy. She did not think him capable of any cruelty, and if he was, she did not care. She would have happily let him destroy her if she were not honour-bound to keep him at arm's length due to their relationships with Candi, whatever they may be.

The spell was broken by a shuffling behind her, and each became aware again of their own presence and insecurities. Candi came over and sat on the couch next to Anna. She said nothing. She leaned over and rested her head on Anna's shoulder. Evelyn got up and took the old tea cups away. They were silent for some time. Anna broke the quiet.

"It was the ghost."

"The ghost? What? Our ghost?"

Anna filled her in on everything that had happened the previous evening that led her to being here, now, in Evelyn's apartment.

"Oh." Candi was silent for a while, then, "I'm sorry I said all that stuff last night. It's none of my business what you do, anyway."

"I wasn't... doing anything. I just needed somewhere to go. And the door was open."

"I see that now."

They sat quiet again.

"I'm not really like that, you know," said Candi. "What you saw last night. That's not me. Maybe it used to be. I'm sorting some things out."

"What time is your lecture, Candide?" Evelyn interrupted.

"I don't have one."

"You do. You told me last night."

"Did I? Oh... Well, it's at eleven, but I obviously can't go. I'll just skip it and make it up later."

"You'll go."

"Evelyn, that's in 20 minutes. I can't go."

"Up."

Evelyn and Candi locked eyes. She let out an exasperated breath and disappeared into his bedroom.

"Anna, what do you have on today?"

"Uh, I think I have a tutorial at two."

"You do. It's mine. Nothing else?"

"I don't think so."

"Have you finished Frankenstein?"

"What? Why?"

"You need it read by this afternoon. Have you finished?"

"No, but I haven't exactly had time…"

"Take mine." He threw the book down on the couch next to her. She took it grudgingly.

"Don't we have more important things to do right now?"

"No, Anna. It's really important you do well at this." She thought it was odd the way his voice softened for just a moment, then he was right back to teacher-voice. "You have to do your best."

Candi reappeared wearing a gorgeous, cream-coloured sweater.

"No," Evelyn said to her. "I'm wearing the cream."

"Ugh, you're impossible!" Candi went back into the room.

"Anna, what do you need from your room? I can get it for you. He should remember me."

It was the first time he had mentioned the ghost that morning.

"Uh, money. I need clothes. I'll get Candi to come in with me."

"Are you sure?"

"Yep."

Candi returned with a different sweater tucked into her skirt. Still gorgeous, of course. "I'll go with you, Anna. But I'm keeping the sweater, Eve."

"Today only," said Evelyn. "I want that back tonight. Okay, here's the plan—"

"Who made you boss?" asked Candi.

"I'm a teacher and you're both students. I have responsibility for both of you."

"Would you stop saying that?" Candi cried. "You know he's only twenty-three," she grumbled to Anna. "He thinks he's so superior."

Evelyn just scowled at her until she was quiet.

"Take Anna and get what you both need. Quickly. Don't go back there today. Candide, you get to your lecture. Don't be late and take proper notes." She sighed heavily. "Anna, I suggest you spend the morning in a cafe or the library. You get that book finished by two, all right? You'll need to start the 1818 edition straight after."

Anna just stared in amazement at the change in both of them. They both acted as though nothing had happened the night before, cheery, professional. Anna wondered how many times they had put on the act for other people.

"Okay, great," he continued, as though they had acquiesced. "I have some things to organise. Anna, I will see you in the tutorial at two. Candi, Anna, we will all meet in the library at 4pm. Now listen, this is important: you were never here. Either of you. Don't let anyone see you on the way out. None of this ever happened."

"Yes, I know the drill. Can I go now?" Candi was looking bored waiting at the door. Anna made her way over, wondering all the while what she had walked into.

Eve checked the hallway, then held the door open for them. "Don't forget—4pm in the library."

"Why are we meeting in the library?" asked Anna.

"Study. We do the séance tonight."

CHAPTER 10

A TURBULENT INTERLUDE

"Now… not a word." And with that, Evelyn shoved Anna and Candi out into the hall and closed the door. They heard the lock click.

"Don't talk about it," warned Candi. "It will hear you."

They stood nervously at Eve's door for a few moments, then walked towards Room 235.

Anna placed her beautiful key in the lock, turned it and the door handle, and pushed the door open wide. The apartment was calm and peaceful. Anna looked around for any sign of the ghost boy. There was none. She pulled Candi's arm, and they walked to the bedroom together. They each gathered enough supplies to last another few nights should they need it and left quickly.

Holding the handrails tight, they quickly descended the stairs and went out into the central courtyard.

"Well, that was terrifying."

"I don't want to do that again." Anna shuddered as she turned back to look at the window. They were relieved to see they were not, as far as they could tell, being watched.

"Anna, I'm really sorry about last night."

"That's all right."

"No, not just what I said. I should never have gone out and left you there by yourself. I just didn't think I would be gone that long. And then one thing led to another and suddenly it was so late. If I had thought any of this might happen, I never would have gone."

"No, Candi, I get it. You have your own life here. You don't need to babysit me. It's not your fault we're in this situation."

"It's a ghost! I knew we had a ghost. I'm sorry and that's all. Ugh, I have to run to this lecture or Eve is gonna kill me. I'll see you at four."

Anna watched Candi into her building, stood, unsure for a moment, then turned towards the cafe. She found a quiet booth in the back corner and pulled out Eve's copy of *Frankenstein*. It was clearly well-loved. She saw the creases where the corners had been turned over to mark their place. She ran her finger along the places he had underlined tracts of text. She lifted the book and breathed deeply. It smelled like any other old book regardless of its ownership, and while this is an eternally comforting and welcoming smell, it was particularly charming that day.

Finding her place in the book, she saw she had three hours to complete 134 pages. That meant she had to read one page per 1 minute and 34 seconds. More, because she must include food and bathroom breaks and taking of notes. She ordered a coffee and breakfast and set to reading. Her fingers traced across each line and her eyes barely left the book for the next three hours.

Then, having completed the book, she sat in stunned silence at its brilliance and let the feeling wash over her. The book truly is a masterpiece. There were so many threads to draw together, so many ideas to reflect upon, and with a jolt, she heard her alarm and found she had no time to do any of this. It was 2pm exactly, so she gathered her belongings and ran back out of the cafe and into the old Ancaster-stone building. On the ground floor, she found Room 1.08. The door was already closed. Late for her first tutorial. Oh well, at least she knew the teacher.

Anna opened the door gently and discovered a small, quiet room, almost completely full, everyone staring up at her. She found Eve and smiled.

"Sorry I'm late. I got it finished just in time."

"Name?" He looked at her with no more acknowledgement than a polite stranger would have.

"Anna. Anna James."

"Thanks for joining us, Anna. Please take a seat." He made a mark on some paper as she drew a spare chair up to the large rectangular table they all sat around.

"Mark, you were saying?" Eve looked over at a young man who sat opposite Anna. Polo shirt. Sweater draped over shoulders, not even ironically. Too much hair gel. Anna took an instant dislike to him.

"I was saying that Frankenstein is the real monster here. The monster is actually the victim."

"And what makes you say Frankenstein was a monster?" Eve replied.

"Well, it's hubris, isn't it?"

"Is it?"

"Obviously. He created this life to play God because he thought he was, basically, a god. The whole book is a warning about how science is bad and we shouldn't be overstepping our bounds and 'playing God'."

"That's not how I read it," ventured Anna, feeling the fury of injustice already making the hairs stand on her neck and attempting to control her tone.

Eve looked up at her to continue.

"I found Victor's motives far more complex than that. Yes, he was a genius, and he was aware of that, but that isn't the reason he created the creature. He created it to save humanity from the pain of loss. After he lost his mother. I felt like his actions came from a place of love and grief. Hubris is the opposite of that, isn't it?"

"That's an interesting reading, Anna, because who else knew the pain of losing a mother?"

"Mary Wollstonecraft Godwin. Because of course this was before she married Shelley..."

"Nicely noted," said Eve.

"But," continued Mark, "he still did choose to play God, and he did turn his back on his creation. Had he not done that, the creature never would have gone bad."

"You don't know that," said Anna.

"Everybody knows that," said Mark. "Frankenstein left, the creature went bad, all the things it did were directly Victor's fault, therefore he's the villain. It's not that difficult."

Anna narrowed her eyes at Mark across the table. "That's a ludicrous oversimplification, Mark. You know, people, especially people who have never had to work or suffer a day in their lives, love to be able to put things in neat little boxes: right and wrong, good and bad. The fact is, sometimes there is no neat little box because sometimes things get messy.

"When you come up against a real challenge in life, not which car to buy, Mark, but a real challenge, sometimes motives get complicated. You don't have to be good or bad to make a mistake and then find yourself in a difficult situation that you can't get out of.

"To label Victor a villain is to deny this—to deny his humanity. Sure, Victor chose to run, before he entered into a couple of months of hallucinations and sickness he could do nothing about, but do you really believe that being raised by a father who hates you and wants to hide you from the world—that is disgusted by your very existence—is going to result in a healthy, happy creature? Do you really believe life is that simple?"

She did not wait for his response.

"No! The tragedy of Victor is that you can have all the promise in the world, do your best, act in a way that you believe is right, and sometimes fate will step in and snatch everything away from you. Just like it did to Mary. Just like it did to her whole family! I mean, the poor woman lost her amazing mum, fell in love with an absolute lech, got kicked out of her home, her baby died, she got stuck in a house with Lord Byron! What woman, and really, no, she was a girl, just a girl! What girl wouldn't rail at the world, rail at the god—a creator who would throw abuse after abuse at her and for what? I'm honestly amazed she was as restrained as she was in this book because I would be one angry woman after all that, and if she wasn't already an atheist, having been raised by and surrounded by atheists, the daily shit she had to put up with would be enough to do it!"

Anna realised, with a hot chest and throbbing temples, she had been ranting again, which she was wont to do when she was deeply interested in something. She only hated when she did it in front of a group of people she barely knew. All eyes were on her, as her tone had been somewhat firm. Furious, even.

Evelyn intervened, his eyes sparkling as he watched her, though she didn't notice because she had found a loose thread on her sleeve, which was evidently fascinating. "I think you're—we're—all going to get a lot out of the 1818 edition of this text. She was far less restrained with her views on many of the points you've touched on."

"Sounds like my kind of woman," Anna mumbled. She looked to Evelyn when he didn't respond and saw him leaning on his arm, covering his mouth in an attempt to stifle a laugh at her final comment. Her eyes grew wide in bashfulness and lust, and she turned her attention back to the thread.

Evelyn coughed slightly, cleared his throat and launched into a long speech in order to run distraction and redirect discussion. "So, this is our first tutorial. From here on in, what I do not want is for people to go looking up study notes before they read the book. That is going to skew your reading here. There are a lot of people out there looking to give you an easy, unequivocal reading of these works. They are selling something that you should not be buying."

Mark glared at Anna and she pretended she hadn't noticed him at all. In fact, she barely had, because Evelyn's voice was soft and confident and when he was talking, he wasn't looking at her, so she could feast her eyes on him with little worry of being caught. Of course, she was blissfully unaware of how very aware Evelyn was of her gaze.

"The classics stay with us for a reason," he continued. "A book doesn't draw people together from vastly different backgrounds over the course of hundreds of years unless it cuts through those differences and reveals a deep, human truth to us. None of these books are going to be an open and shut case, so to speak. And yes, everyone comes at a book differently, but that does not mean you can change the author's intended meaning to suit your vision. Never try to do that. When you give me your essays, I will expect proof from the text, proof from the writer's life and intelligent inference based on both. I am not looking for easy answers. This is Endymion College. I am looking for genuine engagement and understanding. I want you to be in communication with the writer alone. I want you to read deeply. We are not on a search here for a soundbite that we can drop at a dinner party to appear sophisticated. In this class, we are on a search for truth and beauty."

Anna breathed out the words 'truth and beauty' imperceptibly.

This was it. She had achieved her dream. Surely life would be downhill from here, but for now she would bask in every second of this celebration of those most wonderful moments in history when magic had occurred, resulting in a special something humanity could hold, love, learn from, adore, for all eternity.

"Now," Evelyn continued, "let's broach the subject of who this creature really is. Who is this creature with no name, born of death, cast out by a broken father into an unfeeling world, leaving death and destruction in its wake?"

"Mary Wollstonecraft Godwin."

He looked down at his papers to hide his boyish smile. "It's Anna, isn't it?"

"Yes. It's Anna," she smiled.

"I will look forward to your essay."

When Eve looked up at her again, all the closeness and recognition of their intimacy that morning was in his eyes and in the soft flush of his cheek. What Anna did not see, could not hear, was the gentle alarm that started sounding incessantly in the back of Evelyn's mind from that time.

CHAPTER II

PREPARATION

As the tutorial continued, Evelyn, imperceptibly to all but her, grew cooler and cooler in his manner towards Anna. As she left the class, he did not even glance up to acknowledge her. Had she imagined the connection she thought they just shared?

Anna made her way directly to the library and sat, once again, on a large leather lounge in front of the eternally roaring fireplace to write up her discussion notes. Again, she found the library empty, cavernous. Her work took almost the full hour between tutorial and meeting, and she had just closed her notebook and pulled out the 1818 edition of *Frankenstein* when Eve arrived.

He approached her quietly. "Occult section," he whispered.

"Of course there's an occult section," she mumbled. She followed him at some distance, up two flights of stairs, around the winding balcony, past several rows of dusty, clothbound books, until they reached a small alcove where the curling bookshelves formed two crescent moons either side of them. Within was a low table and two leather couches facing one-another.

As long as they remained alone in that space, Evelyn was distant, barely even professionally friendly. He kept his body partially turned away from her at all times and he refused to meet her eye. Several times she felt him looking over at her, but his words and his manner were cold. Even so, she couldn't help but sense a curiosity in him, and she wished he would pick one emotion or the other so she knew where she stood and could react accordingly.

"Anna, can you please take a look through this one? Anything you can find about séances, take it down." He handed her a massive volume titled *Casting Out Devils and Evil Spirits Which Attack Mankind,* and sat opposite her with another large, ancient-looking book.

"So we're really going to do this? Just based on a few books in an old library?"

"This isn't just any old library."

"That's hardly the point."

Still he would not meet her eye. "No, you're right. If you don't want to, we don't have to. It's your apartment now." He continued running his finger down browned pages, searching for something or other, or avoiding her.

Anna opened her own book and flipped through. Advice on different entities that might attach themselves to places or people; a how-to for séances and spirit contact; a list of incantations in various languages for different types of spirits and demons. She turned to a list of warnings. As she glanced up, Eve looked back down at his book. Anna rolled her eyes and went back to her own book. He closed his, stood to get another, and she continued to throw secretive glances in his direction. He had worn the cream sweater. It looked nice. It looked soft. She wondered how many soft sweaters he owned.

"You're late," he said as Candi appeared between the bookshelves. Anna blushed and fixed her eyes on the book again.

"I was busy taking 'proper' notes."

"Here." Eve handed her a book.

Candi sat down next to Anna and held a gigantic bag open for her to look inside. Anna could see a large, white, plastic bottle with a green lid. She slid her finger down the side of the bottle until she could see the inscription: 'SODIUM CHLORIDE'.

"Where?"

"Chem. lab.," Candi whispered.

"But how?"

"Notes!" said Evelyn. He was clearly in no mood for socialising.

"Is he always this much fun?" whispered Anna.

"You have no idea," Candi replied. "But look what else I got."

She pulled up another bag and brought out a ouija board.

"I think you're actually enjoying this," said Anna.

"And!" Candi opened her notebook to reveal a long page of spidery, almost indecipherable writing.

"Is it Latin?"

"It is!"

Anna started to read out loud: "Exorcizamus hanc bestiam in Nomine Patris, et Filii, et Spiritus—"

Candi slammed the book shut. "Anna! Don't you know not to just start reading ancient Latin incantations out loud?"

"But this is talking about an exorcism, isn't it? We just want to communicate with it."

"Can't be too careful."

"You don't think one of us might get possessed?"

"I don't know. I mean, if ghosts exist, then that stands to reason, I suppose."

Anna nodded her understanding. "Then I need to copy it down, too. Just in case."

"Not on paper. They can blow that out of your hands. I'm going to write it on my wrists."

"Look, mine are already full of notes!" Anna held up her arms for Candi to see.

"You are too cute!"

"Oh, stop," Anna laughed.

"It's true. Too cute."

"Would you two stop enjoying this so much?" Evelyn interrupted. "Do you know how to do a séance?"

"I mean, it's not exactly complicated," said Candi.

"Look here, this is a whole list of what not to do. Does your board come with that?"

"You saw my board?"

"It's a toy, Candide."

"They work!"

"How would you know?"

"Seriously, what's the worst that could happen? If it doesn't work, then we just try again tomorrow."

"Just... Could you just check all the warning sections please? Do we need candles? Is that a thing?" Evelyn flipped through his book.

"I don't think so? What's their problem with light, anyway?"

"You know," said Anna, "it's been full daylight every time we've seen him at the window. And if that wasn't a dream the other day, then he appeared to me in daylight. I don't think it bothers him."

"Either way, it will be dark soon. Let's hurry." Eve sat down with a new book and Candi and Anna bent over their own books. Within the hour, they felt they hardly had an understanding of what to do at all.

"They all say something different. This is nonsense." Evelyn was clearly feeling anxious.

"Let's just get on with it," said Candi.

"Okay, I have a list of 'do nots'. Ready?" Both nodded their agreement to Anna's words. She read:

Do not ask for a sign—it gives the entity an invitation to leave the board and control things in your world.

Do not leave the séance or break the circle until you have moved the planchette to goodbye, or the entity can follow you.

Do not give the entity permission to use your body in any way for communication, whether that is for speech or writing.

Do not upset the spirit.

Do not ask it when you are going to die.

Do not trust the spirit. Do not believe anything it tells you.

They all sat quietly for a few moments.

"Are we ready?" asked Evelyn.

"No," said Anna. "We need a leader and a scribe. Only one of us is allowed to talk and ask questions, or supposedly, we will confuse the spirit. And the person writing is not allowed to speak or interrupt."

"All right. I'm leader, Anna is scribe."

"Eve, no."

"Candide, yes."

"The leader needs to be able to focus. You're too anxious."

"What makes you able to focus?"

"Yoga is just meditation with movement." Eve rolled his eyes. "Also, I know more about ghosts than you."

"No, Candide."

"Yes."

"No."

"Yes!"

"No!"

"Eve—"

"No, Candide." His voice was low and firm and Anna thought that was the end of the discussion until, turning away, he finished his thought: "Your parents would never forgive me if anything happened."

"Well, it's a good thing they're not here then, isn't it?" There was a quiver in Candide's voice and she, too, turned away to gather her belongings.

"Candide—"

"No."

She walked out.

"Shit." Eve touched Anna's arm to indicate they should hurry. They gathered their things and followed Candi out of the library. She was halfway across the courtyard when they caught up with her.

"Just stop," Eve said. "You can do it, all right? If it's that important to you. I know you can do it. I'm sorry. You know I'm just trying to look out for you." He put his arms around her and she accepted his peace offering by leaning in. Anna averted her eyes so she didn't have to see the kiss. She only heard it. A sweet, quick peck. A kiss that was undoubtedly an enormous risk to his career for him to give to her right there in the courtyard. A kiss that Anna would have given her right arm for. When he spoke to Candide again, it was only a whisper, but Anna caught every word in the still evening air:

"You know how much I love you, don't you?"

"I do," Candide whispered back.

When Anna looked up again, she saw the way he looked at Candide, so happy, so sweet, so loving. He ruffled her hair affectionately, then spoke normally, softly and like his usual self for the first time that evening. "Wait here for me. Let me get some candles."

He disappeared into the cafe. Anna watched him go, awkwardly, not sure what to say to Candi.

Candi spoke first. "I'm sorry about this. About that whole thing. He just pushes my buttons sometimes. All the time."

"You two have a lot of history, by the sound of it."

"Ah, so he told you about all that." Anna shook her head in the dark, but Candi carried on, unheeding. "Too much history. He treats me like a child." She wiped a tear away from her eye. "But I still love him." She brightened and forced a smile as she said it, and Anna knew it was true. Her own heart sank as she resolved to try to stop thinking thoughts about Candi's boyfriend, or lover, or whatever he was. That was definitely the end of that. Whatever was going on with them, they were in love.

Anna looked up at the apartment. "Is that him?"

"I can't tell. It's so dark inside."

"That's him," said Eve, reappearing with an arm full of candles in small red glasses.

"Did you… Did you steal those?" asked Candi.

"What? No. I just borrowed them."

"Did you ask before you borrowed them?"

"Come on, let's go."

"I'm so impressed!" said Candi.

They made their way, once again, towards the dark hall. Anna kept an eye on the boy as they approached and she had to admit, he did look different to when he appeared at the foot of her bed. He looked sad, or concerned, or worried or something. Ghosts aren't supposed to look happy, she considered, otherwise they wouldn't be here, surely.

Eve passed Anna some candles and took a bag from Candi so they could all hold the handrail as they ascended the stairs.

"What the hell do you have in here?" asked Eve. "It weighs a tonne."

"Girl stuff," replied Candi. Eve sighed heavily, and they climbed up to Room 235. They paused at the door.

"Okay, Candide," said Eve. "Now you know what you're going to say, right?"

"No," said Candi. "I'm just going to wing it."

"Wing it? Are you kidding me?"

Candide started to reply, but Anna cut her off, irritated with their constant squabbling. "Would you two stop already? You're exhausting!"

She shoved the door open and a glass, thrown with great force from across the room, smashed on the doorframe only inches from her face.

CHAPTER 12
A SÉANCE OCCURS

Anna felt Eve's strong arm around her waist pulling her back, and the door slammed shut.

"Shit! You're bleeding. Are you ok?" Eve pushed her hair back from her face to reveal a cut on her left temple. She looked up at his concerned eyes, both excited and annoyed by his closeness, then in quick succession, ashamed and resentful he was making her feel that way. Eve's face betrayed none of these feelings as he looked over the wound. He was calm and genuine and his hand felt good as it remained absent-mindedly on her hip.

She pushed him off roughly. "I'm fine."

"Let's call it off," he said. "It's worse than we thought."

"No!" said Anna. "This is my room, and I'm taking it back. Candide, give me the salt."

Candide poured salt into Anna's hand until it overflowed. Anna shoved her way back through the door. As she did so, she saw the boy standing opposite her. He was not smiling malevolently like last time. He did not look evil now. Anna hesitated for a moment, wondering if she should approach and try to communicate, but a drop of fresh blood on her cheek set her on her guard again. She threw a handful of salt at the boy, who dispersed into the atmosphere on contact.

"It's just like tv!" she said.

"Son of a bitch!" said Candide. They both laughed, slightly hysterically, with relief the tension was broken for a short moment.

"What the hell is wrong with you two?" said Eve.

Anna glared at him.

"Let's get the board set up before he comes back," said Candide. She withdrew it from her bag. In an instant, it was sent flying out of her hands by an invisible force. It smashed into the wall behind Anna but did not break. Anna grabbed it and held tight as she felt something pulling at it. She fought with the thing to hold on until she was shoved violently into the wall and fell to the floor.

"Salt circle!" Anna yelled as Eve helped her to her feet. He ran to where the board lay dropped on the floor as a series of dishes and glasses went flying at him, one after another.

"It's done!" Candide yelled back. Eve and Anna dashed to the safety of the ring with Candide, where they stood, back to back, and looked around. The room was still. The room was silent.

"We just want to talk to you," said Candide. "Please stop throwing things at us."

Still nothing. Silence. They set the board up and lit the candles, looking around uneasily, still breathing heavily. Anna pulled out her fountain pen, spread her paper and nodded to Candide.

"Eve," said Candide, "just put your finger on the planchette and keep it there. No matter what happens, stay calm and don't say anything." He nodded his agreement.

"We know you're here," said Candide. "That much is obvious. We want to communicate with you, with words preferably. We just want to know how we can help you. So, all we ask is that you stop trying to hurt us so we can try to help." She looked around cautiously. "I'm going to break the salt circle now, so you can use this board to talk to us." Eve shook his head, but Anna obediently reached back and ran her finger through the line of salt. Immediately, the planchette moved.

G E T O U T

Candide blanched slightly, but held her composure. "Just talk to us. We want to help you. How can we help you?"

R U N

"No," said Candide.

The word kept repeating

R U N R U N R U N R U N R U N

Candide snatched the planchette off the board. "Not good enough, ghost! We are not going anywhere. Now you can help, or we can call a priest!"

"You're going to piss him off," said Eve.

"You're not allowed to talk," Candide replied.

She slammed the planchette back down, but this time, it stood still. They watched and waited and still nothing happened. "Are you still with us?"

Suddenly, three loud knocks came from behind Candide. With wide eyes and hearts beating fast, all three turned to look.

"The hanging door!" whispered Anna.

Their attention was drawn back to the board as the planchette moved violently to "YES".

"All right then... You're definitely here... Can you tell us your name?"

The planchette moved to "NO".

"Okay, I'm getting annoyed now. This is the last time I'm going to tell you. We want to help you. And we're not going to run. Please, for the last time, tell us what we can do to help."

Y O U C A N D I E

"You can die," whispered Anna with enormous eyes. "Oh wait, is he saying, 'You Candie?'"

"Her name is Candide," Eve said.

"Would you stop with that already?" Candide snapped.

"Well, it is. He would know, wouldn't he?"

"You're not allowed to talk."

"Mmm."

"Yes! My name is Candi!" She raised an eyebrow at Eve. "What is your name?"

The planchette moved again.

Y O U W I L L D I E

They looked at each other.

H O R R I B L Y

All three jumped as they heard a crash directly behind Anna. A large book had fallen from the bookshelf onto the floor. Then another. Then another. The planchette moved again as books continued to fall.

R U N

"No! This is my apartment. You run!"

The remaining books all crashed to the floor at once. The planchette took on rhythmical, circular motions, making an infinity symbol over and over. Then...

Z Y X W V U

"It's just nonsense," said Candide.

T S R Q

Eve turned pale. "It's counting down."

"Move it to goodbye," said Anna. "Now."

P O N M L

"It won't move," said Candide. "We're stopping now!" she yelled. "Goodbye!"

K J I H

"Look. It's outside." Anna pointed to the window where the boy stood, in the air, staring in at them, his eyes keen and his face worried.

"Anna, salt!"

G F E D C

Anna grabbed the huge salt container and began to run salt around the perimeter of the room, pouring as she went.

"Anna, hurry!"

The boy at the window continued to watch, motionless.

B A 0 9

"Goodbye! We are leaving! Eve, push it!"

"I'm trying!"

8 7 6 5

"Almost there," Anna called.

4 3

"Goodbye!"

2 1

"Done!" Anna looked over triumphantly and waited. They all waited. Suddenly the planchette released its power and Candide and Eve pushed it to "goodbye". The boy remained outside, staring all the while. "He's out at least."

They were quiet for a moment, then Candi, her eyes on the boy, broke the tension: "We're going to have to get curtains. Oh, look, he left one book for us."

They saw the only remaining book was the *Necronomicon*.

"The Book of the Dead. At least he has a sense of humour," said Anna. "Do we call a priest now?"

"A priest? No. Why bother? He's out there, we're in here." Candi walked over to the window and put her face almost against the glass, right up next to the boy. The boy stared straight back into her eyes. "Marvellous, isn't it? He can't do a thing." She tapped on the window, then turned back. "Now we finally have our happy home. Who wants a drink?"

Candi disappeared into the kitchen. "Is it just me, or is it hot in here?" she called. Anna watched the ghost warily and Eve said nothing. It was not until Candi returned, carrying three glasses in one hand and a previously opened bottle of wine in the other, that Anna noticed the way Eve was looking at Candi. His eyes were fixed on her, watching her every move intently. Candi blew him a kiss, then pulled the cork out with her teeth. Even Anna had to admit, it was a very attractive move. She flushed red, suddenly back to the reality of Candi and Eve's prior intimacy.

"Uh, Candi, I don't know if I'm comfortable staying here. You know, with him there. Looking at us. Maybe, is there a hotel nearby?"

"No, no, Anna. You have to stay here with us. Look, there's a ghost out there." She put the glasses on the coffee table then threw her arm over Anna's shoulder, her breast pushed into her. She took a drink straight out of the bottle, flexing one hip against Anna as she did so. Anna became aware of a discomforting feeling within herself, one which she had never sensed before around any woman. She looked up at Candi, who looked back down at her with a distinct sparkle in her eye. Then, in one short move, she ran her hand up over Anna's shoulder, along her neck and into her hair. She twisted it around her finger for a second, then yanked Anna's hair back, not so hard that Anna would cry out, but enough to cause a small, thrilling amount of pain. Anna's heart beat hard and she found herself, for the first time, uncomfortably captivated by her roommate, as a tingle went down her spine. "You know," whispered Candide, "I think we could all have a superb time together. Tonight."

She poured out two glasses of wine, handing one to Anna. "Come on! We did it! It's time to celebrate." Anna took a sip, but she felt increasingly uneasy with the way Eve was staring at Candide, neither attracted nor repulsed, just watching, a vaguely puzzled, possibly wary expression on his face.

"You have a drink too, Evie." Candide walked over to Eve and pushed the glass into his chest.

"No," he said.

"Okay." Candide drained the glass, threw it down on the lounge, then slipped her hand under Eve's sweater, running it up over his chest. She attempted to kiss him. He pushed her away.

"What are you doing!"

"Okay. I'm going to go." Anna started looking for her things. "This, uh, really isn't my scene at all. I don't know what's going on with you two, but I don't want anything to do with it."

"Candide, stop it! Anna, I don't…" He stopped mid-speech, his sudden pause attracting Anna's attention. Candide had put her hand back under his shirt and he caught it again, more gently this time, and Anna saw the change come over him in an instant. His face became ashen as he cast his eyes to the floor, and the hand that arrested hers shook slightly. The other moved to his stomach, as though he were going to throw up. His face, when he did look back into Candide's eyes, was horrified. "Oh, Candide," he whispered.

"Oh, I see how it is. She's the one you want?" Candide focused her attention on Anna, who blanched in response. "You know I'm much better looking, right? Still, I think I know what she likes. We can sort something out."

Eve's voice was firm. "Anna, you need to go."

"He's right, Anna. Run along. Leave me with Eve. Maybe come back tomorrow. I'm going to keep him very busy tonight, but we'll see what I can do for you in the morning."

Anna turned away again, taking a few slow steps towards the door... then she pulled up her sleeve and started reading.

"Exorcizamus hanc bestiam in Nomine Patris, et Filii, et Spiritus Sancti..."

Candide made a move towards Anna, and Eve grabbed her and pulled her in tight. Though she struggled hard against him, he held her firmly, looking up at Anna in shock, apprehension, appreciation.

"Quaesumus, Sancte, corpus hoc ab insidiis diaboli defende. Protege adversus spiritus nequitiam et tyrannidem diaboli..."

Candide's words, when they came, were calm and cold. "You're not supposed to be here." Anna looked nervously up at Candi, then forced herself to keep reading.

"Vade Satana, infernales invasores, putrescentiae mentis et omnes legiones diabolicae..."

"I'll be back for you soon, Anna. I know what you want."

"His verbis Satanam sub pedibus nostris opprimimus, ligamus et proicimus in foveam profundam..."

"And next time, I will make sure we have some fun." Anna looked again into the malicious face of the entity, and while unable to name the feeling to herself, she still sensed the unwanted attraction from before. Its eyes burned into her and she found, just for a moment, she wanted it to stay, wanted to get closer, to study the thing. There was a look of recognition on the face and she knew in an instant it knew what she was thinking. Candide started to laugh deeply in a voice not her own. In sudden alarm at herself and at the creature, Anna read louder:

"Expellimus te a nobis immundum spiritum! Pessima bestia, te ad Infernus projicio!"

As she finished the text, Anna saw Candide's eyes change very suddenly, to a look of understanding, or shock, or horror, or all of those things at once. This was not like television. Her body doubled over and she vomited red wine all over the floor, the table, Eve's lovely boots. It looked ghastly. Eve turned pale but stayed close to her, holding her hair up and rubbing her back as she threw up over and over again. She continued to wretch and shake for some time after her stomach was clearly empty. Eventually, she fell back onto Eve, exhausted and out of breath.

Eve turned her face to look at him. "Are you, you?"

"I am," she said, still panting.

"We should get her out of here." Anna moved forward to help Eve pick Candide up.

"Get the book." Candide motioned her head towards the *Necro-nomicon*.

"No!" Eve and Anna spoke in unison.

"We're going to need it," she said.

Eve turned Candide around and held her arms, looking searchingly into her eyes.

"Eve, it's me. Please. We are going to need that book."

He searched her face for a moment longer, then said, "Anna, please bring the book."

Eve helped Candide out the door while Anna grabbed the *Necronomicon* and her apartment key. She glanced back before leaving. The boy at the window had disappeared.

CHAPTER 13
A TERRIBLE MISTAKE

They made their way down the hall and into Eve's apartment, locking the door to Room 244 quickly behind them. Candide collapsed into an armchair. "Is the salt still intact in there?"

"I didn't see," said Anna.

"You're going to have to go back and check."

"It didn't make a difference, though. He was outside the room, outside the salt ring and he still, what? Possessed you? Are we saying 'possessed'?"

"It wasn't him."

"What do you mean?" said Eve.

"He was outside. You saw him. What was in me… it was something different."

Anna and Eve stood frozen to the spot, taking in what she had said.

"So go check the salt!"

Anna made her way to the door.

"Eve, go with her. And don't touch that book again."

"No, I can't leave you here."

"Leave the door open. That's always your rule, isn't it?"

He smiled briefly, reassured by her humour, and walked to the door. He held his hand out for Anna. She gladly took it and they stepped out into the dark hall together. As they got closer to the room, they saw light appear underneath the door. Then off again. Then on again.

Anna pushed her key into the lock as quietly as possible. They opened it slowly so as not to disturb the line of salt. They saw at least one of them had stepped in it on their way out, but it remained unbroken and the door closed again easily, leaving ample space above the barrier.

"Looks like we're okay," he said as they turned back up the hallway.

"For now."

He had not let go her hand this whole time and while she longed for the light and, hopefully, safety of his apartment, she found she did not want to lose the warmth and camaraderie she found in his touch out here in the dark hallway. Yet as they approached the door of the apartment, she gently pulled her hand away, conscious of how Candide might feel about what was, at least to her, their intimacy. Eve gave no sign he had noticed.

When they entered the apartment, they found Candide had already fallen asleep in the armchair, the *Necronomicon* spread out on her lap. Eve placed the book on the coffee table and picked her up. He carried her into his bedroom, laying her down on his bed as Anna pulled back the sheets. She noticed within seconds that it was a relatively spartan space. The bed had been made nicely, though he had not slept there the previous night either. The brown duvet had revealed pale blue linen sheets. They looked gloriously soft to Anna, and she longed to curl up in that bed. Instead, she, with Eve, pulled the blankets up to Candide's chin, and Anna stood back as he tenderly swept the hair away from Candide's face. His hand lingered on her cheek for a moment as he looked at her seriously. She smiled, softly.

"Okay, kiddo?" he asked.

"Okay, Eve." And she snuggled down further to sleep.

Eve held the door open for Anna as they made their way back to the living room.

"Drink?"

"Not red wine, please."

Eve smiled and brought over a bottle of whiskey. "Okay?"

"Very."

He sank into the seat beside her, his leg touching hers. They sat quietly and drank for a time.

"Anna, you were amazing. Really amazing. That was just, in hindsight, such a stupid idea to do that. I had no idea what I was going to do. I don't… I don't like to think what would have happened if you left."

"I only figured it out from your reaction. You knew from the start, didn't you?"

"I think so. She wasn't acting like herself."

He looked at her meaningfully, as though one of the many things Candide had said or done should be forgotten immediately. But which one? "You two must be close," was all she could manage.

"We are. She's impossible, but I'm lucky to have her."

"That's what she said."

He smiled and finished his drink.

"Another one?"

"Why not?"

"Do you want the couch? Or do you want to go in with Candide?"

"Don't you want to go in? It's your bed."

"What? No. No, I'm fine out here."

Anna looked at him doubtfully. "I guess you two are still working stuff out."

"I don't think we'll ever stop 'working stuff out'. Maybe one day."

Anna sipped her drink quietly, still conscious of his leg against hers. Perhaps she was over-tired as the adrenaline dissipated, maybe slightly tipsy too. As she relaxed a little, she mused over her change in feelings towards Eve, the way she had stopped thinking of him so formally as she had only twenty-four hours earlier. She felt like she had a sense of who he was now—warm, sweet, gentle, anxious. She leaned her head back, and though it accidentally found his shoulder, he didn't move away, so neither did she. She felt the rise and fall of his body with his breath and she felt warm and safe and cosy for the first time in a long time. His sweater was exactly as soft as she had imagined it being, and she turned her face slightly to feel its softness on her skin.

They sat silently that way for several minutes, then, "Have you studied Latin?" he asked her.

"Me? No. Just what I come across in the classics."

"Your pronunciation was perfect."

"I didn't want to get it wrong. I wonder if it still works if you don't say it quite right?"

"Can I see?" Eve picked her hand up with his, then placed his other hand on her wrist, moving it softly along the length of her forearm as he pulled her sleeve up to reveal the incantation. She felt his fingertips gently tracing the lines, running across her arm. She looked up at him, his eyes intent on the writing through long lashes, and she revelled in his closeness, breathed in his scent, wanted to grab hold of him and feel the weight of his body on hers. "You've got notes from our class on here, too. I didn't even notice you taking this down... That was so clever..."

Then his hand tightened on her wrist. He paused like that, just for a moment, as though thinking of something else.

Eve kissed her. She felt, in that brilliant second, her entire being melt into him. He was so warm and so soft, and he raised a hand to her cheek as he kissed her. She felt a tingle all down her spine, throughout her entire body. She turned towards him and kissed him back, and she did not want to stop there. It took every ounce of strength in her being to pull back from him.

"Eve, what the fuck?"

He paused for a moment, seemingly shocked, then a look of recognition spread over his face. "Oh God. Oh God, I am so sorry. I totally misread that."

"I'll say!" She cried, duplicitously.

"Oh, ohhhh I didn't mean to..." One recognition on top of another, clouding his handsome face further. "I should never have done that." He stood up and started pacing around the room. "I just forgot for a moment."

"How could you forget? We were just talking—"

"I know! And I am so sorry to put you in that position." He raised a hand to his temple. "I'm your teacher. I'm responsible for you. You're staying in my home. Oh, this is so bad." Anna watched him in silence, confused at where his mind was going. "You know I'm not..." he paused. "You must think I'm some kind of predator."

"No, I—"

"You are vulnerable and I put you in this position. And I have to mark your essays! Ohhhhh, what must you think of me." He walked over to her. "Anna, I will never let anything like that happen again. I promise you are safe with me and I am not like that and whatever feelings or—anything—it's not going to effect your work. Or my work. Or how professional I am. Or I'm supposed to be… Oh God. Do you want to change courses? Should I report this? Should I resign? But if I resign, the course gets cancelled and you can't study Romanticism. This is so bad."

"What about Candi?"

He looked at her, blank. "Candi? Oh shit, yeah, Candi."

"Yeah, Candi. Asleep in your bed."

"Yes! We should definitely check on her. Soon."

"What the hell is wrong with you?"

He paused again. "I don't even know," he said. "I should go."

"You can't go! Go where?"

"It doesn't matter. I'm just going to leave and, Anna, I am so sorry. Maybe we just get past this stuff that's going on, with the ghost and the, whatever she said that was, then we reset. Can we reset? You probably don't trust me at all now, but I will make sure I sort this out."

"Eve, please, I don't want you to go." They stood there, neither sure what to do. "Eve, there's a ghost. Maybe two ghosts? Just stay here, okay? On the couch. We'll forget the whole thing. I'll go in there."

"Anna…"

"What?"

"I just want you to know, I feel terrible. I'm sorry I did that."

She looked at his sad, beautiful, pensive face for a moment, completely unable to reconcile his behaviour with the look there, then said, "Me too."

She went to his room, climbed into his bed, and curled up under his covers next to his on-again-off-again, both of them having declared only a few hours ago they were in love with each other. Anna couldn't even like him as a person—on paper. What kind of man cheats with his sleeping partner in the next room? Or attempts to. But they weren't actually together. Were they? If not now, they soon would be again. And how could he be so disrespectful, as though Anna were some kind of side-piece! She would not lower herself like that and she was angry he was so indecent as to think of her that way.

Yet Anna knew deep down she wanted him desperately.

Guiltily and unwillingly, she dreamed of his kiss through the night, savouring it, convinced, resolved, it would be their first and last.

CHAPTER 14

A SOLID PLAN

The next morning, Anna woke up in Eve's bedroom alone. Making her way into the living room, she discovered Eve and Candide in intimate conversation, hands wrapped around coffee cups in a riveted manner, faces close, looking into each other's eyes. The sunlight streaming through the window illuminated their beautiful faces against the dark green wall behind them, as if in some dramatic renaissance painting. She saw at once Eve's eyes were bloodshot and shiny.

"I can't lose you," she heard him say.

"You never will," Candide replied.

As quiet as she was, they noticed her almost immediately, and it was with a guilty conscience Anna realised she had destroyed this beautiful scene.

Eve looked away from them both immediately. Candide smiled at Anna, genuinely happy to see her, and Anna realised Eve could not have told her what had passed between them. Candide rose up, fresh and beautiful, hair flowing. It was clear she had showered and changed for the day. Anna had not expected her to recover quite so quickly, or so beautifully, from the day before.

"Are you okay?" Anna managed.

"Better than okay. Anna, thank you so much. You saved me. And Eve too." She looked over at him lovingly.

"It was your spell. I'm just glad it worked."

"I really didn't think it would. Or that we would need it, anyway." Candide led her to the couch. "Eve, get coffee. How are you holding up with everything?"

"You're asking me?" said Anna, disconcerted by her sweetness. "How are you holding up?"

"I'm fine. I mean, it's not how I imagined things. But I already have people and a life here. It's all new for you. Are you all right?"

Anna looked away from her, not wanting to show the tears forming in her eyes. She had not expected this kindness, this inclusion, this support. She realised she really wasn't okay, but it also wasn't right for her to put that onto her friend. Her beautiful, kind friend with the cheating boyfriend. She pushed the sadness and fear back down by turning it into anger. She glared at Eve as he handed her the coffee, and he quickly retreated to the kitchenette to move random items around while they talked.

"I'm doing ok, but I need to stop staying here."

"I totally get it. Those two things are still in, or out, or around our apartment."

"I know. I think one of them is trapped in there, by the salt. Candi, I think it's time for that exorcism."

Candide smiled over at Eve, as though she had won some kind of point. "That's exactly what I was thinking. We need a priest. That's a solid plan."

"Do they really still do that?"

"I think they have to? I mean, if you're going to believe in God and Heaven, you have to believe in the other side, right?"

"I guess so. How do we find someone? Is there a neighbourhood church or something?"

"There is! We'll go together. Today okay?"

"No, no," interjected Eve. "Haven't you got work to do? Classes?"

"I have a free day," said Candide.

"Then you should use it to prepare for your other classes," replied Eve.

Anna had had enough. "Stop talking to her like she's a child! Have some respect. She can organise her own life. She certainly doesn't need someone like *you* to do it for her." Candide and Eve were both silenced by the outburst. Anna got up and started looking through her bag to find a change of clothes. "Candi, give me an hour to get ready, okay? And we will go into the village together." Eve said nothing.

"Do you want me to come keep you company in the bathroom? It's pretty spooky. I made Eve come with me this morning."

"No, that's fine. You two have coffee or whatever you're doing."

Anna left the apartment with her things, too upset and angry to be scared. She threw everything down and claimed one of the shower stalls for herself. It had been some time since she had a shower and it felt good to wash away the grime of the past two days. As the hot water relaxed her body, so she began to feel weak. She let her tears fall freely there in the shower, where they would neither be seen nor commented on. She cried until she was exhausted, then she cried some more. Then she felt her strength returning, slowly.

She stood tall, washed herself all over, then stepped out into the cold bathroom, having forgotten where she was. She dressed. She had picked out a nice outfit. Her grey plaid trousers sat perfectly on her hips, a thin black cardigan tucked into them, a belt defining her curves beautifully. She slipped into her thick woollen socks and oxfords and applied light makeup. She did her hair more carefully than usual, for reasons she could not explain to herself, then studied her reflection carefully, taking strength from the woman in the mirror who looked so bright, competent, intelligent. Anna made her way back to the apartment where Eve appeared to be alone.

"Shelley?" she said.

Without a word, he found a small, dog-eared paperback on the shelf and put it on the coffee table. If he noticed how much better she looked now, he made no sign of it. She felt approval of this behaviour, and also shameful disappointment in equal measure. She accepted the book silently, sat on the floor by the coffee table and flipped through it aimlessly, hoping Candide would return to break the silence.

"Anna—" he started.

"No." She cut him off. She did not want to talk about it. She did not want to raise any emotion. She wanted to stay strong, to get through the day, to do what she needed to do to get her life back on track.

"Can we reset?"

She looked up brightly. "We've reset. It's done. I'm not going to say anything."

"Anna, that's not fair. I don't expect you to keep my secret."

"Surely it's better that way. Why would I want to tell anyone, anyway?"

He said nothing.

"Thanks for the book. It's my first Shelley."

"You will love it." She shot him a warning look. "Everyone loves Shelley," he corrected.

Silence again.

"Are there any other books you need?"

"Medieval Lit. is in a reader. I don't suppose you would have that."

"No."

"Introduction to English Lit. is too big. I see it there on your shelf, but I can't cart it around. It will have to wait until my apartment is, um, exorcised, I suppose."

"And your fourth?"

"Modernist Lit."

"Really?"

"I don't know what I was thinking," she laughed. Eve laughed too. "I love Fitzgerald though," she ventured.

His eyes snapped over to her. "I love Fitzgerald too."

Her eyes snapped over to him. "Do you know he adored Keats?"

He was sitting on the floor next to her in an instant and all was forgotten between them for the following swift and life-altering moment:

"I do know that, but a lot of other people don't know that."

"Like, loved Keats."

"He understood it all completely, as though it were in his bones."

"It's incredible, isn't it? It's in every word. Every second you're experiencing both things, Keats and Fitzgerald all in there at once. Who else could have done that?"

"No one else! It's in every sentence, down to the grammatical structure, but it's more than that—"

"Yes! It's the very essence. It's the soul. It's almost like you can reach out and touch it."

"Yes! But you never can. You never can because that in itself—"

"That's the very essence of Keats! You can't touch it. But you can."

"Yes!"

"You know, I came to Fitzgerald before Keats—"

"Don't we all?"

"Right? But anyway, I loved it, of course, but then when I discovered Keats, I finally understood."

"A whole new world opens up. And it's so, so beautiful."

"It does! And it is. And I, before Keats, I always thought it was his love for Zelda, that desperate, elusive something—"

"It was! It must have been. But it's both. Who could have understood Keats better on that level? It was different with Fanny Brawne, but he knew the whole time he would die."

"And Scott must have believed the same thing about he and Zelda. And counted every second…"

"You feel it, don't you? That something slipping away even while you hold it."

"Yes! It's like you have this person, this great love before you, and it's not unrequited—"

"No! It's so real and it's right there—"

"Yes! You can reach out and touch it, but you know you can never hold on to it. You know always. Every beautiful moment is suffused with the pain of that imminent parting."

"'The sweetness of the pain…'"

"'Give me those lips again…'"

They looked into one another's eyes. They froze. Eve looked as though he were about to throw up. Anna felt the same. They both crashed back into the room.

"I have to go over there." He stood up and walked back to the kitchenette to stand around awkwardly again. She did not say a word, just sat and caught her breath. He was it. He was everything. She could not, would not, look up. Neither would he.

"What a mess!" Candi reappeared with an armful of bedding, which she dumped on the floor. "You'll have to get these washed. Sorry. Possession is gross. Oh, and here's your sweater." She threw it down, crumpled, sticky, and smelly.

He watched on, doubtfully. "You can keep that one."

"Yes!" She stuffed it in her bag. "Ready to go, Anna?" Anna nodded her approval and busied herself with her own bag so as not to interrupt their goodbye, but there was none. Neither Anna nor Evelyn acknowledged one another in the least as they departed. She and Candide stepped out into the hall without another word.

They approached the top of the stairs and their apartment door quietly. All was still. They turned to descend the staircase and jumped as a huge bang sounded on their apartment door, as though something had been thrown at it, hard.

"Thing's pissed," said Candide.

"Sounds like," replied Anna.

They opted to take coffee away from the cafe and walk down the hill and into the village. It was a beautiful, crisp autumn day. The sun was still low in the sky and there was a refreshing chill in the air. Not enough to need a coat; just enough to feel a tingle on their cheeks as they walked across the field. The second spring had brought forth a multitude of yellow and white flowers that littered the clearing. Crisp autumn leaves were strewn across their path and Anna delighted in crushing them as she walked.

She was not so much lost in thought as lost in a daze, not really wanting to think at all, just wanting to be empty for a while, to suffuse the interior with the beauty of the exterior and nothing else. She let all the crushing beauty of a fleeting autumn fill her up and quite forgot she was with Candide at all, who also seemed preoccupied. Candide eventually broke the calm.

"I had no control over anything last night," she said. "It was really weird. I have no real sense of what it was, or what it wanted. I was just, kind of, watching. I wasn't even scared. Just kind of… sedated. And I could feel it moving my body, but it was like being half asleep." Anna said nothing. Candi went on, "You know on tv, someone who gets possessed seems to have knowledge of the thing? What it wanted or what it even was. I don't even know."

"Do you think that's better or worse?"

"I honestly don't know." They walked on. "I just wish I knew if the salt really worked or was it that boy doing it all?"

"He was watching the whole time."

"I know. I remember I had to walk right over to him. It makes me shudder now, but last night I just looked at him."

"It's kind of reassuring to know a possessed person isn't suffering."

"Not until afterwards, anyway. I don't know what it would have done, but I think it would have been bad. Really bad."

"Let's just get this priest and not think about it. As far as we know, it can't leave our apartment, or near it at least."

They came to the small village. It was like a time capsule, and if not for nice, neat, modern cars, it was as though nothing had touched the place in the last 200 years. Picture perfect gardens, old signage immaculately maintained, antique shops and old bookstores lined the streets. The local church was the tallest building in the town and it was easy to find their way by following the steeple through the winding streets. They smelled the incense on approach and stopped at the door.

"I'm not religious," said Anna. "Is this okay to do?"

"I mean, why not? It's all the same supernatural thing, isn't it?"

"I guess so?" They entered, and a sensor alerted whomever may be in attendance to their entry. They waited uncomfortably by the doorway. An old man came out to greet them.

"We need an exorcism," said Anna, once niceties were out of the way.

"An exorcism? For you?"

"No, no, for our house."

"Your house? What makes you think so?"

"It's definitely haunted. We saw the ghost."

"Numerous times," interjected Candi.

"And it possessed her," said Anna. Candi nodded in agreement. The priest looked her up and down. "But we cleared her, and now we need our apartment exorcised. We don't know how to get rid of it."

"Or them."

"Them. We think there might be two. We think one is a ghost."

"A ghost won't possess you," said the priest.

"You think it's a demon?" said Candi, horrified but clearly also excited.

"Yes, if it can possess, it must be a demon. But you are clearly not possessed now," he said, "or you would not be able to cross this threshold."

"That's really good to know," said Candi. "On tv they can lie dormant, you know, for years sometimes."

"No, no, you just come to the church, you can check. But what you need now is not an exorcism. You need a 'Negative Energy Clearing'."

"Well, all right then. When can we do that?"

"I am booked out all week. I assume you want it done soon?"

"We were hoping today, even?"

"Okay! I will send Joe."

"Joe?"

"Joe!" The priest clapped his hands as he called out.

They waited, Anna and Candi feeling quietly awkward, the priest chatting about the lovely autumn weather.

"Ah, here he is now. This is Joe. He is the curate here."

Anna felt her stomach twist and untwist itself and tried valiantly to force herself to maintain her dignity as he appeared before them. Joe was tall, handsome, beautiful. He held out his well-manicured hand and as Anna took it, she felt how soft and strong it was. Only hours earlier, she thought she would never be able to look at a man who wasn't Evelyn Worthing. In an instant, she was cured.

Introductions were made. His name was Joe Bruno. He was lovely.

"Joe, these young ladies need a Negative Energy Clearing. A ghost and perhaps a demon, too. Over at the university. Can you do it today?"

"I can." He thought for a moment. "How would 2pm be?"

"Uh, fine. Any time that suits you." Anna coloured and giggled stupidly as she rambled out her reply.

"All right. Father Milton will get your details and I will see you then. It's so nice to meet you both." Again Joe shook hands with Candide and Anna, and with that he disappeared back into the darkness of the church.

"Okay, now there is just the matter of payment," said the priest.

"Payment?"

"Yes, that is $297, plus tax, so all together that comes to $326.70." Anna and Candi looked at one another. "It's usually more," he explained. "We have a sale on this week."

"Oh. That's lucky. Right. I'll pay," said Candi.

"No, no, let me," said Anna.

"It's all right. I'll get it from Eve later. He won't mind."

"Oh. Okay."

CHAPTER 15
A WELCOME VISITOR

As it was only 11am, and as Candi and Anna were both yet to eat, they decided to get lunch in the village. They wandered through the narrow, curving streets until they found a book-shop-come-cafe. Making their way through winding stacks of dusty books, they eventually found themselves outside in a leafy courtyard, overgrown with ivy, allowing only a light dapple of sunshine on either of their faces. They each ordered a meal and more coffee before Candide started the conversation.

"Does this mean we can relax now?"

"I don't know. They seemed very organised. Like they do this all the time?"

"How many genuine ghost slash demon hauntings can there be? There's only the university and the village."

"Bad ju-ju in this area?"

"You wouldn't know to look at it, would you?"

"No. I had no idea it would be so beautiful. Did you live here when you were off campus?"

"No, I lived in town. It's nothing like this." They were both quiet for a while, enjoying their coffee. "Anna, do you think it's because we're not religious?"

"Being haunted? No. Demons love Christians."

"You think so?"

"Yeah, they love all that stuff. Good and evil. They live for each other." Anna took another sip, looked around the courtyard, then, as casually as she could manage, "I don't think my lack of religion gives me much of a chance with the hot priest, though."

Candide looked up. "The curate?"

"Yes, the hot curate. I'm not really sure what the difference is."

"But I thought—"

"What?" Anna met her eye, perhaps too directly.

"I thought you might already have something going on."

So Candi had picked up on the tension between herself and Eve. "Me? No! No, I'm not interested in anyone right now. Hot curates only."

"Really? There's nothing at all going on? You can tell me—if you want to. I can keep a secret."

"There's nothing to tell. I only started here two days ago. I haven't had a chance to meet anyone. No one worth my time, anyway."

Candi's eyes flashed. "Worth your time?"

"I mean… no one who would be, uh, appropriate. And available. And, listen," she looked seriously at Candide and controlled her speech: "I am not interested in anyone at university. No one. I am not going to pursue anyone there. It's absolutely not something I would ever do. Okay?"

Candi looked confused now, hurt even, but to Anna's relief, she let it go. Still, Anna felt as though there were a shift in the atmosphere between them from that time. As they ate lunch, the conversation was light and inconsequential, and by the time they left the cafe, they were hardly talking at all.

The walk back to the apartment was long and awkward. Anna felt intensely that she had ruined everything, and this made her even angrier at Eve for messing up their burgeoning friendship. When they finally arrived back at his apartment, they found he was out, and Candi was clearly still not in the mood to sit and talk with her. "Do you mind if we just study for a while?"

"No, not at all."

"Okay, good. You're all right out here? I'll take the bedroom." She turned to go.

"Candi, are we ok?"

"Yep. Why wouldn't we be okay?"

"I don't know. You just seem, kind of, annoyed with me."

Candide was still, thinking, then she put a soft, reassuring smile on her face. "I think I just need a rest. I'm tired from everything. I'll be back to normal soon."

Anna nodded and Candi disappeared into the bedroom.

Anna tried to keep herself occupied by looking at Eve's books, but she was too anxious to settle with one. Candi must have some idea what had happened. If only Eve hadn't kissed her! She knew even as the thought occurred to her how unfair it was. She had wanted him to kiss her. She had willed him to kiss her. She had kissed him back. She wasn't thinking about Candi any more than he was, and her friend had every right to be upset with her. Then, to top it all off, she had been dishonest when she had the opportunity to smooth things over.

She suddenly felt sick at the idea that perhaps Eve had been honest with Candi and she had forgiven him already. That made Anna a straight-up liar in Candi's eyes. Or worse, made it look like she was covering up because she still intended to carry on with Eve behind Candi's back.

Or, Anna considered, perhaps Candi just had other things going on that did not involve Anna or Eve, and perhaps she should stop being so self-absorbed…

At that moment, Eve came in, leaving the door wide open behind him.

"No priest?"

"He'll be here soon. At two."

"Candide?"

"'Candi' is in the bedroom."

"Eve?" Candi called.

"Yep."

"Eve, I need three-hundred dollars." Eve sighed and made his way into the bedroom.

A moment later, Anna heard a sound in the hall. A woman's face. A beautiful woman she vaguely recognised from around the campus. "Hi, uh…"

"Is he expecting you?" Anna gave her a cold stare, blank except for one judgmental raised eyebrow.

"No, a friend told me…"

"Professor Worthing doesn't allow students to visit his home. You understand, I'm sure. You will have to wait until the tutorial."

"Okay…" She made to leave, then turned back. "Are you waiting for him?"

"I'm in the study group."

The woman fixed her with her own incredulous look. "Study group for one?"

The audacity! Anna fought to keep control of herself. "I'm afraid study group is full this year. Maybe next year?"

"Maybe. Maybe not." The woman looked her over then reluctantly departed.

Eve returned. "Who was that?"

"Some girl. Wanting to ask you questions." She was quiet for a moment, but found she couldn't let it go. "How often *do* you entertain your students here?"

"I usually avoid it at all costs."

"Yet they come."

He looked sharply over at her. "I can't help that."

"Can't you?"

"No. It's not like I tell people where I live. They just seem to find it."

"They don't seem to have much trouble."

"Why do you care?"

"I don't. It's just annoying having to get rid of your admirers."

"They're just random students."

"Come on. I'm sure there's a reason you're in the habit of keeping the door open when you have students over. Just for female students, I presume. Make it seem like it's all above board. Yet the bedroom door is closed…"

He blanched, shocked at her open accusation. "I don't think I like what you're implying."

"I don't think I like what you're doing." She felt tears welling up and tried to force them back down.

Eve sat down near her, but Anna didn't look up. He spoke more softly. "I don't sleep with my students, if that's what you're getting at."

"Could have fooled me."

"Is that seriously what you think of me?"

She said nothing.

"Last night was a mistake. I don't do that. I would never do something like that."

"Except last night."

"I said I'm sorry!"

"And today? And tomorrow? Or is Candi not taking any of your classes this year?"

"What!"

"Excuse me." They looked up to see the curate at the door. "Anna, isn't it?"

"Yes!" She got up. "Eve, this is Joe. He's going to fix the apartment for us."

Eve walked over to Joe. Their hands met. They touched, perhaps a little longer than necessary as introductions were made, and Anna couldn't be sure, but she thought she noticed a light, pleasant, pink colouring suddenly brighten Joe's features softly and to great advantage.

Anna was struck anew by how handsome they both were. Even though she was instantly attracted to Joe, she was still surprised to see how well he looked next to Eve, who was, to her, immaculate. She racked her brain trying to remember which members of which churches were allowed to have relationships with women, but alas, her religious education had been poor. She figured it was probably a moot point, but given any interest in Evelyn Worthing must now be at rest, it couldn't hurt to indulge in a little fantasy. Perhaps it would even help. Regardless, she was aware of every movement, every mannerism, every tone, every single thing Evelyn did, even if she forced her eyes away from him every time she realised she was looking again.

Joe sat on the couch next to Eve. Anna fetched Candi and they took an armchair each. The curate first took down full details about the history of the apartment, of which they knew very little, their experiences with the entity, details of their incantation.

"From what you have told me," Joe said in his soft, Italian accent, "we are dealing with two separate entities. I don't think the little boy means to hurt you. What you saw in your dream, in your bedroom —that was not the boy. It was something else pretending to be the boy. The being that possessed you, it was something more powerful. That one is a demon, not a ghost. So, here's the problem: we need to let the little boy back in. He means you no harm, and we must find what attaches him to the building to set him free. Until we do, you have to live with him. But I don't think you will see him much once the demon is gone. I think the demon has upset him.

"Now, this demon is not your friend. I don't know why he is here or what he wants with you. I think he must like one of you, or he would have killed you all last night. Do not play with the ouija!"

He looked around at them all sternly before continuing.

"I'm guessing the demon was probably planning to stay around for some time; play with you, torment you. Demons enjoy this kind of thing. He would want to take all your energies. Your happiness, your fear, your anxiety, your sexual energy. University is a great place for this sort of thing. He will inspire the fear in you himself, but the rest—he just follows wherever it is strong. This may be what made him notice you. You have a ghost in your building and this means everything is already heightened. Then we have relationships start and bam! It's a perfect storm."

Anna, Eve and Candi sat wide-eyed, taking in all the information. Candi tried to catch the eyes of both Eve and Anna, but they avoided her gaze.

"I know where you got this spell. I watch this too. This Dean? Dean?" Candide and Anna nodded slowly. "He is very good. But now you probably think you can kill this demon. You cannot kill a demon. There are no magic guns, no knives, no ancient religious relics that will do that for you. There is no green tea to let you see, no whistle to make him come, you understand?"

Anna and Candi exchanged knowing, impressed glances. Eve listened attentively.

"If you were able to cast this demon out of Candi, I do not think he can be very powerful. That or he didn't put up a fight for some reason. The spell you used is very good, but most likely, it was just playing with you. It knows it can get more energy from you if it waits. Did it say some things to you? Some things that build tension? Besides the fear."

They were all quiet, no one wanting to talk first.

"I can guess the kinds of things it said. Demons are like this. He probably just needs to be released now because he is trapped in the apartment. If we can get him out, I will put a warding spell on your building, and that will keep you safe inside. That will let you sleep in your own beds. He will not be able to feed on your energy anymore and he will go away, eventually."

"To haunt someone else?" Anna asked.

"No. Like I said, I think this demon, for whatever reason, likes one of you. Or all of you. I don't know why. It will be weak from being on this spiritual plane for so long, so if you continue to starve it of energy, it will go back to where it came from."

"And where's that?"

"Hell."

"Hell?"

"Hell."

"It just popped up from Hell?"

"It's what demons do. They come here from time to time to feed, cause trouble, reap souls. That's why I'm here. I try to reduce the harm they do, but they will always do some harm. This is just life."

He opened a small wooden box and began to remove each item, explaining what they were and what he would do with them. Inside he had sage for burning, holy water for sprinkling, and some sort of red liquid in a vial that he said was very precious. He said he would use it to seal the building.

"I will say some incantations and I will drive the thing out. You three, you must stay here. I will give you a charm each while you wait." He pulled three small, wooden tokens from his box, handing one to each of them. "You hold these tight and you do not let them go until I come back. When I break the salt, he will want to come for you. This will protect you from him until I am done. Okay?"

They nodded.

"Okay. I'm going to go now. You wait and be quiet." He paused. "You two," he pointed a finger back and forth between Anna and Eve, "I don't know what's going on between you, but if you cannot talk without fighting, then do not talk." Eve looked at Anna but her eyes went involuntarily to Candide who sat back in her chair looking curiously at Anna. The curate continued, "I know it's hard, but try not to create any strong tensions, okay? It gives him energy. I don't want him to have strength over me. I want you all to wait here, quietly, until I return."

The curate then closed his box, set some sage on fire, and started walking down the hall to their apartment, chanting something in Latin.

CHAPTER 16

STRONG TENSIONS

They waited without a sound until they heard the door of Room 235 click shut behind the curate, then they waited some more.

Anna's heart was on fire after Joe's final comments, but she tried to quell the intensity of feeling within her. Candide, a sly smile on her face, broke the silence. "This should be interesting. Well, if no one has any burning desires they want to discuss—I mean," she laughed, "you know what I mean… then maybe we brighten the place up a bit while we wait." Candide must feel quite confident in her relationship with Eve to joke so openly about it. Or perhaps it was a challenge. To Anna? To both of them? Candide set about turning on lamps as they had only now noticed the gathering gloom. "Eve, get us some tea, won't you?"

"I guess I can't make it to the library after all," said Anna, as casually as possible. "Do you think this sort of thing takes long? I have a class at 9am."

"What is it?" asked Eve.

"Gothic in art."

"Got it," said Eve, moving to his well-stocked bookshelf.

"Don't you ever get rid of old books?" asked Candide.

"Never," he replied. "It all ties in together, anyway. Who's your first artist?"

"Um," Anna checked her wrist. "Henri Fuseli. *The Nightmare*."

"En-ri," corrected Eve.

"En-ri," Anna repeated quietly.

"Are you kidding?" laughed Candide.

"What? What's wrong?" said Eve.

"Well… it's 'charged'."

"'Charged'?" asked Anna. "How charged can it be? It's just a picture."

"I mean, maybe save it for tomorrow," said Candide. "Or later. Maybe not right now."

"Candide," said Eve, "it's fine."

"Is it, Eve? Right now?" She looked at him meaningfully.

He made no more response than to roll his eyes and take the book over to Anna. She ran her finger down the index and turned to the appropriate page. "Ohhh." She feasted her eyes on the woman before her. She was on her bed, her back arched and her eyes closed, as if in some kind of erotic ecstasy, her thin nightgown showing every curve of her body, stretched out all in white, lost in unconscious pleasure.

"She looks to be having a nice dream, doesn't she?" Candide was over Anna's shoulder now. Anna didn't look up, so as to hide her flushed cheeks. "I did Gothic in Art last year too. That lecturer—"

"No, Candide." Eve said.

"It's just Anna," Candide mumbled.

"No." They exchanged vexed glances and Candide clearly lost the battle of wills because she sat back down and picked up a book while Eve continued making tea.

"Anyway, I know all about it," she said, "in case you want to discuss it. Later." Candide and Eve carried on as though the interaction had never happened.

"Anna, does it remind you of a scene in Frankenstein?" Eve's voice shifted seamlessly into lecture mode.

"You know, it actually does," Anna replied.

"Mary Wollstonecraft Shelley knew this painting intimately. Both her parents were at one time friends with Fuseli, and he did a portrait of her mother." He held a cup out for her. Taking it carefully, she was forced to brush his fingers. She pulled away slightly, spilling a little of the tea on the rug.

"Sorry."

"I'll get it," he said.

"Wollstonecraft had an affair with him, didn't she?" interjected Candide. Anna looked at her for an explanation. "Women's Lit." Anna nodded.

"That has been the narrative for a long time," replied Eve. "It isn't true, though. Wollstonecraft wasn't yet in a relationship. She was young and independent, she was an absolute powerhouse, and he was already married. Wollstonecraft saw the relationship as purely platonic, but, perhaps given he, uh, had an eye for the ladies, his wife didn't take to their friendship too well."

"No, I should think not," said Anna.

"Wollstonecraft proposed," continued Eve, "she could actually live in their house with them, and they, Wollstonecraft and Fuseli, could carry on their friendship, their 'meeting of minds' with no marital strings attached. Meanwhile, she thought Fuseli's wife should have no concerns about her husband because Wollstonecraft had no intention of breaking up their marriage."

"Sounds like someone spent too much time in France," laughed Candide. "They were much more open to having a second woman in tow. Oh, Anna, I was going to ask, will you take French Lit. this year?"

"I was planning to. Will you?"

"Yes! Let's be study buddies."

"Okay, let's!" Anna was delighted at the notion of their bonding over scandalous French novels.

"Have you got another elective, Candide?" asked Eve. "Make sure you cover all your core subjects."

"Could you stop being a dad for just five minutes? I have enough to do French Lit. in the fourth term and Gothic Lit. next term. Will you get sick of me being in all your classes?"

He smiled. "Never. You do what you want. It will be fun having you both in my class, anyway."

Anna blanched slightly. "You're teaching *both* those classes?" She did not mention her over-excited, bank-account-crippling expenditure on the prettiest editions of every book required for Gothic Literature that meant she was now absolutely compelled to take the course.

"I am," he said, then almost apologetically, "It's not for a long time."

"So many mistresses in French Lit.," Candide continued, unchecked by either of their blushes. "I love it. Get the business of marriage out of the way and you can still have your pleasure on the side."

"I suppose it might have been a good thing, as a society back then, to be able to say, 'okay, we married for money or family, but we're not in love, so let's accept it, get the job done, then we can see other people'." Anna's mind suddenly switched from fiction back to reality, and her tone changed accordingly. "It's all the dishonesty and lies involved in affairs that are so damaging." She looked over at Eve, but he made no indication he understood her deeper meaning.

"There are certainly many examples of wives and mistresses becoming good friends throughout history," Eve said. "Especially in France."

"I think it would be fine if everyone was comfortable with what was going on," said Anna, more pointedly, "but I wouldn't want to share."

"Wouldn't you?" asked Candide. "What if the one you wanted was already taken, but his wife offered him up to you, for as long as you wanted, only he must return to her each night?"

Unsure if Candide had meant to imply anything beyond what was said, Anna chose her words carefully: "To share the marriage bed? How is it love if he's still producing children with the wife to cement that marriage? If he can think about her like that, he can't really be interested in me. So I wouldn't want him."

"You don't think a man can love two people at once?" asked Eve, still leaning against the kitchen bench drinking tea, in no way indicating discomfort with the conversation.

"No, I don't. Not real love anyway. The man in question owes the first woman respect enough to stick to their deal and not embarrass her publicly, but the other woman—she is always taking half of what she could have. It may be devastating for them both that they met too late, when one had already committed to someone else, but if they cannot really, truly be together, well, I would not want any part of it. I would feel it was disrespectful for a man to even suggest it to me. And I would not destroy the happiness of another woman so selfishly, even if it were just an illusion."

"And what do you think of Mary Wollstonecraft's actions, then?" asked Candide.

"I think Wollstonecraft was idealistic. I'm sure she truly believed what she was saying at the time. She wouldn't be the first woman in history to think a man genuinely respected her, only to find out later he just wanted sex." She felt herself getting angry now, not understanding why Eve would keep the conversation going on for so long, acting as though he didn't understand the subtext, both of them knowing he had kissed her only the night before. "It seems her daughter put that to the test, too. And that worked out horribly for her. Percy Shelley seemed so clever and dashing, but he was just another one of those guys."

"What guys?" asked Eve.

She shot him a filthy, accusatory look. "I'm sure you know."

"I don't," he said, now staring hard into his tea, motionless, listening intently, having finally sensed the change in her.

"You know, the hot, smart, older, academic guy coming on to various women who don't know better yet so he can sleep around with everyone in sight?" At that he did look up, and she locked eyes with him, both silent, neither of them continuing the sentiment. For a moment, she felt satisfied the blow had landed as she intended. A moment later, she felt annoyed with herself for deliberately creating such an intense atmosphere. The very next moment, she felt regret at the look of mortification and guilt she saw on his face.

Candide looked from one to the other, then ventured, "It certainly makes you wonder how things might have gone had Mary Wollstonecraft lived."

"I can't imagine we would have Frankenstein," said Anna, quietly.

"No, but it makes you wonder what else might she have done under her mother's guidance."

"I doubt Wollstonecraft would have allowed Percy in the house, for one thing. I'm sure she would have seen him coming a mile away."

"Do you think he was really sleeping with her and her step-sister that whole time?" asked Candide.

Anna made no reply, feeling too ignorant of the topic to be able to comment.

"Probably," said Eve, filling the silence cautiously. "Claire is believed to have had a child by him."

"That's awful," said Anna. "I knew they were sleeping together, but I didn't know that…"

"There's a lot more to the story. We've only looked at their lives up until Frankenstein. We'll do Percy Shelley next week."

"I know," said Anna.

"It's funny, isn't it," said Candide. "Mary Wollstonecraft Godwin was one of the most enlightened women of her age, or, I suppose she was just a girl really, and Percy was able to use it against her to allow him to sleep around in the name of freedom. How is it that men always seem to find a way to use empowerment to play women off against one another?"

"If it helps, Percy wasn't particularly happy either," said Eve.

"Yes, but it was his fault and he could have stopped all of it," said Anna.

"Could he? Once he ran off with two girls and started affairs with them both, there wasn't much chance of going back."

Anna's eyes flashed. "Are you excusing him?"

"Not at all. He treated Mary and Claire terribly. And Harriet, the wife he abandoned for them. He was a mess, though. I don't think he was capable of seeing the possibility of the carnage before it happened. I feel like Percy would never have been truly happy anywhere, and that just made him, kind of, wreck everything as he went along. It would be an entirely different story if society, marriage laws, all that kind of thing had been different at the time. They were stuck with each other once he set everything in motion. And you know, so much of Frankenstein is dissecting that society that made them all so miserable. They were all really out of step with the time in which they lived."

"I suppose you're right about that."

"It makes great literature, though."

"It does," conceded Anna. Eve put his cup down on the bench and moved to sit in the armchair opposite her with some novel or other which Anna was unable to make out the title of.

All were quiet for a time. Anna traced her eyes over the pictures in front of her and played with a pencil that lay on the coffee table. She did not look up or address her question specifically to anyone, but she quietly asked, "Do you think he loved them both?"

"No," said Eve, after a moment's reflection. "I think he truly loved Mary. I think he messed up really badly, and that damaged her and their relationship irreparably. I think he was one of the few people in the world who saw her for what she really was: brilliant, strong, intelligent, original, deeply talented. And I think," Anna felt his eyes on her, his words gentle and low, "he was sincerely sorry for what he did. And I think he would have taken it back and begged her to start over, if that was at all possible, rather than lose her friendship and respect."

She looked up at him and her own eyes sparkled in the gentle lamp-light. In spite of herself, she felt her anger melt away at his soft voice, in his soft sweater, speaking romantic words in a melancholy tone.

"You will just have to read his poetry and tell me what you think," he said.

"I will."

"I know you will. I like that about you." He smiled at her and she smiled back, having quite forgotten Candide, who was intently watching both sets of eyes and expressions. Anna looked up to her and, catching her eye briefly, cast her own eyes back down to the book, feeling ashamed, only to be greeted with the image of the prone body in delight. She blushed and forced her eyes to the floor until she sensed the others had returned to their reading.

She had sworn only minutes ago her infatuation was through, yet she could feel herself falling for him more every moment they spent together. She knew what had happened wasn't entirely Eve's fault. She just had to control herself and make sure it never happened again. Once she had her apartment back, she would stop seeing Eve outside of tutorials and lectures. She would take care not to meet him in the hall and she would avoid him in the courtyard. After Gothic Literature, she would not take another of his classes. She felt a pang at the loss of French Literature, but she would just have to study it on her own. Or borrow Candi's notes. And she would ban Candi, somehow, from bringing him to the apartment. Eve and Anna would become strangers.

She stole another look at him, leaning over his book, the yellow light illuminating the tips of his hair around his thoughtful face.

On the other hand, she was here to learn. And he was a damn good teacher. And a damn good-looking one. With so many soft sweaters and no doubt a beautiful body underneath. His bare feet stretched out on the carpet were lovely, his legs perfectly formed; she imagined the line of his belly meeting his hips under his clothes. Her mind went places she did not want it to go, so she dragged her eyes back to the page in front of her, this woman no doubt dreaming of a lover she too desperately wanted in her bed, caught in a moment of pure passion, no reality to interfere with her desires. Anna looked back at the floor but could not stop the flashes of what it might be like to be in bed with Eve and she involuntarily let out a gasp. Eve and Candide both looked over at her. "Sorry... uh... paper cut." She stuck her finger in her mouth. "Ouch."

"It's all over." The curate appeared at the door smiling, making them all jump. "Your apartment is clean."

They all got up from their seats to thank him. "No problem at all. It's what I do. You shouldn't have any trouble now. If you do, well, this is all the church can do for you. I'm sure it's fine, though."

"Finally you can have your apartment back," Anna said to Eve.

"Ah, but there is one more thing," the curate interjected. "This apartment—the energy here—it's not good."

Their faces fell. "It's not?"

"No. You have all been here too long. It's too 'charged' in here. This apartment needs clearing too, but you see," he pointed to the dark window, "it's getting very late. I can't do it now."

"Okay. I can drive you into the village if you'd like?" said Eve. "I'll find a place to stay in there."

"No, no. Those charms I gave you are not strong enough. He has your energy and we don't want him to lock onto you just yet. You will have to spend the night in the warded space. You don't mind sleeping in their apartment, do you? I'm out of supplies."

Eve sighed. "Is this really happening?"

"Eve, it's fine," said Candide. "Isn't it, Anna?"

"Yes! Yes, of course. You've done so much for us. Come stay." She hoped she hid her misgivings in her overly cheery response.

"You don't have a choice, I'm afraid," said the curate. "Do you want to be possessed? You might not get it out so easily next time. Now, please put your charms in the box for me." He opened the box in a gingerly manner and placed it on the table for them. They each dropped their charm in and he snapped it closed. "Thank you. And the last thing." He reached into his bag. "This is holy wine. It is blessed. It comes as part of the Negative Energy Clearing package. You must take this back with you, and you must toast to the success! It is the blood, not the body, but the blood, you understand? Eat some bread or something. It will help complete the warding. Once you're back in the apartment, you can talk as much as you like about any tense issues. I will be back tomorrow to clear this apartment. Everybody out now." They gathered their things.

Candi quickly retrieved the *Necronomicon* from the bedroom.

"Oh no, not this one," said the curate. "This book is very bad. Very dangerous. You should not touch this. Even touching it is enough to release the bad energy of the book. Put it here on the table and leave it. I will fix it tomorrow."

"Uh, okay then." She put the book down, clearly more than a little annoyed.

"Oh! Fuseli!" He looked over at the picture still open on the table. "This one is very sexy. Did you know he was a man of the cloth too? A very naughty man. He drew some *very* naughty pictures. But we are all the same, the men of the cloth. Under this, we have the same feelings as you. It doesn't matter if it's a man or a woman or both— we do not lose our desire just because we wear the cloth." He laughed a little too loudly at his own comment and they all looked at each other awkwardly, laughing politely, Anna blushing. "Okay, let's go now!" He clapped his hands and ushered them out of the room, following them down the dark hallway, pausing at the top of the stairs.

"Ladies, he's very beautiful, am I right?" Joe bumped Eve playfully with his shoulder. "He's like a painting. No fighting over him! Just study…" Eve cracked a cheeky smile at Joe, and Anna wanted to stomp her foot in frustration. Was no one immune? Again Joe laughed at his own joke, then turned to descend the stairs, Anna resenting the warmth of the light blush she sensed on Evelyn the entire time. They watched until they heard the door close behind Joe.

"I forgot something." Candi ran down the hall to Eve's room. Eve and Anna stood in the dark, saying nothing to one another, wondering how long Candi would be. Seconds that felt like aeons later, she returned, and they all faced the door of Room 235 together.

CHAPTER 17

REVEALING CONVERSATIONS

As they opened the door slowly, nothing happened. The line of salt at their feet was broken, but there was no other sign of the incidents that had led up to this moment. The books were all back on the bookshelf, the candles sitting in an innocuous row on the dining table, no smashed glass or smashed plates, no red-wine vomit on the floor, which they were all openly relieved and surprised about.

Their eyes were drawn to a large symbol upon the ceiling in whatever the red liquid in the curate's box had been. In every corner of the room was a smaller version of the same symbol. Anna looked to the window, half expecting to see the boy, but he was not there. Uneasily, they went over the apartment looking for signs something was wrong. Nothing was. In fact, the curate had even turned on the heating and the room felt warm and cosy and comforting.

Sitting down, the three found they had little to say. Having been driven together by a shared aim and shared trauma for several days, they were unsure how to start to begin again. Small talk seemed too small, and they were exhausted at the thought of demons and ghosts.

Candide was the one to speak, eventually. "I don't want to be the person to suggest it, because last time I suggested wine, things were weird, but the curate said it was important we drink it together."

Eve picked up the bottle. "Should be good for three-hundred dollars." He disappeared into the kitchen.

"Listen," said Anna, quickly, "I'll take the couch so you and Eve can have the bedroom."

Candide's smile froze on her face. "What? Why would I want you to do that?"

"Well… I just thought… you might want some time alone. You know, together."

"Oh no. Ohhhhh no. Oh. Eve!"

"Just a minute."

"Didn't you tell Anna about us?"

"What?"

"About us! Oh God, Anna, you thought we were together?"

"You thought we were together!" Eve reappeared.

"I thought maybe…" said Anna, increasingly embarrassed.

"No! No, he's my… What even are you Eve?"

He snorted as he placed the open bottle and three glasses on the table. "Keeper?"

She glared at him. "Babysitter. Ex-babysitter and contemporary hanger-on."

"Your babysitter! He's like, two years older than you!"

"Right? Can you imagine how irritating that was? Why didn't you tell her, Eve?"

"I thought you told her! You live together."

"Hardly. I thought you would have said something the other night. Jeez, what you must have thought of me turning up at his apartment drunk like that."

"I just thought you had some kind of history," Anna mumbled.

"Well, we do, but not like that."

"So, the other night…" Eve trailed off, and perhaps to save one or both of them the embarrassment of finishing the thought, he disappeared back into the other room, empty-handed, only to return moments later, still empty-handed. Anna said nothing as realisation upon realisation washed over her. He had kissed her because he liked her. Genuinely. He was not the sleazy professor. He was totally unattached and not cheating at all. She had spent the day attacking him like an insane person for absolutely no reason whatsoever. And then the kicker: she had been given one golden opportunity to have a relationship with the man of her dreams and she had blown it. Unequivocally. He had sworn he would never kiss her again, and he had been painfully true to his word since that very moment. Her stomach sank and her pale hand was slightly shaky as she reached for the wine glass he now held out to her.

"Eve, I'm sorry."

"It's okay." His smile looked forced and his eyes had no sparkle to them, meeting hers only fleetingly. The realisation was clearly dawning on him too, how she had judged his behaviour the last few days, and she could see his mind at work tracing over the conversations, accusations, every time he might have set a foot out of place to give her the wrong impression. She began to understand how genuine, how open he was in his expression, now that any impropriety she might have formerly charged him with was gone.

"Anna, I just didn't realise. It must have been so weird for you," said Candide.

"No, no, it's fine." Anna wanted to burst into tears and beg Eve for forgiveness. "Can we just talk about something else? How did you meet, anyway?"

Candide seemed to understand the tension between the two and filled the space with more than her share of light talk as Eve sat at the table setting fire to a candle. "Our mothers were best friends even before we were born. They went to university together. Here. We've always been together, haven't we, Eve? He's like my older brother." She looked at him adoringly. Anna wondered how she ever could have seen anything else there.

"And what, two years apart?"

"Three," corrected Eve.

"Same difference," said Candide.

"Not when you're a kid," he replied. "She doesn't remember half of what she put me through."

"I wasn't that bad."

"You were the worst possible kid a babysitter could ever have," he laughed.

"How old were you when you started looking after her?" asked Anna.

"Seven, I think?"

"Seriously? You had to look after a four-year-old by yourself and you were only seven? For how long?"

Candide's expression as she looked at Eve signalled to Anna she was touching on something she perhaps shouldn't. Eve reached for the bottle and topped up their glasses, apparently not bothered. "Our parents were pretty unusual." Anna locked the word "were" away, remembering not to press that point tonight.

"Yeah, they had a lot going on," was the non-committal response from Candide.

Eve stared into the flame of the candle, clearly still not ready to face Anna, but willing to talk. "They were in this paranormal club—"

"Eve, you just broke the first rule of paranormal club," said Candide, a sudden edge to her voice drawing Anna's attention.

Eve continued, undaunted. "It meant they had to be out at night. A lot. I don't know what was so interesting about it all. I mean, I guess I do now, given what just happened to us. I can't imagine why you would go looking for that, though. Especially when you've got kids at home."

"We had some good times though, didn't we?" Candide reached out for his hand. He squeezed it. Anna knew it was both an affirmation and a warning for Eve to not overstep what was appropriate for her to hear.

"It was the best," he smiled. "I wouldn't trade it for anything."

"What about your parents, Anna?" Candide asked.

Although it was only fair she should share something with them, Anna wasn't ready. "Just normal parents. Boring normal parents. No paranormal clubs. That sounds so fascinating."

Eve continued, "Yeah, we ended up—"

"Eve, Stop." Candide looked at him with her steady eyes, all the humour gone from them for that moment. "That's not yours, that's mine."

"You're right," he replied, then he sipped his wine and concentrated on twisting the stem of the glass back and forth, back and forth.

Candide's demeanour changed again, back to her light and sweet usual self. "Anyway, it wasn't just that. His mum always had something big going on. The best parties, the best adventures. My mother followed her around like a pet."

"So did our dads," said Eve. "I remember your dad told me once, if you ever meet an intellectual who is as beautiful as she is smart, you'll follow her to the end of the Earth. I always thought it was such a stupid, irresponsible way to think. I wonder now though…" He smiled softly as he continued gazing into the candlelight and

Anna furrowed her brow, wondering just how many beautiful, intellectual women attended Endymion College. She considered herself to be neither of those things, though she relentlessly pursued the opportunity to become the latter, at the very least.

"His mum is incredible," said Candide. "She's a big deal around here. I'm sure you know all about Lady Adeline Worthing, though."

Anna froze as she was bringing the glass to her lips. "Wait, what? Like the statue?" Anna's eyes shot across to Eve, who coloured, but he still did not look back at her.

Candide nodded proudly. "She owns half the campus."

Anna felt her defences go up immediately. "So you're…"

"Rich kids?" Candide laughed. "Not me. Evie is, though, aren't you, Evie?"

"I'm not like them." His tone was gentle yet resolute. "Her title comes from marriage. She didn't grow up like that."

"He's really not," said Candide. "That woman made us both work for this."

"She made you work too?"

"Yes, well, when my parents died, she took me in. She's my godmother. But I don't get my inheritance, which is actually just their life insurance, until I hit twenty-one. So she made me work in a coffee shop to buy my own clothes, my car, anything I needed, and then she had me tutored relentlessly by Eve every spare minute. He got me in." She smiled over at him again.

"You would have gotten in without my help."

"I seriously doubt that."

"She never gives herself enough credit," said Eve.

"Yes, well, if I blow the scholarship, she's certainly not going to buy me a place or pull any strings on *my* behalf."

The implication was clear. Eve addressed Anna, half apologetically, "You don't get to be a professor at my age without someone pulling a few strings."

"She gave you the job?"

"She did."

"He's perfectly qualified," Candide said defensively.

"Except I haven't finished my PhD."

"That hardly matters."

"Try telling the rest of the staff that."

"Who cares what they think? You're almost done, anyway."

"What? Already?" asked Anna.

He blushed a little more. "I finished school early."

"Genius child," explained Candide.

"Oh," said Anna.

"More like, wealthy, pushy mother pulling strings," said Eve.

"It doesn't matter how you got here," said Candide. "You're still the best teacher they have."

"I can believe that," said Anna, a light blush rising to her own cheek at the attempted peace-offering. Then turning to Candide, "But she won't do that for you?"

"Well, I'm not her kid. I also think she's harder on me because I'm a woman. She had to make it on her own and now she expects the same from me."

"She sounds very impressive," said Anna.

"She's a drug addict," said Eve, his tone still quiet and gentle, without a hint of bitterness.

"Eve!" Candide cried. "Don't say that!"

"It's true," he said. "I don't mean it in a bad way, but it's misrepresentative to paint her like she's perfect. She's far from it."

"Eve—"

"She self-medicates. I think there's some sort of neurodiversity going on. Of course, she would never get tested. But then why would she? You don't need to when you're rich. You just become 'eccentric'."

"But she's a professor, isn't she? How could she do that with those sorts of... challenges?"

Eve looked confused at Anna's response. "That's pretty standard for people who have the necessary skills. If you're lucky enough to have a deep passion for something that universities revere, then it's the perfect place to hide in plain sight. People will often attribute intense passion to genius if they don't know. But then people who don't have intense passion never really can understand intense passion."

Anna thought of her own home life. "You think she uses drugs to... what? Calm her mind? Concentrate?"

"Both? She says the legal ones aren't any better—"

"They're probably less likely to kill you," Anna replied.

"Yes, and they are absolutely life-changing, in a good way, if they work for you, but she says they're less effective than whatever she's using that particular week, which, I mean, I think she could just make more of an effort with it all, really."

"Eve, I don't think she would want you talking about her like that." Candide was clearly getting annoyed with their unguarded conversation.

"It's just Anna," Eve replied softly.

Anna wasn't sure how to take being 'just Anna'. It felt very different when it came from Candide. Clearly, Anna's opinion of Eve's mother didn't matter to him. Perhaps she didn't matter either, she considered. But then he did look at her, finally, and smiled his winning smile, and she and any ice between them melted in an instant. He was noticeably lighter, as though he had said something he needed Anna to hear, though Anna couldn't imagine why any of what was said should be of particular import to her.

"Oh yeah, Anna, don't tell anyone about us, okay?" said Candi. "Everyone here knows who Eve is, but not about me. And you of all people know, well, what people would think. Plus, his mum says I can't use him to get ahead."

"Sounds kind of harsh."

"You don't know the half of it."

"Oh. Okay then." Anna sighed. It was a lot to take in at once. "I could really use a cigarette," she said. "But I'm not going out there in the dark by myself."

"Anna, that's a terrible habit," said Candi.

Eve laughed.

"What?"

"Listen to you telling people about bad habits."

She sent him an innocent smile. "I told you I would do better this year."

"You're exemplary."

"Thank you."

Eve turned to Anna. "You know, there are no smoke alarms in this building."

"Seriously?"

"Terrible, isn't it?"

"You can't smoke in here," said Candide. "I'll want one. At least go over to a window or something."

"Can I come?" said Eve.

"Of course." Anna's stomach tightened with excitement at the thought of a close, quiet moment with Eve... but where?

The hanging door.

She couldn't. She shouldn't. Yet he was so beautiful and it would be such a lovely, dark, confined space and so romantic and he would be impressed with her having a special key and this might somehow fascinate him enough to sit closer to her...

She made a move for the hanging door.

"You won't get it open," Eve said. "The key has been missing for years."

"You mean this key?" She pulled the beautiful skeleton key triumphantly from her pocket.

Eve's response was low and serious and not at all what she had hoped for. "How did you get that?"

"The guy at the office gave it to me."

"Guy? What guy?" His gaze had become hard, cold, and deeply unsettling, in a way she had never seen before.

"I don't know. Some guy."

"What was he like?"

"I don't know. Some guy."

"Anna, did he have a scar?"

"What?!"

"A scar under his right eyebrow? Did he have one? It's very important!"

"No! What kind of bizarre gothic fantasy world are you living in?"

Somewhat checked by her comment, he became calmer, though still strangely perturbed by the new information. "There's not usually a guy in the office, is all..."

Anna was annoyed by his impertinence. "He was just some guy. I didn't pay much attention, but I didn't see any scar—"

"Are you sure?"

"Yes!"

"One-hundred percent?"

"Eve, yes! I assumed he was just a student working part-time or something. How can it matter?" Anna could have described the incredibly handsome man from head to toe down to his perfume had she needed to, yet she shied away from letting Eve know any more about him, so vehement was his reaction to the very thought of this man.

"It's just odd," Eve relented.

"Is it?"

"It is." He watched as Anna put the key in the lock of the old door and it swung wide open. "Huh. I honestly wasn't sure that would work. You shouldn't have that." Anna chose not to say anything, but remained wary of the darkness that clouded his lovely face. They stood in the opening looking down and he seemed to make an effort to pull himself together. "That's a really long way down," he said pointlessly.

"We're fine. We'll just dangle our legs." And she did so, sitting right on the edge, supported by the old stonework that had been in place for hundreds of years. Eve sat facing her, his back against the stone wall of the doorway, one leg dangling down into the darkness, the other knee up, his foot almost touching her leg. She was conscious of his proximity and hoped he would make contact, though she did not dare do so herself. She lit two cigarettes and passed him one. "I didn't think you'd be a smoker," she said.

"I bet you didn't," he smiled. "It's only when I drink wine." He took a drag on his cigarette and she noticed the elegant way he held it, his hand upturned, thumb balancing the cigarette carelessly between two fingers. "This is a weird doorway," he said.

"Weird how?"

"It's set really deep. It's set back maybe two or three feet? That's weird for a doorway, right? Why did they set the door back like that? And why is this stone wall so thick, do you think?"

"I don't know. I hadn't thought about it."

He breathed a plume of smoke out into the night with his beautiful lips. "This whole building is really odd. There's something about it I can't put my finger on. Like I'm missing something. Especially in here. Does it ever strike you as odd?"

"I've hardly had a chance to look at the place. I only spent one night here." She wondered what it was he really wanted to say about the building, the key, the man in the office, something he had started a few nights ago. She pulled a leg up and turned to face him, waiting. "Eve?"

He leaned his head back against the wall and met her eye, calmly, happily now. "So why literature?" He clearly didn't want to talk about whatever was going on.

"It's the only thing I ever loved."

"The only thing?" He raised an eyebrow and blew out another puff of smoke. "You never had a fish?"

"I never had a fish."

"Not normal parents, then."

"No, not normal parents," she blushed, hiding in the luxurious, dark folds of hair about her face.

"That's okay."

"Is it?"

"It is."

Then she looked into his calm, patient eyes and, without planning to share even a little of her history, blurted out, "I had a brochure...

that I loved." And it was with relief that she saw neither ridicule nor contempt in his expression, only that his face lit up in response to her comment.

"A brochure?"

"For Endymion College. It was… besides my books, it was… I used to daydream about coming here a lot. A lot. It was the only thing I ever wanted, to come here and study literature." She shied away from his now serious, searching look. "It probably seems a bit ridiculous, I guess, obsessing over a brochure like that—"

"It doesn't. Not to me."

"It just seemed so nice. And it is. Excepts for ghosts and things. I still think I'm very lucky."

"Don't be self-deprecating about it," he said. "It wasn't luck. It's a really big achievement to get a scholarship here. And whatever happens next… Anna, whatever happens, in the future, I mean, you can always remember that. You did something incredible. And you got the one thing you wanted. I think you must be very smart and very…"

They locked eyes as he assessed her, a slightly arch tilt appearing at the corner of his lips.

"Determined."

She met him on equal ground. "You have no idea how true that is."

Then his face cracked into a full smile and he was utterly spectacular, and she wanted more than anything to kiss him again.

Eve's lovely hand tapped the ash off his cigarette into the abyss and he drained his wine glass gracefully. "Candide! More wine!"

"Get it yourself, you lazy bastard," she called back.

He smiled again, and they sat in silence, Anna sipping her wine, both enjoying being with the other, neither of them saying anything at all for the next few minutes, nor did they make any attempt to move, beyond Eve stretching his leg slightly and his shoe coming to rest gently against Anna's. Neither let the other know they had noticed the contact, but they both silently savoured the moment.

"I'll get it," called Candide, resigned.

"Another cigarette?"

"Definitely."

She passed him another and watched the red glow from the fire illuminate his face. How easy he was becoming with her, how delightfully tipsy he was. "Why literature for you?"

"Because it's one of many loves—but my best love."

"I love that."

"Anna..."

"Yes?"

"Do you know you're the only scholarship student here this year?" He searched her face in the half-light as she replied.

"What? No!" She could not, nor did she attempt to hide her shock as her stomach tightened into a sick knot at the thought of how close she must have come to missing out entirely. "But that... Surely that's... Why would they only give out one place?"

"They didn't give out any places this year at all," he said.

"That makes no sense."

"I agree." Still he watched her reactions intently.

"Well, what am I doing here? I did the application, I did all the forms, the essays, everything. I've got the acceptance letter. I've got a key!"

"I know. I read your essay. 'The Passion of Keats'."

"You did?"

"It was really good."

"I know." She raised an incredulous eyebrow. "You're not supposed to be able to access my application, are you?"

"I didn't. Your essay was mysteriously placed on my desk."

"But why? Did you need to approve it—because you teach Romanticism?"

"Not at all. I have no idea how it came to me. I thought you sent it to me, but I didn't know why you would do that. Perhaps I shouldn't have read it, but once I started reading I couldn't stop. And I loved it. And I wanted to meet you. And then I found out you were the only scholarship student in a year there were no scholarships. And then you turned up in this room where you're not supposed to be, with a key you're not supposed to have. And then, your very first day here, you ran straight into my arms..." He trailed off and stared down into the nothingness outside their room. She saw his expression harden and noted his foot pull back, as though he dare not be too close to her.

"Eve, I think you really need to tell me what's going on."

"I don't know what's going on," he said, and raised one beautiful finger to his beautiful lips to signify Candide's approach.

"Fine, I'll have one," she said.

"No, Candide, you quit," Eve said, quickly.

"Do you see what I'm dealing with?"

Anna passed her a cigarette.

"You two are going to be a terrible influence on each other. I can feel it," said Eve.

"For sure we are," said Anna.

They sat in the cold evening air, looking over the pitch-black forest, and talked and drank deep into the night. Eve and Candide were both in good spirits, enjoying reminiscing about their past with Anna, and all three felt the tension of the past week slip away.

Throughout the evening Anna received the distinct impression it had been some time since Candide and Evelyn socialised with a third party. There must have been at least a dozen occasions one censored the other by words or looks. Anna heard no lack of amusing anecdotes, but they did not talk of their parents again that night. They did not explain how their bond had become so very intense and they did not talk about paranormal club.

A few times, Anna found Eve watching her when she was talking to Candide, but his gaze rarely lingered long enough for her to catch it. She wanted to decipher the various mysteries he had been alluding to, but as the evening progressed, wine and conversation made it all seem less important than it had earlier in the evening. She was here, now, at her dream university with her bright, gorgeous, fascinating new friends.

As the night went on, the only difficulty she dwelt on was how to clear the air with Eve once and for all. She wanted to apologise for everything she had said. Incrementally, the hope had been building that perhaps all was not lost. Perhaps this could be salvaged. She had a bond with him and if only they could talk freely, or recreate the atmosphere of the previous night, perhaps they could move on to something special. Yet he was careful not to come too close, never flirting, never touching her unless their hands brushed as they passed one another wine and cigarettes, both always aware the other's lips had touched that same cigarette or glass only moments earlier.

As tired as she was, Anna stayed awake, enjoying Candide's company but hoping she would tire first so Anna could be completely alone with Eve. She nursed the small amount of wine left in her glass after the third bottle was empty. Eventually Candide announced she was going to bed.

"I'll just finish this and be in," said Anna. She caught Eve's eye briefly, but he looked away again.

Candide left. They sat for a few short moments, then, "Goodnight, Anna. It's been really nice." He moved to the couch and lay down with his head on the pillow, as if going straight to sleep. Anna didn't want to follow uninvited, so she stayed awkwardly in the doorway, watching the stars, hoping he would say something else. He did not.

"Eve, can I just say I'm sorry?" He sat up again and sighed. She came and sat, also on the couch, but perched on the very edge.

"Don't apologise. It was the wrong thing to do. It won't happen again."

"No, it wasn't wrong—now I know you weren't with Candi."

"It was wrong, though. I'm still your teacher, even if it doesn't feel like it. I don't know why I did it. I would understand if you wanted to make a complaint about it. And if you do, I'll be honest about what happened. I'll take full responsibility."

"I don't want to complain about you, Eve."

"That's exactly the problem. You should want to complain about me. If you were a few years older, you would understand how awful that was. I'm supposed to have a duty of care to you and I breached that."

"What if I want you to breach it?" She caught him off-guard with her direct comment, and slightly shocked herself, yet she tried not to let it show. For a moment she saw how undecided he was, that if she pounced now, he would be helpless to resist her. It was but a split second and by the time she mustered up the courage to make her move, she saw the delight in his eyes had given way to resolve.

"Eve—"

His voice was serious as he cut her off. "Anna, I had a really nice time tonight, but… I grew up in this environment. I've spent my life watching creepy old professors—grown adults—hitting on teenagers." He paused, averting his eyes before he continued. "That includes my father… and I never want to be like that."

There it was. A good, solid reason. An impenetrable boundary. At the time, all Anna saw was the boundary, and it did not occur to her that Evelyn had chosen her, of all people, to tell one of his most closely held, most miserable secrets.

"You're not like that."

"Not until last night, no. But I won't ever do anything like that again. It's a personal rule, and I broke it. Once. I hope we can be friends."

"We are friends."

"Then I'm very lucky." This should have been the natural end of the conversation, but she lingered awkwardly. She felt him slipping away. She wanted to move closer, to touch his hand, to tell him actually no, she wanted, she demanded more than friendship, but she knew it wouldn't be right. She didn't know what to say, so she didn't say anything.

"Hopefully I'll be out of your way tomorrow," he said.

"You're not in my way."

"I shouldn't be here. I need to get back to my own apartment. We need to get back to our own lives."

It was a comment she felt in her stomach. "Oh... I understand..."

"Goodnight, Anna." His face was still kind, but the distance he put between them had become palpable.

"Goodnight, Eve." She made her way to her own bed more deflated and disappointed even than she had felt the night before, back when she had the luxury of believing she could never have had Evelyn Worthing.

CHAPTER 18
A PROBLEM

Anna had no idea how long she had been asleep when she felt Eve come to her. It was pitch black, clouds hiding any illumination the moon may have offered. She could sense his warmth and closeness against her skin. She felt his soft kiss on her cheek once, then again. She reached out her arms up to pull him closer and kissed him full on the lips. He pushed her blanket back, climbed in close to her, and pressed his body against hers. She ran her hands under his clothes, feeling his well-formed muscles, and pulled his soft sweater off. They both continued to undress, his lips pressed against hers all the while and she delighted in the weight of him all over her, breathed in his scent, felt the texture of his hair between her fingers as she pulled at it, revelled in every inch of him. She thought of nothing else in this moment, nothing but wanting Eve. He leaned over her and she wrapped her legs tight around him. The clouds parted, and the moon shone full on his face.

She made the horrifying discovery!

Staring down, with a lascivious smile, was the face of Joe Bruno. He laughed at her revelation and she, in turn, screamed, kicking him with all her strength to get him off her. He thrust her arms back violently and kissed her neck, her shoulders, her lips, enjoying his power over her while she struggled as hard as she could under his wicked grip.

Anna opened her eyes to bright sunlight streaming through her apartment window and sat bolt upright in panic, covered in sweat, gasping for air. Candide's bed was empty and Eve was no longer on the couch. She jumped as the alarm went off next to her. She turned it off and fell back down on her bed.

What kind of messed up dream was that? Was it all a dream? Was Eve ever there? It felt so incredibly real. She was still fully dressed. There was no way it could have happened. Yet she still felt Eve's kisses all over. Shamefully, she still felt Joe's kisses, too. Even more shamefully, she was aware of savouring the feeling of both.

She dragged herself out of bed. Candide was reading at the table, her yoga mat unfurled behind her. Eve was nowhere to be seen.

"Has he left already?"

"Yes. Busy day, apparently."

"Oh. Me too. I should get ready for my lecture."

"Are you okay?"

"Yes. Fine. Why?"

"You just… You seem kind of rattled. No more nightmares?"

"No, no ghosts." Anna forced a smile. "Just adjusting to daytime." She hastened down the hall to shower. Walking past Eve's door, she slowed, but saw no sign of anyone inside. Reluctantly, she showered, dressed, and made her way back to her apartment. Candi had left by then, so she gathered her things and made her way to the lecture theatre, stopping only to have her mug filled with fresh coffee on the way.

She, like the other students, did not sit front and centre this time. She had no desire to be acknowledged or talked to by anyone, the forced socialisation of the past few days beginning to weigh heavily on one who was ordinarily introverted, so she chose a seat towards the back, near the far end of a central row, a few seats away from the aisle. The theatre soon filled up, and she was surrounded by students on either side, though she successfully spurned any possible advances of friendship by burying herself in a book with a scowl on her face.

The lecturer arrived. She was a striking woman, mid-forties perhaps. Quite beautiful. She introduced herself, welcomed them to the course, and began her oration on Henri Fuseli. Indeed, he was a minister. He was of the type that was allowed to marry. Even so, as a young man, he had fallen hard for a woman who did not return his affection, and he became obsessed with her for some time. This adoration influenced his art and so much of what we see today is erotically charged with his longing for a woman he could not have.

The lights dimmed, and the lecturer turned on a screen. Up sprung *The Nightmare* by Henri Fuseli. Anna was glad of the darkness as she blushed at the remembrance of her dream the night before, the tense confines of Evelyn's apartment yesterday, her daydreams of him. The lecturer described in thorough terms Anna's own under-standing that this woman before her lay in some sort of erotic ecstasy, dreaming of her own beloved.

"But," the teacher continued, "we see here a nightmare, represented by this, well, mare. Things are not as they appear. This perfect vision of happiness is going to be derailed before the climax."

Anna sat straight in her chair, the similarities between the painting and her nightmare the previous night closing in on her.

"Here lies the promise of a beautiful sexual experience with her lover, but before it can be realised, with the intrusion of another man, the dream turns into a nightmare."

Anna, now frightened, turning pale, became vaguely conscious of a feeling of being watched in the dark theatre.

"This demon that sits on her chest is an incubus. It is a demon that comes in the night, follows her breath as she dreams of her lover, absorbs her sexual energy, and replaces it with nightmares. The incubus will come to her every night, filling her mind with passionate visions, sleeping with her over and over, drawing away all her energy, leaving her spent, exhausted, eventually wasting away to nothing."

Already scared and sickened, Anna reluctantly scanned the room, the backs of heads bathed in darkness, and only in her second search of the area did she see the small white face at the base of the stairs, watching her. It was the face of the child that haunted their apartment.

Anna shuddered in horror and looked around the theatre. No one else seemed to notice it.

"The incubus wants to dominate her. He will either steal her energy or impregnate her with his child. Which did Fuseli want to do? Probably both." Everyone laughed. No one saw the child. Anna's heart beat loudly as a cold sweat broke out on her hands and face.

The ghost moved its mouth, shifting as if to speak, but in a manner that was completely unnatural. The black mouth contorted itself almost side to side rather than up and down, as though the jaw were broken or damaged, or as though the thing did not know how to manoeuvre a human mouth to make words. She snatched her bag from the floor, but when she looked up again, the thing was no longer there. Her eyes searched in between the rows of heads, all silently, stupidly, staring forward.

The pale face appeared. The creature was moving. It was low down, watching her. She realised, with creeping horror, the thing was crawling. It was crawling, and it was climbing the stairs, one by one, hands first. Yet its head, not looking where it was going, was locked onto her, always still and never shifting even as its body twisted painfully and it continued its excruciating movement towards her. Anna was frozen in horror as she watched this slow procession up the aisle. It came and it came and it did not stop. Then, as it reached the end of her row, it stood tall. She could see it as clear as day now, yet no one else seemed to notice it. Surely they would soon notice and help her. Someone would scream—someone would run out of the room.

The creature's mouth began to move again, in that same strange manner. Was he talking? Was he gasping for air? Anna saw the flash as his wet, black tongue reflected what little light there was from the projected image at the front of the room. Gaining some awareness, Anna pulled her bag in tight, prepared to stand, but she was not prepared for what the creature did next.

Leaning forward, it started to crawl, hands on the legs of the students in front of her, its black fingertips and broken nails gripping tight the knees and thighs of each one, who showed no recognition of its intrusion. Over each one, it crawled, sometimes slipping down and crawling back up. Anna wanted very consciously to flee now, to get away from the thing, but just like in the apartment, she felt herself trapped, unable to move.

Closer and closer it came, and she was unable to even turn her head away, or close her eyes. She could smell its rotting breath as its mouth still opened and closed, see the greenish wet mould in its hair, see, for the first time, a black ring of long marks, as if from fingers, pressed down and black on the neck.

The thing came and her knee was next. It reached out for her. She struggled and she moaned because she could not scream and she wanted to cry out, but she could not. The child proceeded regardless. The grip was tight and skeletal. She felt hard bones dig into her leg as the emaciated frame supported itself. She wanted to cry as one of those dangling, black fingernails caught in the fabric of her pants and ripped off the fingernail entirely. He took that hand and placed it on her shoulder. He put his face in front of Anna's and he sat on her, legs wrapped around her waist as a small child sits on his mother. He moved his expressionless face ever closer to Anna's, still talking, always talking, mud, water, dirt spilling from the open mouth all over her and she could feel the moisture from the water and the filth soak through her clothes and into her skin and at last Anna could scream. She cried out in fear and loathing at the wet, rotting thing on top of her, and suddenly the room was ablaze with light. Every student in the theatre was staring at her. The child was gone.

"Eyes to the front!" yelled the professor, and most of the students did as told, but several, especially in Anna's vicinity, remained gawking, whispering, occasionally giggling. "Meth," said one student to another, who nodded wisely, as though it were the most obvious and only possible reason for this outburst. She jumped as the man next to her touched her hand. He pulled it from his coat, which she had not realised she was gripping.

Anna continued to breathe heavily, unsure if she could trust that she was awake. She continued to hold her bag close to her, but she could not bring herself to stand and leave the theatre, nor to stay and concentrate. She refused to make even more of a spectacle of herself by leaving. But the thing had been there. Right there with her—on top of her—and it could still be there. She looked around nervously for it, studying every inch of the room, but she could see nothing. Perhaps it was behind her. Perhaps it was under the chairs, behind her feet, and would reach forth and grab her ankle at any moment. She shuddered again but sat dead still, her legs locked in place, staring forward.

After what felt like an eternity, the lecture was finally over. The students made their way to the front, and she held back, wanting to be one of the last out rather than reveal herself fully to the crowd. When she finally walked down the stairs, she saw the professor raise her eyes and take note of her, but she did not say anything and Anna was glad of it.

On leaving the room, she followed the crowd out to the bright, sunny courtyard. Rather than go back to her apartment alone, she made for the cafe, attempting to disappear into a dark booth to wait for her next lecture. As she wound her way around the side of the bar and towards the back wall, she saw Candide.

Candide looked up at her as she approached. "We've got a problem," she said.

CHAPTER 19

DEMON STUFF

"You saw him too?" Anna sat down.

"Saw who?"

"The ghost."

"The what?"

"The ghost!"

"Anna, what are you talking about? What ghost?"

She stared at Candide in disbelief. "The ghost who haunts our apartment. The little boy! The ghost!"

"You mean the demon?"

"No! I mean the ghost! Candide…" Anna's eyes started to water, though she was trying valiantly to hold her composure.

Seeing this, Candide came instantly over to the other side of the booth and linked her arm through Anna's, her leg touching Anna's leg. "Oh! Oh, Anna, I'm so sorry. It just—I don't know how I forgot, just for a moment… You saw him? When?"

"In my lecture."

"What? How is that possible?"

"I don't know, but it wasn't like before. He was... powerful."

"How do you mean?"

"I mean he was there, in the lecture theatre and he came right over to me and he sat on me and it was so horrible. He had total control over me, like in my dream, and no one else could see him. It was like a nightmare, but I don't even know if it was. Candi, it was a 9am lecture. How can I have fallen asleep?"

Candi didn't miss a beat. "I don't think you did."

"You don't?"

"No. He sat on you?"

"Yes, it was so awful. I could feel him. His skin and how wet he was. And he was talking, but I couldn't hear anything and I don't know what he wanted. Why would he be there?"

"Because he can't go home."

"He can't? But isn't that a good thing?"

"Apparently not. I think he's locked out of his home and he's probably desperate to get back in."

"But we moved the salt."

"It's not the salt, it's the warding."

"I thought that was for demons, or whatever that thing was."

"That's the problem. Look here." Candide cast her eye around the cafe to make sure no one could see, and then she reached down under the table and pulled up the *Necronomicon*.

"Candi, no, you shouldn't have that!"

"Shouldn't I?"

"No! The priest said."

"Curate. Look here." Candi turned the book over and Anna saw someone had carved a large symbol all over the back of the book. "You see this symbol?" Anna nodded. "Now look here." Candide opened the book and looked through it expertly, as though she was already intimately familiar with its contents. She turned to a page inside that had an image of the same symbol.

"I can't read it," said Anna. "It's Greek?"

"Ancient Greek," said Candide. "This says these are all the symbols that can be used to ward off a demon. Just like the one on the back, and here." She opened the front cover to reveal the symbol inscribed again on the inside. She closed the book and looked at Anna. "I have been studying this book since we found it. Anna, this isn't some cute reproduction: this book is the real deal."

"The real Necronomicon? Are you kidding me?" She pulled her hand back, knowing the cover was said to be made from human skin. "It can't be. What's it doing in our apartment?"

"I don't know. What I do know is that this is the one book that demon couldn't remove from our shelf the other night. It's perfectly warded. He can't touch it."

"Huh. They should do that on tv. It would save so much trouble."

"Right? Anyway, the symbol on our ceiling is not the symbol on this book. That symbol is not for blocking demons."

"Seriously?"

"Seriously. Ghost boy can't get back in because the curate has warded him out."

"Okay. And that's bad because... he can now follow us somehow?"

"It's bad because the demon can still get in."

"Oh shit."

"And the boy can follow you. And I don't know how he's doing that. A ghost shouldn't be able to do that according to this book."

"I can't believe that's the real deal. Are you sure?"

"I'm sure. Look at this writing. It's human blood, you know."

"Of course I know," said Anna.

"The question is, why didn't the curate ward off the demon?"

"Perhaps he didn't know the difference. Not everyone has the real Necronomicon."

"No one does. Except us. I thought it was a myth, but here it is. It has to be the most powerful book of the dark arts, demonology, magic—everything! How on Earth did the Book of the Dead end up here?"

"We can't keep it."

"What? Of course we can!"

Anna shook her head. "Candi, it's dangerous."

"Only in the wrong hands. Do you think I'm going to become a necromancer?"

"That's not what I mean. Surely there's a reason that thing is warded for demons."

"Yes. They want it. Why wouldn't they? There's so much juicy stuff in here. Also, without this, I would have had no idea the demon could still get into our apartment."

"So we need to go ward our apartment."

"Yes, but it's not that easy."

"Of course not."

"That red liquid the curate had was a special concoction of, well, a whole bunch of things. We need that. So we need to find Joe, or go see that old priest, and get some of that."

Anna recalled her unsettling dream from the night before. "Can't we just make it ourselves?"

"No, it takes months to make. I mean, I guess we could maybe buy some somewhere else, but the church is probably our best bet. Joe was supposed to be coming back to fix Eve's apartment today, so maybe we can catch him. You won't mind seeing the hot curate again, will you?"

"No, I..." Anna searched for the words. "Can we just leave him a note or something? I don't think we should be hanging around there if the demon knows where to find us."

"Oh... You don't want to say hi?"

"I'm not really interested now..."

"I didn't think you would be."

"What do you mean?"

"Nothing. Just, things change, right?"

Anna left the sentiment hanging in the air as they ate breakfast and left the cafe. It was to their great relief that they were able to get into Eve's unlocked apartment and leave a note on the coffee table asking the curate to find them in the library. They left a note on their own apartment door telling Eve to stay out, then resolved to spend the afternoon in demon-study.

Having wound their way to the back of the library, and found themselves quite alone in the occult section, Candide set down her books and papers and opened the *Necronomicon*, translating and writing out several tracts, should it be necessary for them to refer to later. Anna searched the collection until she had found several books on demonology. She read through them for some time before sighing heavily. "Everything here is so contradictory. I don't know what to believe."

"It's thousands of years of history all rolled into one. And thousands of different demons. And they are all going to react differently depending on what they want from you. There's no one right answer."

"What does this demon want? Is there anything we can do until we can ward it off?"

"I wish I knew. This book says they all feed on some kind of energy. Positive or negative energy. I mean, it makes sense it would be drawn to us, like Joe was saying yesterday."

"I don't feel like we're especially different from any other students here."

"You don't?"

"Well, no, I mean, if we didn't have a ghost. And the Necronomicon wasn't in our apartment."

"We get along well, don't we?"

"We do, yeah. Kind of, suspiciously well, come to think of it."

"But I don't think it's just the weird situation. I feel like you and I have a kind of..."

Anna nodded. "It's a kind of affinity. An understanding. I feel the same."

"I've been thinking about that. Anna, I don't know much about your past, and you don't know that much about mine. Or Eve's."

"I thought we cleared all that last night."

"We did. At least the part about Eve and me. You know now that would never happen. Ever. But that's a whole other element here." Anna said nothing. "No need to discuss that whole thing, but... I don't know if you realised when we were talking the other day..."

"When?" asked Anna.

"At the cafe."

"When you got mad at me?"

"Yeah. Not mad, exactly."

"I just… It was a weird situation."

"I don't know if you understood," Candide said. "I thought there was an implication…"

"What?"

Candide looked like she wanted to say more, but she chose not to. "Anyway, I think maybe we have all come with our own history and baggage, which is, well, maybe more than a lot of the rich kids at this school come with. Rich kids studying non-arts subjects, you know."

"Rich kids who paid their way in."

"Yes. So there's maybe that added element of… passion… in our apartment, you know?"

"We're not the only scholarship students here, though."

"No, but maybe the only ones with a haunted apartment, a Necro-nomicon, this weird bond and other, you know, passionate interests."

They went back to their books for a while, until Candide said, "I just can't figure out why it didn't come for us last night. It's weird. We weren't expecting it at all, we were drinking, then we all went to sleep thinking we were safe. Why do you think it stayed away?"

It took Anna almost a full minute to respond as she tried to decide how to answer. "Candi?"

"Mmm?"

"Do you have anything about an incubus in there?" Candide looked over at her suspiciously. "You know, Fuseli. Since we're here, anyway. Just curious."

"Mmm. Let me see." She searched through her book and after some time: "Well, they're just demons. They're not a sex-demon, like people seem to think. They're just ordinary demons who steal sexual energy."

"By giving people dreams?"

"Yes and no. It can influence your dreams, whisper ideas to you, and feed on your energy if you're having a very nice dream, like the woman in the picture."

"Or?"

"Or it will actually have sex with you."

Anna turned pale. "It can just come into your bed?"

"Well, what it wants is passionate sex—consensual sex. So maybe you're the kind of person who would happily take a demon sex-buddy—no problem. It will still drain your essential energy until you die, but you will do it willingly."

"Ew."

"Yes. Otherwise, it has two options."

Anna listened uneasily.

"It can possess someone it thinks you might like, or…"

"Or?"

"Or it will kill them and reanimate their body to sleep with you, so, like, you won't know you're sleeping with a corpse."

"Candi, that's messed up."

"Apparently you can tell, though, because their penis is cold."

"What the hell, Candi!"

"I'm just reading."

"That's messed up!"

"So messed up. There's more. The incubus is also the succubus. It's the same thing, it just changes its form to appeal to whomever it's with. It will take on the form of your lover in a dream, and then take on your form to appear to your lover and have you both dream about good times together."

"It all seems like a lot of work. Surely it could get energy just hanging around a place like this, people meeting and hooking up everywhere."

"This says there's more energy in unrequited passion. It's chasing that desire, that longing, the buildup, if you will, and the eventual... you know."

Anna smiled. "So that's why these things tend to bother lone lovers rather than feed off the sexual energy of a married couple."

"Apparently, yes. Nowadays, most people who like each other tend to just sleep together immediately, unless there's something keeping them apart. I guess a drunken one-night stand just isn't as, er, energising."

"So basically if there's no unrequited sexual energy, an incubus, or succubus, has no desire to stay and feed and it will leave you alone."

"Correct! But if there is unrequited sexual energy then it *will* stay and feed off it until it knows you will soon be together and then it will kill the person you love, possess their body, then either steal your life energy with sex or impregnate you with a demon child and disappear leaving you a single mum to a half-demon baby."

There was a pregnant pause...

"Candi, I had a dream."

"I figured as much."

"What do I do?"

"I guess that depends who the dream was about."

"It was about more than one person."

"Oh. That's hot. But oh. Okay. Do... you want to tell me? Or maybe not..."

"Okay, so it was Eve..."

"I knew it!"

"And Joe."

"And Joe? As in the hot curate?"

"Yes." Anna was flushed with embarrassment, hiding her face in her hands.

"Oh my God. That's a dream. So that's why you don't want to see him?"

"It was really vivid."

"Lucky you."

"So, if it was just me having the dream, then we can assume it's just my issue, but if either of them had the same dream…"

"Then we have an incubus. And you know what that means, right?"

"I do."

"We have to go find Eve," Candide said, at the exact same moment Anna breathed:

"I have to sleep with Eve."

"What?" said Candide.

"What?" said Eve.

CHAPTER 20
AN AWKWARD INTERACTION

Candide burst out laughing. "Eve, Anna needs to talk to you about something."

"Candi!" said Anna.

"Time is of the essence. I'm doing a coffee run. We're going to need it."

"No, stay, Candide, I'll go for coffee," said Eve.

"No. And it's Candi."

Quietly, "'Candi', I need you to stay."

"Would you stop being a teacher for one minute? It's a public place, anyway. And this is important. Demon stuff."

"Candi, no, please stay," begged Anna.

"Anna, he's like my brother. I just… I just can't." She disappeared into a sea of books and Eve sat down opposite Anna, who was still curled up on the couch, her jumper pulled over her knees as though protecting herself from the shameful conversation to come. Her heart pounded and she would have happily been torn limb from limb by the demon rather than have the following discussion.

"What is it, Anna?" He seemed distracted, distant, as though he had, in his mind at least, put a significant amount of distance between them since the night before.

"So, it's about the demon."

"Yes?"

Silence.

"Okay, what about the demon?" Eve's irritated tone just made it more difficult for Anna to start the conversation.

"Eve, are you upset with me?"

He sighed. "No, I'm not upset with you. I'm just... I'm trying to adjust."

"I thought we were going to be friends?"

"Anna, we are. It's just… It's nothing. Tell me what you were going to say."

"Eve, the last few days have been really intense, and I have to ask you something weird. Personal. And I don't want you to get the wrong idea, but it really is important that I ask you."

Eve just looked at her, waiting for her to continue.

"So. Um. Have you had any dreams lately?"

He flushed. "Dreams? What kind of dreams? Like dreams about a demon?"

"Kind of. Uh, you know. Dreams about... someone... you might... be with…"

"With someone?"

"Like, at night. *With* them."

"Oh." His eyes widened. "You mean like…"

"Yeah, like that kind of dream."

"Anna, why the hell would you ask me that? That's personal."

"No, it's not for me! It's a demon thing."

"It's a demon thing? Since when?"

"Like an incubus thing. We were reading the Necronomicon—"

"Why were you reading the Necronomicon? Does she have the Necronomicon?"

"Yes…"

"You're not supposed to *touch* the Necronomicon."

"It's not as bad as you think."

"How do you know that?"

"Look, she's got it, we were reading it, and, I, we, need to know if you had a sex dream." She could have died of embarrassment forcing the words out.

"You *need* to know?"

"It's not because we *want* to know. Just that you could be in danger. And if you are, it's my fault. And Joe…"

"What about Joe?"

"He might be in danger, too. I am so uncomfortable about this and I didn't want to have to ask and I know it's none of my business, unless…"

"Unless what?"

"Unless the dream… was about me…"

He paused, only fleetingly. "This is so inappropriate. I can't discuss this with you."

"It will come for you and it will kill you." She felt her chest tighten and her voice started to lose its strength. "I don't want you to get hurt. And, Eve... I've had a really bad day and I just need you to... to stop what you're doing and go back to being Eve right now. Eve like you are when... when you're not like this."

It wasn't the way she said it. It wasn't that she was vulnerable or brave in that moment. It wasn't even that she looked particularly alluring to him on that huge leather sofa, surrounded by thousands of old books, her hair shining softly around her big eyes in the gentle lamplight. Without meaning to, she had communicated very directly to Eve that she deserved the personal right to expect the best from him, as though it were unspoken but known between them to be an absolute truth. Although she could not bring herself to meet his eye, had she done so she would have caught the subtle change in his expression and demeanour which indicated that, unbeknownst to both of them, he had become in that instant permanently attached to her. She felt the atmosphere soften.

"I'm sorry," he said.

"Just... Just nod if it was about me and we won't talk about it ever again."

She looked up now as Eve cast his eyes to the floor and nodded slightly.

"Okay then. I also had a dream," she said quietly. "And that means we're in trouble."

"And what about Joe?"

"I don't know." She looked away. "I mean, unless you dreamed about him too, I guess it's not an issue?"

There was no reply. Anna's eyes shot back over to Eve, who kept his down. "Did you dream about Joe? Like that?"

"I mean, it's just a dream."

"Oh... but... did you..."

"Can we stop already?"

"I just need to…"

"Yes! Maybe. It was just a dream."

"Okay. Okay then. So we need to find Joe, too. And make a plan."

Candi returned, handing out the coffee. "I've got that covered. As you say, we need to find Joe."

"How much did you hear?" asked Eve.

"Oh, only that bit," she smiled. "We need to get the sealing fluid and we need to ward our apartment straight away."

"I thought Joe did that yesterday," said Eve.

"He did not. He just sealed the ghost out," Anna replied. "He can follow me now."

"Ghost? There's a ghost now?"

"Eve—"

"Anyway," Candide continued, "we're not going to wait. Let's go to the village right now, get Joe, get the fluid and fix this. And there's one more thing we need to do. And you're not going to like it. At all."

Anna looked anxiously between Eve and Candide. "It's not…"

"You wish!" laughed Candide. Anna blushed. "No, we're going to have to seal ourselves."

"What?"

"What?"

"Like with the symbols?" asked Anna.

"Yes, like that. But, um, you know how only some things work, like you can't just draw it on with a pen or something?"

"Yes…"

"It needs to be *in* the skin."

"Like a tattoo?"

"Kind of. But deeper. And more permanent."

"Are you… Are you suggesting we carve demon symbols into our skin?" asked Eve.

"Not for fun."

"No, I'm not going to do that! How did I get stuck with you two?"

"It wasn't my idea," said Anna.

"But are you going to let her do this?"

"What else can we do?"

"Not just do whatever Candide says."

"Eve, that's hardly fair," said Candide.

"We're going to go find Joe. We'll go to the church and wait for him. And I'm getting a refund." Eve picked up his satchel and threw his scarf around his neck as a definitive end to the conversation.

Anna and Candide packed their belongings, picked up their coffee cups and followed him out of the library, out of the building and across the field. All was bathed in glorious autumn sunshine and had it been any other day, they would have thrown in classes for the afternoon to lay in the field together, enjoying their youth and freedom. As it was, even with the sinking realisation that they were all in increasing danger, the crushing beauty of the moment was not lost on any of them. Perhaps it was even intensified by the thought they each secretly had that they may not live to see another day like it.

CHAPTER 21

A DEADLY SURPRISE

The village was as beautiful as it had ever been as they arrived in the early afternoon. They wound their way to the church as directly as possible and waited for the sound of the motion detector to bring someone.

No one came.

They waited and set off the sensor again and still no one came.

"Is that weird?"

"I don't know. Do they just leave churches open for people?"

"We should look around," said Eve.

"Are we allowed to?"

"It's important."

So they did. They walked together down the central aisle of the church. At the far right was a small, old, wooden door, which they opened to find a narrow sort of alleyway behind it. It was clearly ancient and made of stone from floor to ceiling, worn down underfoot, uncarpeted. Gas lights flickered in the dark, providing only a small amount of light. They followed the passageway cautiously as it curved around to the left and into almost absolute darkness. Eventually, they reached a cold, damp stone wall, then as their eyes adjusted, they realised there was another door on their right. The heavy wooden door was held shut by an old-fashioned metal latch. It made a screech as Eve lifted it from its metal fastener.

Suddenly their eyes were flooded again with bright daylight and as they adjusted, they found a beautiful courtyard, immaculately manicured, grape vines turning bright orange and red, dropping their leaves and filtering the autumn sunlight over granite cobblestones. Ahead of them was a small, two story dwelling, no doubt centuries old, but clearly well-loved and well cared for.

As they approached, they all admired the picturesque scene, wild roses growing up the side of the stone building, giving way to an astounding rainbow display of Boston ivy.

The old wooden door was painted a cheerful bright red and the gold lion's-head door knocker made a reassuring sound as it tapped against its metal plate. Yet, all three felt a queasy sensation as the door swung open, unbidden.

"Do we go in?" whispered Eve.

"Hello?" Candide stepped forward and pushed the door wide open. "Hello? Are you there, father?"

She went in. Eve and Anna followed, feeling they had no other option, though they both would have preferred to stay outside. In front of them was a staircase, presumably leading up to the bedrooms. To their left was a low-beamed ceiling hanging over a heavily decorated but tidy little living room. Behind that was what appeared to be a bright kitchen, half hidden by a partitioning wall.

On the left side of the room, bathed in bright sunshine, was a table set with tea. "It's still hot," said Anna. "He can't be far away. Should we wait here?"

"Hello?" Candide called again. She advanced towards the kitchen area and stopped. "Oh God."

"What?"

"Oh God. Oh. Don't come in here." She was pale and already visibly shaking.

Anna and Eve ran to her, and they all stood stock still, staring at the kitchen table. There, in the centre of the table, was the decapitated head of the priest. There was a large carving knife sticking out from between his eyes, eyes which were open, staring, as though the last thing he saw in this life was frightening enough to mark him for eternity. They saw a trail of blood leading from the table, along the floor and out the open kitchen door. Candide stepped unsteadily to the window and looked through.

"The rest of him is out there," she whispered.

Anna touched Eve's arm. "Eve, the tea is still hot."

Eve turned pale and grabbed her hand. "Candide," he whispered. "He's here. We need to go."

Candide nodded, but advanced further towards the back door. Stepping gingerly over the blood, she pulled her hand up into her sleeve and used it to quietly pull the door closed and lock it. She then walked to the kitchen drawer and pulled out what must have been the second largest knife in the house. She nodded again, and they ran out of the cottage, through the small courtyard and bolted the church door behind them, running back through the stone passageway and into the church in what seemed like seconds.

"It can't get us in here, can it?" asked Anna.

"I don't know," said Candide.

"What the hell is this thing?" Anna said.

"We don't know that was the demon," said Eve.

"What? Who else would it be?"

"I don't know. People kill people all the time."

"Priests?"

"Yes!"

"We need to call the police."

"There's a phone at the front," said Candi.

"I'll call," said Anna. "Check we're safe in here."

"Okay, we bolt the front door and wait for the cops," said Candide. She and Eve set about securing every door and window and alcove until Anna returned.

"The village police will be here in ten minutes. Now listen: we came to find Joe because I'm Catholic... It's Catholic, right?"

Eve and Candi nodded.

"Okay, so he blessed our new apartment yesterday, and I wanted to thank him. You two just came for a walk. We thought we heard someone at the back of the church and went to look for him and the rest we can be pretty honest about. No demon stuff, no ghost stuff. Everyone understand?"

"Yes."

"Yes."

"Okay. Then we hole up here in the church until Joe comes back so that thing can't get to us."

"Anna," said Candide. "Don't... Don't you think Joe could be involved?"

"What? No! Why? How could he be? He's a priest."

"Curate. It's weird though, isn't it? He didn't do the seals, and he isn't here, and now this priest, who he knows, is dead."

"Why would he kill the priest?"

"It makes sense," said Eve. "Is there anyone else in town who can stop a demon?"

"And then there's the dream," said Candide.

"But... Poor Joe. That's awful."

"Poor priest," said Candide, her voice thin and wavering. "It's just so hideous."

It was the first time Anna had seen Candide give way to any sort of real fragility. Even when she was fighting with Eve, even when she cried, she was always strong. Anna reached for her hand in an instant and squeezed it tight. "Push it down and don't think about it. It didn't happen until you know you're safe."

Candide knew at once Anna spoke with experience, and though her years of therapy had taught her Anna's was a dangerous route to take, she realised at once she was in the presence of a survivor.

CHAPTER 22

THE FIRST CUT IS THE DEEPEST

C andide continued to hold Anna's hand, and they sat in silence in the church until the police arrived.

They were taken aside, and they each gave statements separately.

They were told the church was now a crime scene and they must leave.

"Well, there goes that plan," said Anna once they were safely out of earshot. "We can't go home. He'll find us there."

Candide looked at Anna uneasily. Anna understood and though she was daunted by the task ahead, she was feeling as strong as she ever had and was ready for the next step.

"Eve," said Candide, "get us a room at that inn, would you?"

Eve, clearly rattled, only nodded and disappeared between hanging baskets of beautiful flowers and old wooden tables into a dark stone building down the street.

"Anna, how much did you tell him?"

"Maybe not as much as I should have. I told him we're in danger, but I don't think he fully understands why. Or how bad it is."

"Well, shit. He's not going to want to get warded."

"We'll just have to talk him round."

Eve came back with their key, and they made their way inside. As they did, Candide said something to the barman, and they made their way up to the room.

"It was the only one available," Eve said, looking around apologetically.

The room was decorative to the point of ridiculousness, especially given their current predicament. There was a double bed covered in a pink floral quilt. Its dark-green wrought-iron bedhead, tipped with gold, leaned uneasily against red and green floral wallpaper. On either side of the bed was a small set of drawers topped with green prismatic-glass lampshades. Eve switched them on, throwing a sickly green light across the gaudy, paisley, green carpet. There was a small table with two chairs under a tall window that overlooked the street.

They all jumped as they heard a knock at the door, but Candide appeared to be expecting it. She calmly received the bucket of ice and bottle of whiskey with three glasses and set them down on the table.

"Drinks?" asked Eve. "Really?" Yet he did not protest as Candide pushed a glass with a large pour into his hand.

"Eve," she said. "There's something you need to know."

"I know," he said.

"No, I don't think—"

"I know," he said.

Candide looked up at Anna, who stared at the floor uncomfortably.

"Okay, so you know it's coming for you…"

"And Anna. And anyone who gets in its way, apparently." He drank the large portion of whiskey and Candide refilled his glass. Eve moved up to the head of the bed and started messing with the ugly lampshade.

Candide and Anna sat opposite one another at the table and drained their glasses. As the warm flush of whiskey ran through them, so their camaraderie grew. Anna grabbed the whiskey bottle and refilled Candide's glass, then her own. "You know, it's been really nice knowing you."

"You too." They held up their glasses, then emptied them again. "It's really not such a bad way to go out," Candide mused as she refilled the glasses.

"Killed by a demon?"

"It could be worse. I don't want to die of cancer, or a car crash, or boredom. It was brief, but it was passionate!"

"I'll drink to that," said Anna, and they did. She refilled their glasses. "We lived our lives—this last week of our lives—to the fullest!"

"That we did!" And they drank again. Candi refilled their glasses.

"We can't help," slightly slurring now, "if we are passionate people."

"We can't help it."

"We can't help if demons love that shit."

"Nope. You and I—we were always going to go down in a blaze of glory. I could feel it."

"No one's going down in a blaze of glory," Eve laughed. Candide refilled his glass, then sat down closer to Anna.

"I have to wonder," she whispered, "if I hadn't been here, if all this tension would have been, um, resolved."

"I guess we'll never know. I'm glad you were here, though." They emptied their glasses again and were silent for a while. "Candi, I don't want to die."

"Neither do I. And I keep thinking about Joe. When he comes for us, are we going to have to kill him?"

"Candi…" Anna gasped.

"We have to be realistic. We can't ward our apartment. Even if we could, we can't hide there forever. We're going to have to fight him. And he's in there."

"We don't even know for sure he's possessed."

"No, but if he is, he will come for us."

Anna was silent for a while, then continued in a hushed tone, "I wonder if it's keeping him fed. His body. How long can a possession go on for? Do they just let the body die while its 'soul', I guess, is inside, watching? Starving."

"I don't know. I guess that depends how bad it wants to keep the body. But I think we both know it's not *his* body it wants."

"Would it still want to do that, though? I mean, the jig is up. We both know what… what it would do if it had one of us. But we wouldn't do that anyway… now… probably…"

"All right, Anna, let's do it," said Eve.

"What?" Anna looked over at Eve as he pulled his sweater off. Illuminated by the sublime golden beams of sunset, it was the first time she saw his body exposed. He was more beautiful than she could have imagined. She saw his well-built chest, the veins running down the interior of his beautifully made upper arms, his pale forearms, those elegant fingers. She saw the line of hair running all the way down the midline, past his belly button… His glasses were still on and his hair was pushed carelessly to the side and it curled deliciously around his cheekbones. She noted, almost subconsciously, the complete lack of self-awareness with which he moved, with which he held himself, a confidence that came from a lack of concern for anything but that which he had turned his mind to. She knew instinctively that would make him an incomparable lover. It was a vision she had not been prepared for and she quite lost herself just looking at him, her heart beating fast, imagining her hands on his body, what she would do first…

It was only the matter of a moment before he spoke again, though she felt she had been staring for some time. "I know it's a lot to ask." He came closer, and she sensed the heat from his body on her skin. She stood up close to him.

He reached past her, his chest brushing her arm, as he picked up the whiskey bottle. He took a large drink, then he poured some whiskey in his hand and rubbed it over a sharp shard of green glass he had managed to free from the lamp. "Will this work?" She stood looking blankly at the glass for a moment. "She only talks about Bon Jovi when she's drunk, so I don't trust her to do it."

"Oh shit," said Anna.

"Or do you want to go first?"

"No. No. I'll do you. I'll do your… uh… warding," Anna mumbled, lightly mortified.

"Which one is it, Candide?"

Attempting to stifle her sniggering, Candide pulled out the *Necronom-icon* and found the appropriate page. "This one should do it."

Eve looked at the picture doubtfully. "It's quite… intricate… isn't it…"

"Sorry."

"Okay, then. Let's get it over."

Anna became aware that her hand had started to shake. "Where? Are you sure you want me to?"

"Is that okay?"

She nodded.

"I guess, here." He put his hand up to his chest.

"Mmhmm. Um. Sit down." Anna felt every fibre of her body tightening into a sick knot. A light sweat broke out on her arms, her neck, her temple. She would not, could not say no. She would take this glass and cut the skin of this dear, lovely, beautiful man she adored, and she would not let him see how sick or sad she felt about doing it.

He sat in the chair where she had just been. Not sure how to get close enough to get purchase on his skin, she found herself obliged to push his legs apart and sit between them. She felt the rough woven wool of his trousers chafe the underside of her arms, so she sat up tall on her knees. She placed her hand on his naked chest for the first time. His skin was warm and soft and firm and she felt his heart beat strong. She put the glass to his chest.

"I can't," said Candide.

"Book, Candide," said Anna.

"Here." She placed it on the floor beside Anna.

"And it doesn't matter what order I do it in?"

"No, this says it just needs to look like this."

"Okay."

"Anna?"

"Yes?"

"Don't make it too small, okay?" And she went to the far side of the bed and telephoned down to the bar to order more whiskey.

Anna took a deep breath to prepare herself. "Eve... I'm really sorry I have to do this." She looked up and saw his face was perfectly calm.

"Me too," he said, and he smiled reassuringly.

He placed his hand on hers and pushed it down. Together, they made the first cut. She felt him tense, heard him breathe harder, felt the sweat break out on his body. He held tight to the arms of the chair as she continued the motion of the glass, but he did not pull away from her. She made more cuts. She saw the blood run down from his chest, over his belly button, and start to pool along the line of his belt. There was so much blood.

She cut him again. More blood than she had expected. She felt panic rising within and saw her tears fall, creating tiny pale pink streams that wound their way down and around the curves of his lovely body. "I'm so sorry, Eve," she whispered. "I'm so sorry." The whole day was closing in on her. She had been able to block it out in the talking and the drinking and the planning, but now, with his eyes on her, destroying his perfect form, the last lovely, perfect thing in her life, she felt weak and exhausted and helpless.

She was almost limp as Eve lifted her up onto his leg and pulled her in close, where she nestled her head into his neck and cried freely as he held onto her, stroking her hair and resting his head on hers until he felt her body become calm again. "I should never have asked you," he said. "I'm sorry. You seemed like you were doing okay."

"I always seem like I'm doing okay," she whispered. He understood. He understood in a way no one else could have. His gentle hand on her chin lifted her face up and as her sad eyes met his, she saw he understood. And they reached for one another and they kissed. Anna knew she would never again find another person in this world she could love the way she would love Eve, and she knew, on some level, he now belonged to her, as much as she did to him, whether he would accept that or not.

She felt Eve's hand reach for the glass and she pulled it away. "Anna, I'll finish it," he said.

"No. I want to." She meant it.

She shifted to his other leg and set the glass firmly against his chest. His arm wrapped around her waist, she felt his grip tighten on her delightfully with each stroke of the blade. She carved his skin, deep, in neat slices. She felt his other hand on her neck, in her hair, and he watched her all the while, mesmerised, his breath sharp at every cut, his heart beating hard under her other hand, his hand on her thigh now, his fingers deep in her flesh. Anna removed her shirt and wiped away the blood, over his chest, over his belly, along the line of his belt.

She picked up her glass of whiskey and looked into his enraptured grey eyes, in which she saw she was the only thing that existed for him now. She claimed her victory.

She poured the alcohol over the open wound and pushed gently but firmly on his chest as his body arched, writhed, in response to her action. Breathing hard and covered in sweat, he gazed at her, standing tall over him, a soft smile about her lips. She kissed him again.

They both knew from that time that nothing would ever be the same between them.

CHAPTER 23

SALVATION

Anna doused the shard of glass in whiskey and handed it to Eve. She turned the other chair backwards and straddled it with her back to him, and waited. Eve's hand was hot and delightful on her back as he pulled down her bra strap. Just as he touched the blade to her skin, they heard the screaming. The sound of loud, terrified wailing came from below them. Screeching, crying, begging—then nothing.

None of them moved. They did not make a sound. The inn was completely silent and still. Candide looked to the door to see it was locked and glanced meaningfully at Eve, who silently pushed the *Necronomicon* into a bag and gathered their other necessary belongings. Then they heard it.

Thud!

There was a heavy step on the stairs in the hall.

Thud!

It was deliberately measured and slow, as if to intimidate them.

Thud!

It worked.

Thud!

"Get ready to go," said Candide. She advanced towards the bed and pulled a pillowcase from the bedspread.

Thud!

She ripped it in half and grabbed the new whiskey bottle from the bedside table.

Thud!

She shoved the pillowcase into the bottle. "Anna, lighter!"

Thud!

"Candi, no."

Thud!

"Now, Anna."

Thud!

"You can't! Joe is still in there."

Thud!

"Only if I have to."

Thud!

"Anna, give it to me!"

Thud!

Pushing down all her humanity into her guts, Anna took the lighter from her pocket and threw it to Candide.

Thud!

"Did you soak it?" said Eve.

Thud!

"No! Do you think I'm an idiot?" came the reply.

Thud!

Candide lit the rag on fire.

Nothing. No sound. No more thuds.

The rag burned as they all stood tense, waiting.

"Where is it?"

"We've got to open the door," said Eve.

"No!"

"You can't just let it burn! We have to go."

"Oh, shit."

Eve grabbed the bag with the book and stood next to the door. He locked eyes with Candide. "On three," he mouthed silently. She nodded. "One, two, three." Eve flung the door open wide. They looked out into the darkness of the hall. Nothing. Silence.

Cautiously, they approached. Candide felt her hand become uncomfortably hot as the fire grew, moving ever closer to the alcohol.

The hall was dimmer than their own room had been, but still light enough to see there was no one else with them. Candide led them down the stairs. Eve and Anna followed reluctantly, not convinced it was the right thing to do, but not wanting to be left behind in the dark, either.

They made their way downstairs as quietly as possible, each of them knowing it was pointless trying to be silent because the thing must have known they were there already. They turned a corner into the bar.

"Holy shit," said Candide.

The lights were still on, the music was still playing, and everyone was dead. Each and every person who had been at the bar that night was lying, eyes wide open in terror, staring blankly across the room. The barman's head was sitting grotesquely on the bar, removed from his body. Their eyes followed the line of blood that ran from his freshly hewn head to the very edge of the bar, making a sickly noise as it drip-drip-dripped into the already-soaked carpet. One man at a table had clearly had his glass mug broken with the force of his face being repeatedly smashed into it until it became a permanent part of him. Another was missing his eyes entirely, his unseeing face pointing at them accusingly. Although there was a good deal of blood on the floor, the walls, and the tables, they did not have time to discover how the others had been murdered.

Thud!

"He's on the stairs," said Anna.

"How?" said Candi.

Anna ran to the door and flung it open. "Come on!" To her disbelief, neither Eve nor Candide came. Candide stood at the bottom of the stairs, the bottle ready to launch.

Thud!

Eve started rifling through the pockets of the dead. He quickly pulled out every set of keys he could find.

Thud!

"Let's go!" Anna yelled. Eve searched a final set of pockets, accidentally sending the still-warm corpse sprawling on the sticky floor. He ran to Candide, burning his hand as they removed the rag from the bottle. All retreated to the safety of the street.

Thud, thud, thud, thud! It was now moving faster down the stairs. They slammed the door behind them and instinctively ran across the road to the church.

"There's no way in," said Anna.

"Is this hallowed ground or something?" said Candide.

"I don't know. I don't think we can take the chance."

"Take," said Eve, handing them each the keys he had stolen. He started clicking the buttons, and they did the same. They ran down the street clicking as they went, trying each car they came across in the village.

"This is hopeless," said Candide. "Everyone will have walked to the inn."

"I don't have any other ideas," said Eve. "If we go into a house, that thing will kill whoever lives there."

They heard the doors of the pub crash open.

"Down here," whispered Anna. "Run!"

They moved quickly and quietly down the side of a house and through the back garden. They jumped a fence and, finding themselves in a new garden, ran towards the front of the house. They had arrived in a small, dark, cul-de-sac where there was but one car on the street. "All right, this one," said Eve, looking around. He passed his keys to Candide while Anna aimed hers at the car, clicking each button desperately. Eve walked around the car, picked up a rock from a garden and smashed the passenger side window.

"Eve!" said Anna.

He reached through and unlocked the other doors, then climbed into the driver's side seat. "Get in."

Candide did so without hesitation, but Anna remained on the street. "We don't have time to mess around with—" She heard a crack. Eve had already reached under the dash and ripped it open. She climbed into the car.

"Light!" said Eve. Candide held the lighter close as he pulled the wires out and, using the shard of glass from his pocket, started stripping them.

"What the f—" Anna's sentence was cut off by the engine starting. Eve hit the accelerator.

"Eve, the lock," said Candide.

"Shit. Hold on." He yanked the wheel hard and sharp to the right, breaking the steering-wheel lock.

"1986 Nissan…" said Candide.

"Right?"

"What are the chances?"

"Right?" Eve laughed.

"Can I just say you're both way more relaxed about this than I thought you would be?" Anna said.

Slightly panicked looks were exchanged between Eve and Candide.

"Whiskey," said Candide. "Lots of whiskey."

"Mmm," said Anna, watching them exchange another worried glance.

"Did anyone see if that was Joe?" asked Eve.

"I couldn't tell," said Candide.

"That was really too close," Anna replied. "My God, those poor people. Were they all dead?"

"I think so," Eve said.

"It's so horrible. Why would it do that? Just to get to us?"

"Eve, where are we going?" Candide asked.

"I don't know. The apartment?"

"Not yet. We need to be able to make a seal. Can we find a church?"

"At this time of night?"

"Don't Christians pray at night?

"No. They sleep. While we get chased by demons."

"One demon."

"One is enough."

"And it got Joe anyway, didn't it?"

"Maybe. Probably. Good point."

"Eve, where's the glass?"

"On the floor somewhere, I think."

Candide fumbled around for it, then climbed into the backseat with Anna.

"Anna, I think we should get on with it."

Anna felt a wave of nausea come over her as she realised what Candide meant. "Oh. Oh no. Not here…"

"Candide, no!" Eve said.

"It's you he wants," Candide said to Anna. "And he will catch up with us, eventually."

"Shit…" Anna knew Candide was right. Her mind quickly raced through all the possibilities and she concluded, like Candide must have, there was no way they would be able to feel safe unless they were all warded. "Can I have that?"

Candide passed her the whiskey bottle. She took a large drink.

"Absolutely not!" said Eve. "You are not doing that in a moving car."

"Eve, it's a goddamn demon," Candide replied. "You don't know what it's going to do. It could possess anyone. It might just jump in here right now and possess Anna. Or me."

"How is that even possible?"

"How is any of this possible? Anna, turn around, shirt off."

"Shit, no! Fine, just wait a second. I'll pull the car over," Eve said.

"No!" Anna and Candide yelled simultaneously.

"I feel much safer moving with you driving. Okay, Eve?" said Anna, taking her shirt off again.

"No, not okay!"

"No choice, Eve," she said.

"Keep it steady," called Candide. "Ready?"

"Ready."

Anna turned her back to Candide and leaned her head against the window. Candide pushed her spare hand firmly into Anna's back to keep her still, then brought the glass down to her skin.

"Oh wait, I need the book."

"Are you serious right now?" Eve threw the bags back to Candide.

"Lights on too, please." Eve sighed heavily as he reluctantly did as he was asked. Candide found the page in the book. "Are we ready?"

"I'm ready."

Candide pushed Anna hard against the window and made the first cut. Anna closed her eyes tight. She knew that crying out would only make it harder for Candide, and for Eve, who kept looking in the rearview mirror anxiously, so she tried to push the pain down and save everything for later.

She felt the familiar feeling of herself going numb, just as she had learned to do when she was a child. Her mind drifted, and she sunk into the darkness of the road, the white stripes going by so quickly they almost formed one line. The sound of the tires on the road lulled her and in her drunken state of disassociation, she felt almost nothing.

She wondered vaguely, as she stared through the cold glass, how many times a person can disassociate without losing themselves entirely. Is it time-limited? Do you eventually fade away forever? Do you lose all ability to feel or love or engage with the world around you? With the people you love?

Then she thought about Eve and Candide. She thought about feeling very real love and passion and excitement, the first she had known outside of books for many long years. And now, here she was feeling nothing again. Sinking back into that well-known and thoroughly despised emptiness that had always punctuated her life. And she hated it. And suddenly, she felt the glass deeper than ever and she cried out.

"Are you doing okay?" said Candide.

Anna let a few tears fall. "I'm good," she said. "Are we almost there?"

"Very nearly. Drink?"

"Yes." Anna took another sip of whiskey and held the bottle close to her as she pushed her head against the window. Candide finished slicing Anna's skin.

"All done. Do you want me to…"

"No. I can do it," said Anna. She rested the bottle on her shoulder and poured a trickle of whiskey down her back. She cried out in pain as she felt the searing heat of the alcohol pouring into the fresh wound.

Eve reached a hand back and touched her knee. She squeezed his hand tight, then sat up tall. "All right, Candide. Your turn."

"Look, there's a church," said Eve.

"Oh, thank God," said Candide.

"Seriously?" said Anna.

Candide laughed. Eve drove up on the pavement, pulling up next to the door. They rattled the huge wooden doors, but they were shut up tight.

"Hello?" Eve called. He walked around the church, looking for a way in. Candide and Anna grabbed the *Necronomicon*, whiskey and glass and ran after him.

The building was far bigger than the village church. It was made of heavy chunks of bluestone, set off with sandstone detail. It towered above them and as they traced along the side of the wall, it seemed to go on forever. Finally, reaching the back, they were illuminated by the multi-coloured rays of a gigantic stained-glass window. It depicted a skeleton, standing tall and eyeing them with two beady eyes in its stricken face, holding a yellow mass that was dripping with sparkling red blood. Yellow and orange and red and brown, it looked like a vision of Hell. They stood still for a moment, taking in the horrific vision.

Anna broke the silence. "What's it holding?"

"He's holding his skin," said Eve. "That's Saint Bartholomew. He was flayed alive."

"Oh," said Anna. Then, after a short pause, "You know, that's kind of…"

"Apt?"

"Apt."

"It's apt," Candide agreed.

"Anna," said Eve. "Do you think you could fit through that space— that really big swathe of skin there?" He grabbed the bottle of whiskey from Candide and took a large drink. He passed it to Anna.

"Maybe. It looks pretty big." She took a sip from the bottle and passed it back to Eve.

"Drink?" he said, passing the bottle to Candide. She too accepted the bottle, then passed it back to Eve. He finished what was left. "Well, all right then," he said. And with that, he flung the bottle and landed a blow exactly on the largest glass panel in the window.

Bright light streamed out of the church as a shower of yellow glass shards fell sparkling to the ground in front of them.

"Eve!" Candide cried, clearly delighted, but Anna was already at the wall waiting for Eve to lift her up. He pulled off his sweater, groaning in pain as the dried blood sticking it to his chest ripped his wound open afresh. He gave it to her to use to protect her from the broken glass she was about to clamber over, but she insisted it was far too nice to be used in such a manner. He declared that it was ruined already, citing blood stains on pale blue. She declared that it could and should be saved because it was really a lovely thing. "Hurry up!" yelled Candide.

Anna put her hands on Eve's shoulders, and he put his around her waist. She pushed hard against him as he lifted her up. With sturdy oxfords, black today, she kicked at the opening where stubborn shards of jagged glass still clung on tight to the wrought iron that held the window together. She pulled herself through gingerly. It was a long drop down into the church below and she did not want to slide on the shards of glass covering the floor. She pulled her legs up into a crouching position and aimed for the altar.

With a crash she found her target, sending flowers, candlesticks, relics, all manner of religious iconography smashing to the floor. "Shit!" She got up and ran to the front of the church. To her relief, the doors were only held closed by a large plank of wood. Using all her strength, she pushed it up and out of the huge brackets that held it in place and sent it crashing to the floor.

Seconds later, Candide and Eve arrived.

"You are completely amazing, Anna, do you know that?" As he said it, Eve grabbed her around the waist and pulled her close, planting a kiss on her cheek. Anna said nothing, being too surprised and utterly smitten at the change in him. She proudly ushered them into the church, and they all pushed the doors closed behind them.

"We did it!" said Candide. "Holy shit, we actually did it."

"Woah, this place is huge," said Eve, moving forward.

They stepped around the corner, and a wide atrium opened in front of them. Rows and rows of wooden pews were hung over with gigantic, wrought-iron candelabras dangling from the high ceiling. The ceiling itself was painted with bright, gaudy images of characters, presumably, Anna supposed, from the Bible.

As they walked forward, the pulpit rose up in front of them. Dark mahogany, it was carved with all manner of bizarre animal images —cats, rabbits, dogs, and other strange creatures, half-animal, half-human.

To their right was the altar Anna had desecrated, the floor wet with water from the vases she had upended. They curved around behind the pulpit where they found a door. "This has to be it," said Candide.

"I'll get a candle," said Anna. She found a dry one on the floor and Candide lit it with the cigarette lighter. Passing through the door, they found a small office.

They searched the room, opening one filing cabinet after another, rifling through the drawers of a desk. Candide lifted the lace cloth off a table at the back of the room. "Look!" she shouted. She pulled the cloth off and sent a large wooden cross and several pictures of Jesus Christ smashing to the ground. "It's locked."

Anna picked up the cross. "Stand back." Eve and Candide took a step away from the box as Anna brought the huge cross down, smashing the lock off the box and splitting the cross in two. She discarded the pieces, and they flipped the lid open. Inside, they saw ancient texts, strange relics, bizarre artefacts. "Careful. These look important," said Anna. They placed each item delicately on the desk behind them. Eventually, they found a small wooden box at the bottom, just like the one Joe had brought to Eve's apartment. "This is it!"

They opened the box and found several vials of the precious red liquid inside.

"Is that all?" asked Candide doubtfully.

"Looks like," said Anna. "Will it be enough for the apartment?"

"It will have to be," said Candide. "All right. That means it's my turn now."

"Oh. Oh no."

"Yep. Let's get it done before we leave the church. He won't find us here, but come daylight someone is going to come open this place up. We have to be gone."

Anna looked around the office. There was a large glass and wood cabinet none of them had paid much attention to in their previous search. "That's where they keep the wine!" said Anna triumphantly.

Eve looked over the labels. "Some of this is really old. I wonder what it's worth."

"Or if it's any good," said Anna.

"Just take the oldest one." Candide took three silver chalices from the box while Eve grabbed a bottle from 1967 and they made their way back out into the church.

"I suppose this is as good a place as any," said Candide, climbing up onto the white cloth of the altar. She took her shirt off and lay her beautiful body out long. "Which of you is less drunk now?"

"I'll do it," said Eve.

Anna knew he would not soon recover from the deliberate mutilation of the best friend he had spent most of his life caring for. "No, I'm very sober now," she lied. "Plus I have experience. I'll do it." Anna dipped the green shard of glass into her cup of wine.

Eve looked over at her. "Anna—"

"I want to do it. Go sit." There was a quick exchange of looks between Anna and Evelyn, and in that she convinced him he should not try to overrule her.

And so they sat in the church, bathed in the light of a thousand fake, flickering candles, chatting, drinking sacramental wine, as the

Necronomicon sat open in front of them. Anna carved the demon-warding symbol into Candide's back, staining the white altar-cloth red with the blood of her closest friend, as her own blood continued to trickle slowly down her back. Although their night was long, their wine was very good and they all openly enjoyed the experience far more than they would ever admit to anyone who wasn't there that night.

CHAPTER 24

CONFESSION

C andide had eventually fallen asleep where she lay on the table. Anna sat by her, stroking her hair gently while she recovered from the warding. Anna watched the various shades of gold, champagne and honeycomb as they ran through her fingers, and found herself mesmerised by how beautiful it all was. How jealous she had been only a few days prior; how that had all changed now. All she saw now was her lovely, smart, caring friend, and she wanted her to be successful, and she wanted her to be beautiful, and she wanted nothing but good things for them both.

She daydreamed, as she played with the soft hair, about how wonderful things might be. How if none of this had happened she might not have this bond with Candide, but from here, maybe they would settle into that life she had dreamed of; nights of wine snuck into the library to drink by the roaring fire, reading their books quietly together, long conversations about the greatest minds and greatest works in history. Or perhaps Candi would want to go back to her old life, to those friends she was out drinking with only a few nights earlier. It was a lifetime ago.

Eve sat on a pew, smoking a cigarette and staring off into space, a silver chalice of wine balanced on the seat next to him. He looked as though he, too, were lost in a daydream. He didn't notice as Anna traced her eyes over his chest, still bleeding from where she had warded him, followed the arch of his elegant wrist as he held his cigarette, memorised the shape of his lips as he let go a breath of smoke. He looked glorious.

Anna suddenly became crushingly aware of how she must look by comparison, also covered in blood, but her hair a mess, wearing only a bra on her top half. She looked down at her stomach, protruding over her trousers in her thoughtlessness. She straightened her back, adjusted what clothing she had, and wrapped her arms around herself.

Her movement must have caught his attention, because she glanced up to see Eve looking back at her. Their eyes locked for a moment and he turned away, flushed. She did the same, recognising at once that no man had ever looked at her quite like that before.

An awkward moment of silence passed until he chivalrously filled it. "It is good wine." Picking up the silver goblet, he said, "I feel like we're justified in taking this, but if we took a bottle home for later, it would be stealing."

"I think if they knew what we've been through, they would want us to have it," Anna replied.

Their eyes met again. Another moment of silence.

"You seem like you're holding up pretty well, considering everything," he said.

"I don't want to talk about it. I don't think I can keep it up if I think about it too much."

"Then we won't."

She came over and sat on the pew next to him.

"Thanks for taking care of her," he said. "I'm not sure I could bring myself to do it."

"I know."

"Wine?"

"Mmm."

He emptied the bottle into the silver cup and passed it to her with the cigarette.

"When she was little," he said, looking over at Candide, "maybe four or five, our parents all went out for the night and left me in charge, as usual. They told me not to let her on the top bunk, but I was a kid, and she was Candide, and she was always like this, so I let her... She fell, of course. She broke her collarbone. I had to go and call the ambulance while she sat on the floor screaming for her mother, begging me not to leave her. Then I sat on hold to the restaurant, while she cried and cried for me. Then I waited with her until they came. And then I got the blame for it all."

"Eve, that's horrible!"

"I know. I knew it even then. The next week they all went out again anyway. I had to look after her, give her pain medication and antibi- otics. I had to pick the movies to help her stay calm. If she had nightmares because I picked the wrong one, that was my fault, too." His eyes remained on Candide, worried, the memories clearly still fresh in his mind.

"They sound awful," Anna said, holding back what she truly thought.

"They weren't. I think. Maybe they were. I don't know. I think they just weren't ready for kids. Whatever my mother came up with, they all went along with it. They didn't know she was manic at the time, of course. They just put it down to the 'intensity of genius'. Anyway," he sighed and smiled and finally looked over at her, "the point is, Candide and I have been through... a lot together. A lot. I know it seems weird how we are with each other, but we pretty much brought each other up. To tell the truth, it feels almost like I've been conditioned to take care of her. And she doesn't bring it up much, but she's still trying to get over losing her parents. And everything else. It's just… Thanks for putting up with us. How we are together. No one else… Not many people could, or would, kind of, slot in so easily, as you have." He blushed a little, stumbling over whatever he was trying to get out, finishing with a non-committal, "I'm happy she has you."

Anna smiled back at him with a raised eyebrow as she passed the cigarette over. "You're happy I'm in Candide's life?"

"I am."

"Is that all?"

"No." Even so, even as he blushed a shade darker and looked away, he declined to say more.

She assessed his discomfort and pushed forward, undaunted. "Candide told me about the trouble she had last year, with a teacher. She didn't say who it was, though. I thought for a while it was you…"

The look of mortification on his face made her regret her comment immediately. "You did?"

"Just for a while."

He was quiet for a moment, looking around the church, going over their history in his mind. "Well, that explains a lot."

"Sorry."

"No… That really explains a lot." He looked back at her in confusion. "I don't know if it makes me feel better or worse knowing that's what you thought."

"It seems so ridiculous now," she laughed.

"Seriously, it's fine." And he smiled again, resigned. "I'm appalled at how it all must have looked to you. That's exactly why she and I need to keep some distance. Candide isn't going to get the opportunities I get. She made one stupid mistake last year and now she's had to change her major. She's already given up on what she really wanted."

"What? I thought it was always languages."

"No, I bet she told you that, though. It was supposed to be art history."

"Oh. Oh…"

"And it's worse than she even realises. She just sees the students, hears what they say about her. She has no idea what the staff say about her."

"But… that's awful!"

"That's awful. She has all this waiting for her. People who judge her, people who won't believe she did her own work, people who think they can get her to do anything for a good grade. I've heard them say truly horrible things. Not least of all that hideous woman."

"I hope you said something."

"I did. Which didn't go well. I'm trying to convince her to change back to art history, but she's still mortified. Maybe next year."

Anna took the cigarette back from him, puffed out a cloud of smoke and redirected the conversation. "You can't look after her forever, you know. She's an adult now."

"I know. And the first year out, that happened. I'm trying my best to let her be, but… It's been hard."

"And now all this."

"And now all this, with a ghost and a demon and this church—"

"And this." She caught him with her dark eyes and whatever he might have been about to say next froze on his lips. He took the cigarette she handed him and put it out in the empty wine bottle.

She heard it sizzle and watched the smoke slowly dissipate into nothingness, and she waited, and still he said nothing.

They sat that way, quiet for a while, then they felt the atmosphere shift with each and every second they remained silent together, becoming heavier, more urgent. Anna chanced another look up at him, and he down at her, and they both smiled and looked away again.

"It's cold," she said, and shifted herself over against him.

"Should I find my sweater?" he replied, casting his eyes around.

"No," she said, watching him steadily. He smiled bashfully, but still he put his arm around her and rubbed hers for warmth. She felt the heat from his body, smelled his scent, and she leaned in closer, though she knew he meant his touch more as a friendly, brotherly touch than she would have liked. She found her body fit perfectly with his, her every curve moulded exactly as if for the sole purpose of allowing it to be closer to him.

She looked down at his hand on her arm and compared how big it was to hers. His fingernails were dirty and dried blood stained his skin, but the fingers were long and manly and beautifully formed. Slowly, tentatively, she let her fingers brush his, tracing her fingertips along the very edges of his.

At that, his grip tightened a little. He shifted his gaze down again, and she felt his breath warm on her cheek. He slid his hand softly up her arm, over her naked shoulder, up the back of her neck, and lost it in her hair. She felt a delightful shiver right down to her toes as he played with the strands. Her stomach tightened into a delicious knot and her heart pounded in her chest as his other hand reached across and turned her face gently up to his. Their lips met. The kiss in the church was long and sweet and easily the most holy experience Anna had ever had. Then they looked into one another's eyes for a brief moment, both lost in complete adoration of the other, then his face fell, and he pulled away from her and leaned forward, burying his face in his hands.

"What the hell is wrong with me?" he muttered. "It's like I can't be alone with you for five minutes without kissing you."

Anna turned cold with his words, steeled for what was bound to come next. "Eve, don't do that."

"Do what?"

"What I think you're about to do."

"Anna—"

"No. I'm not listening to you."

"Anna—"

"I thought things had changed."

"Things have changed."

"You just kissed me! You kissed me three times tonight!"

"I know. I know. I'm sorry! I got caught up in the moment and—"

"That's bullshit."

"That's not bullshit! I just…"

"Just what!"

"I shouldn't have kissed you. I'm sorry. You're right. Some things have changed, a lot has changed, but some things haven't and we can't do this. That… was a shitty thing to do, and I just… I wasn't thinking about how things are, when I did that, just then…"

"And how is that, exactly, 'the way things are'?"

"Anna—"

"No. I want you to tell me. I don't understand anything that's happening in my life right now. My apartment and my scholarship and, God, everything! But I thought I knew what was going on here at least… and apparently I don't. So please, could you just explain to me—"

"Fine. I'll... I'll be honest with you." He took a moment to gather his thoughts, then, "I just met you and you are... You seem to be my perfect match in every way possible, and I can't do a thing about it. And it's awful. And I feel awful about it. I don't know how this happened or why, because you're not even supposed to be here—"

Her voice came soft and sweet. "I'm your perfect match?"

He reacted in kind. "Is that excessive?"

"Not for us, no."

"See, it's that, right there. You know exactly what I mean."

She took his hand and wound his arm back around her. He didn't resist, leaning his body in close against her. He thought for a time and said, as much to himself as to Anna, "What kind of relationship would we be able to have, anyway? We could never tell anyone. It would be all stolen kisses in dark hallways, secret meetings in crumbling towers, hastily penned Keats secreted in ancient stonework for one another to find." He laughed softly. "Nothing like normal people have."

A light sweat broke out on Anna's hands and along her arms. She shifted in her seat slightly and raised her eyes up to Eve appreciatively. He looked away to hide his smile. "Stop it."

"Stop what?"

"Are you flirting with me right now?"

"You're flirting with me!"

"Am not!"

"That was definitely flirting, so I'm not not flirting."

"Damn it, Anna. I'm supposed to be putting an end to this. That's the opposite of what I want right now." She put her hand on his knee. "Stop it!"

"Are you saying you can't resist me?"

"I'm finding it incredibly hard."

She moved her hand up to his thigh. "Incredibly hard, did you say?"

He pulled her hand off his leg. "Anna James, we're in church." She laughed and leaned back into the pew. "You're not even taking this seriously," he said, trying not to laugh himself.

"Okay, let's be serious. Is that really all it is? Tell me honestly: if I quit Endymion tomorrow, would things be different?"

He was shocked she had even uttered the words. "You wouldn't quit Endymion!"

"No, of course I wouldn't. Not for you or any other man. Hypothetically, would that change things?"

The silence fell heavily over them both, and for Anna, it felt like it would never end. Eve made no motion, no sign he was making a life-altering decision that would seal both their fates. She became increasingly nervous as the seconds passed, until eventually…

"No."

No longer did he joke, and no longer did his eyes sparkle like they had moments earlier, like they were wont to do almost every time he was in her presence, though neither had yet realised that. "No, Anna, things wouldn't be different. I can't have a relationship with you, or anyone else, and that's all there is to it." She sensed she had accidentally stumbled on something new. Something, whatever it was, that had suddenly made his resolve completely clear and firm in his mind.

"Is there more than you've told me?"

"Yes."

"Will you tell me?"

"No."

"And that's it?"

"Yes."

She stomped her foot on the floor and Candide's sleeping body flinched at the loud noise that echoed through the church. "Then you know what? Stop kissing me. And stop putting your arm around me." She shoved him off. "And stop saying nice things and looking at me like—like every time you look at me! Because if you don't like me—"

"Anna, I like you. So much. I like you more than I can put into words."

She looked at him in disbelief. "Why the hell would you tell me that?"

"Because it's true! You wanted me to be honest with you—"

"Your honesty is making me feel like shit, Eve! Keep it to yourself and tell me you don't like me, like a normal person would. Tell me it would never work out and have done with it. And then I'll go and pretend none of this happened. None of this was real. And we'll be strangers again and, eventually, I will be fine with this."

"That's not what I want!"

"That's what I want! I can't have someone like you in my life, telling me you want me, but you won't have me. How did you think that was going to go, telling me something like that?"

"I didn't think—"

"No, you didn't think."

"What I think is…" He sighed and put his hand up to his forehead and rubbed it. "I think I'm falling in love with you, Anna."

The anger went out of her in an instant. "What?"

He continued his stream of thought unchecked by her plea for repetition of the previous sentiment: "And I just met you, and that's ridiculous. I hardly know you, you hardly know me, we're in this weird situation… and I can't do a thing about it… and if I do this wrong… you'll never like me the way I like you… and you're not supposed to like me the way I like you! So I shouldn't even think about that. But I do. A lot. And it's awful. This whole thing is awful—"

"Eve…"

"What?"

"You're waffling."

"I am. Sorry."

She fixed her bright, clear eyes on him. "It's very sexy."

He laughed again, in spite of everything. "Stop it! I'm supposed to be breaking up with you."

She shrugged. "You can't break up with me if you won't start seeing me in the first place."

"Anna, be realistic. When we go back, and this is over, we're not Eve and Anna who fight demons, or steal cars or desecrate churches. We're Eve and Anna, who are neighbours at Endymion College, and I'm your teacher. And you're my student. Everything I just told you about Candide—that's what would be waiting for you if people found out we were in a relationship. And then there's everything else. And this isn't how I want things to be, but it's how they are."

"So what happens now? We just carry on living down the hall from each other like you didn't just tell me all these things? We live separate lives, and what, see other people?"

"If that's what you want. I don't want anyone else. I think you should, though."

"You want me to see other people?"

"Yes."

"But not you…"

"Yes."

"And you don't want to see other people?"

"No."

"And what if I fall in love with someone else and this, whatever this is, this never happens?"

"Then I'll go and read sad poetry alone in my room."

She felt a smile soften both her face and her heart considerably. "Is that very different to now?"

"Not really, no."

"You're a really strange person, Evelyn."

"So are you, Anna."

There really was no point discussing it any further. He was sweet and playful and funny again, but he was firm and clear too, and despite his waffling and poorly ordered thoughts and excuses, she believed every word he said. "Just... Eve, if this is how it's going to be, please don't say those nice things to me anymore. And please don't touch me like you do. Not ever again unless you mean it. You of all people should know, touch has a memory—"

"I don't want to kill it, Anna. And I don't want to be free." Perhaps it had been a test and Evelyn didn't miss a beat. She knew he was right, and that he was undeniably her perfect match: her other half. It was the first time she had felt unable to control her tears during the entire conversation and she turned her face away to hide from him. He dealt the killing blow. "I want to be with you and I can't. It's just how things are. I'm sorry. Maybe I shouldn't have told you that, but I don't want you to think that's... I don't want you to think I wasn't genuine. Or that you were wrong about any of this. Because I really wish things were different."

They were both quiet again for a few moments until he said, "Do you hate me?"

"No. I don't hate you. That's the weirdest... nicest... stupidest rejection I've ever had."

"It's not a rejection."

"Don't say things like that, Eve!"

He reached out a hand for hers. "Don't," she said, breathing in his scent and his warmth and his closeness for the last time. She wiped away a final, silent tear, hoping Eve wouldn't notice, then she pushed all the emotion deep down inside her where she couldn't feel it, and it was all over.

She looked up at the smashed, stained-glass window, shimmering in the first rays of sunshine. "We have to go. Is the car going to work?"

"It should do."

"Okay. Let's go fight a demon."

Anna avoided Eve's worried glances, and they didn't speak to each other at all as they gathered their belongings. They picked up the box with the warding fluid, they packed the *Necronomicon*, and Anna took another bottle of very old wine after all. Eve wrapped the linen around Candide as she slept, then he gently woke her, whispering something or other in her ear. He picked her up, still wrapped in the cloth, and they made their way out of the church, Candide resting her head sleepily on Eve's shoulder. He placed her in the back seat and closed the door behind her. Anna skirted the car, looking forward to a long, silent drive where she could stare out the window and quietly hate herself and wonder why things always went so completely wrong no matter what she touched, but then she was called back to reality by Eve's voice.

"Are we okay?"

It was a stupid question really, but it wasn't the words she noticed. She looked at him, and had it been anyone else, perhaps she wouldn't have been okay. But he adored her. She could see it right there on his face. Whatever was going on, she suddenly realised it wasn't her at all, and it wasn't Eve either, and there was something that, just for a moment, she recognised as pure and light and beautiful and utterly untouchable between them. She thought he recognised it too.

"We're okay," she replied, and they exchanged melancholy, hopeful, tired smiles over the car. Anna climbed in next to Candide, and by the time Anna fastened Candide's seatbelt around her, Eve had the car running again.

CHAPTER 25
BURNING UP

"Are we going straight back to the apartment?" asked Anna.

"Yes," said Candide, yawning. "We'll go in, ward the shit out of that place, then figure out how to exorcise Joe."

"It's going to be harder than last time. Eve could just hold you while I said the words. Joe looks really strong." Eve's eyes flicked over to Anna as she said it. "What? He looks strong."

"Yeah, no, he does," Eve conceded. "He's a good-looking sort of guy."

"That's not my point."

"Still. He is. Really good looking, actually."

"Anyway," interjected Candide, "I don't think we can count on him keeping still for us. Maybe we can knock him out."

"Knock him out?" Eve said. "This isn't a movie, Candide. We could give him brain damage. Or kill him."

"If it's even Joe," said Anna.

"Yeah," said Candide. "What if it's not even Joe? It could be anyone. Oh God, if it's not Joe, he's probably just finding out about the priest being murdered."

"And if it is," Anna replied, "he had to watch himself murder him."

"And all those other people."

"What does that even do to a person?"

"Would he even want to live?"

Eve looked askance at Candide. "That's not our decision to make."

"No, I'm just philosophising," she replied.

"I mean, he's with the church," Anna said. "They have these kits everywhere. They must, sort of, expect this, just as a part of life. Do they do some kind of training, like emotional preparation for what to do when you get possessed and kill a bunch of people?"

"I wonder," Candide replied. "That's a serious workplace health and safety issue."

"Still, they didn't take it too seriously the other day. It's a demon. Do you usually just send one random guy to fight off a maniacal demon?"

"Do you feel like demons are maniacal by definition?"

"And we're here," said Eve.

"Where?"

"We're about three blocks from the university. We'll dump the car here. I need your tablecloth."

"It's a bit bloody," said Candide. She passed it to Eve and put her shirt back on as he wiped the car over with the white portion of the cloth. "For fingerprints? I think it's already covered in our DNA."

"Yeah, but I'm hoping they'll never get around to testing it," he replied.

"That only works for rape kits," Candide said. "We should burn it."

"How the hell are we going to burn it?"

"Or we could drive it off a bridge."

"What bridge? We have to get back. It's already daylight and we look like members of a satanic cult who just murdered a bunch of people." Candide and Anna shrugged in reluctant agreement with his statement. He continued, "We don't know who that thing is going to kill next. We have to stop it."

"No, Eve," said Anna, "Candide's right. We have to burn it. There's a pub full of dead people and a stolen car. Testing this thing is going to be top priority."

"How can we burn it?"

"Drive us to the field."

"It's right by our home, Anna."

"Do you have a better idea, Eve?"

"No, but I don't think—"

"Move it!"

Eve started the car again and after a short, silent drive, they parked in the centre of the damp, grassy field and surrounded the car.

"Pop the cap," Anna said.

Eve did so a little reluctantly.

Anna took the cloth, doused in Candide's blood, and stuffed it into the petrol tank until it became soaked with petrol.

"It won't work," said Candide. "No oxygen in there."

"I know," Anna replied.

"Also, it's the gas that combusts, not the liquid."

"I know that, Candide! Go away! Run to those trees and hide. We'll have to sneak back through the forest."

"Anna, let me do it," said Eve.

"No! It's my idea. Go away."

"Come on, Anna."

"Hurry up! I don't want to get caught."

He remained for a moment, uncertain, but Candide pulled on his arm and led him away. Anna pulled the cloth from the petrol tank and wiped it, dripping, all over the interior of the car. She spread it over the steering wheel and driver's seat and as far into the back as it would reach. She opened each window part-way before closing the doors, then she clicked the flame alight and threw the lighter through a window. The entire car was aflame in an instant. By the time she reached the safety of the forest with Eve and Candide, her first attempt at stolen vehicle arson had become a roaring success.

"You're amazing," said Candide.

"It was your idea," Anna blushed.

"She's right," said Eve. "You're incredible." He reached for her hand but she pulled hers away and led them along the treeline until they came out onto the pavement behind their building. They looked up at the hanging door.

"There's no way we can reach it," said Anna. "We have to go around."

"All right. Listen, it's vital no one sees us."

"This again, Eve?" said Anna.

"Not this again. You're covered in blood and you smell of gasoline."

"Well, you're not looking so hot yourself," she said, knowing it was a bald-faced lie.

"Hurry up!" said Candide. "The car will blow as soon as the air gets through to the tank."

They traced along the back of the building and around the side. The courtyard was deserted. They bolted into the apartment building and just made the base of the stairs when they heard the explosion.

"Shit! Run! Run!"

Anna got her key into the lock as they heard voices, and doors opening and closing downstairs.

"Hurry up!"

"I am!" Anna pushed the door wide open, and they all tumbled in. Eve's fingers were caught in the door in an attempt to stop the noise of it closing in such a hurry.

"Oh shit, are you okay?"

"Yeah," he laughed. "I'll be fine."

"We made it!" said Candide.

"I can't believe we made it!" said Anna.

"Can we please eat before we do the next thing?" said Eve. "I can't remember the last time I ate."

"Neither!" said Anna.

"Let's look in the kitchen." Candide started towards the kitchen, then froze. She traced her steps backwards as Joe Bruno advanced slowly out of the kitchen.

"Finally," he said, throwing Anna's copy of *Frankenstein* down onto the coffee table. "It's a good story, but I'm ready for something... a little more... violent."

CHAPTER 26

OH SHIT!

Joe stood before them, pale and gaunt, eyes sunken and dark. His black cloth was muddy and his face, hands and white collar were stained dark with dried blood. He stood unnaturally tall and erect given his clearly diminished state. Overall, he gave the air of a corpse recently given the ability to walk.

"Welcome home," he said. "I have been waiting for you."

They stood where they were, all three of them speechless, none of them sure what to say or do.

"You were hungry? Go make some food. Go. I can wait. I want to talk to you all. But this 'Joe', I can feel him screaming inside. He screams that he is hungry, too. He needs to eat. Make something for him. You." He pointed to Anna. "You go make it. And no funny stuff. If you do anything to this body, your poor friend suffers."

Anna, unsure, started to break away from the group, but Eve grabbed her hand, which she was happy to take this time.

"No, no. You let her go. Or I will kill you all." He clicked his fingers. "Just like that."

Anna squeezed Eve's hand and slipped away. She poked around in the kitchen cupboards for something fast and, without thinking too thoroughly about the nutritional value, she emptied several packets of ramen into a large pot to cook. She filled four glasses with water and returned to the living room to see Eve and Candide sitting uncomfortably on the couch. She put the glasses on the table.

"Thank you," said Joe. "Now," he picked up the glass, "I will drink this and your friend will not die today." He drank the water. "And the food?"

"It's coming," said Anna.

"Ah, good girl. You sit right there." She sat on the armchair as directed. "We have so much to talk about, but we will wait until we eat, all right? This Joe is very noisy. Not like you." He nodded towards Candide. "I think you enjoyed it, didn't you? Sometimes it's nice not to have to think for a while." She only watched with frightened eyes and made no reply.

"The three of you have been very busy making marks on each other. You probably think I can't kill you now. I am very sorry to have to tell you: that is not correct," he laughed. "Your little marks have made it hard for me to touch you with my bare hands, but I don't need to touch you to kill you. I can just pick up this coffee table and bam! I can smash it into your heads again and again and you will be pulp on the floor. It's very easy for me to kill you still. But! Is that food ready yet?"

Anna, pale and heart beating fast, returned to the kitchen to fetch it. She put the four bowls down on the table with shaking hands and sat again in the armchair opposite Joe. Candide still clutched the bags containing the *Necronomicon* and the items they had taken from the church, nestling them as safely as possible between herself and Eve.

"Eat," said Joe with his mouth already full. Anna, Eve and Candide did not move. "Oh, I always forget," he laughed. "Humans never seem to want to eat when demons come to dinner. Still, you should.

I am going to make a deal with you, so I won't have to kill you today. You will be hungry if you decide to live."

"What do you want?" asked Evelyn.

"Ah, I am so glad you asked! That book you have there, in that bag. I want it."

"The Necronomicon?"

"Yes."

"That's all?"

"Yes. That's all."

"And you'll just leave us alone? And go away?"

"Yes."

"Joe too?"

"Yes, Joe too. You can have him back."

Anna, Eve and Candide looked at one another, unsure what to do.

"I know," said Joe. "It seems too good to be true, doesn't it? But for all the things demons do, once we make a deal, we stick to it." He put the bowl carefully down on the table. "This," he motioned to the empty bowl, "is a sign of my good faith to you. I did this for your friend."

"But all those people…" said Anna.

"All the people I killed?" He looked at her, expressionless.

"Why did you do it?"

"Isn't it obvious? I didn't want you to get the warding fluid, so I killed the priest. Those people in the inn? I killed them for fun. And because I knew it would scare you. Did it scare you?" They looked on in horror as he snickered to himself. "The truth is, I like it here in this nice apartment. I like you all! And I really want that book. I couldn't let you ward this room before I got it, so I killed people."

He looked over at Eve. "Also, I thought to myself, if I could have that exquisite body, I could have a lot of fun and look good at the same time! But then you warded it, so I guess you get to keep it."

"So you did want him all along! And the dreams..." said Anna.

"The dreams?" asked Joe.

Eve and Anna exchanged abashed glances across the coffee table.

"Oh, you think I'm an incubus? Is that why you cut each other up?" He clapped his hands and laughed as the two uncomfortably forced their eyes anywhere but towards each other. "Wonderful! Wonderful! No, I didn't give you the dreams, but please know, I would have had a wonderful time with you, Anna, in his body. You would have had a wonderful time, too." Now she did look up and locked eyes with the demon. "Then I would have had him watch, helpless, as I pulled out your teeth, one by one, with his bare hands. Then we would have pulled your fingernails off, one by one, then your toenails! And then, I would swap bodies, and we would carry on doing that, and other things, until you were both dead. Or maybe I would have let him live. Can you imagine how he would suffer the rest of his life with that memory? Exquisite! Ah, it is a lot for me to give up, but I want the book, so I have to make that sacrifice. Give me the book and I will, regretfully, let you all go."

The three remained silent, wan and sickened by his comments, unable to respond, the horrific imagery playing out in each of their minds.

"Okay," he sighed, "now I am getting bored and I feel like I want to kill you all again. So! Before I get carried away, take the book from that bag, rip the cover off, and give it to me."

"What do you want it for?" asked Candide.

"The Book of the Dead? As you can see, you have only had it a few days and you're already warded. Imagine if everyone had a copy of the book? Imagine if someone like Joe had the book? No, no. That means no more fun for me and my kind. We so rarely visit these days as it is. I only came because I sensed the book was here."

"You just came for the book? Nothing else?"

"Of course. Oh!" He giggled and put his hand to his face in mock embarrassment. "Oh, you thought I came for you? Like you are all some sort of chosen ones? No, you are nothing to me. I sensed the book was here, and I was waiting, haunting you just a little bit, and then voila! You had your little séance, it opened the gateway, and I just stepped through. Your little friend tried to warn you though, didn't he? 'Run!' he said. You did not listen. And now he is suffering too." Candide and Eve screwed up their faces in confusion at his comments, but again he fixed Anna with his gaze. "They don't remember him, but you do, don't you? And it makes you feel so very alone, like when you were a child, when these two don't understand you. You should learn not to be so trusting of them. They don't trust you and they are lying to you."

"Anna—" Evelyn started. The demon cut him short.

"Shut your mouth or I will kill you." His eye shot back to Anna. "It's a shame. If I possessed you that first day, I think we could have seduced them both, don't you? And then, who knows... Alas, she is far prettier, so I thought I had a better chance inside her. We demons cannot know everything. Most things, though, we know. That's why you should always listen to me, Anna. I think we would be good together. But anyway, it was fun while it lasted. Now you, Candide, is it? You take your pretty hands, rip the cover off that book and give it to me, and I will go."

"No."

"I'm sorry. It sounded like you said 'no'."

"I said n—"

"But I know you didn't say no, because this boy..." He walked over to the heavy bookshelf and with one hand sent it crashing down onto the floor, blocking the doorway. All three jumped up from their chairs, looking for and failing to find any sort of weapon more powerful than a scented candle or a paperback in their sparsely if exquisitely decorated apartment. The demon walked back over to the coffee table and kicked it over, sending bowls and noodles smashing to the floor. He ripped one leg away from it. "This boy…" He approached Eve, who was backed into the wall as Joe cracked the wooden leg in two with his bare hands, leaving a sharp stake, which he extended out and under Eve's chin. "I will skin this beautiful boy alive."

"No!" cried Candide.

"Oh yes!" He ripped the stake down Eve's neck and across his still-naked chest, which dripped fresh blood as the weapon left its mark. Eve pushed the stake away and with a quick flip of his hand, Joe drove the stake directly through the centre of Eve's palm, impaling it against the wall. Eve screamed in pain, Anna and Candide in horror.

Joe raised his voice above them. "Believe me, I don't need to touch you myself to skin you alive. Would you believe it's even more painful that way?" Joe wrenched the stake out of Eve's hand. He turned, and in one fast movement, threw the stake directly into Anna's shoulder. She fell to the floor in a spatter of blood. Eve launched himself at Joe, who easily threw him over his shoulder and into Anna, cracking the stake and embedding it further still into her shoulder.

"When I skin your friend alive," Joe said, walking towards Candide, "the ward comes off. Then I will use his body, without any skin, of course, to kill her. Slowly. She won't like that. And you will, eventually, do whatever I say. But then it will be too late for your friends. Sit!" Candide obediently returned to the couch, and Joe sat back down in the armchair. "Now, you see, this is a lot of work for me. Skin him, kill her, torture you with his dead body. And the screams! People will come running. I will have to kill each and every one of them. Except Joe. I will let him live. He suffers more that way. Have you ever seen a man of the cloth struggle with whether to kill himself or not? It is sublime. And let me tell you, he already has a lot of issues. But, I digress. You can choose all this pain, all this suffering, or... you take the cover off that book, give the book to me, I disappear out of your lives and you never hear from me again."

As Joe was talking to Candide, Anna took Eve's good hand and guided it up her back to where half the stake remained embedded deeply in her shoulder. Breathing heavily with the pain, she nodded at him. His eyes widened, and he shook his head. "Do it," she whispered. She saw him furrow his brow and close his eyes in an attempt to block out reality for a brief moment and then she stared straight forward at Joe as Eve's hand tightened on the stake. He pulled as hard as he could and she did not make a sound as the muscle and shattered bone let go of the weapon. Eve put his arm around her and pulled her in close, thinking she had only wanted the stake removed from her shoulder. She reached for the bloody weapon and held it tight.

"Now, you tell me," Joe leaned in close to Candide, "do you want to watch your friends die this morning?"

"I don't." Candide unzipped the bag containing the *Necronomicon*.

"Don't give it to him," said Anna.

"Your friend here," smiled Joe. "She likes the pain. Don't you, Anna?" As his eyes burned into her, she felt a powerful revulsion at the strange attraction rising inside her, even as the man she adored held her close, his own blood mingling with hers. She broke the look and stared at the floor, deeply ashamed, terrified, and even now pushing her attraction away as best she could.

The demon's focus returned to Candide. "Do you know who does not like the pain? Your parents." Candide froze. "For four years we have kept them right by each other. They never see each other, but they hear the screams. And of course, like most human souls, after four years of this, we thought they were broken. But no. You should have seen their faces when I said I have been inside you."

"No..." It was barely more than a whisper.

"Yes. When I told them I knew your thoughts, the way you still hate them, the betrayal you feel, how you probably would not save them even if you knew they were there... And now you do."

"Candide, you know he's lying," said Eve.

"I have changed my mind." The demon looked at Eve with his piercing eyes and nodded towards Anna. "I won't kill you. I will break one of her fingers every time you speak. How do you think that would feel?"

Eve shuddered, remaining silent as he wrapped his arms even tighter around Anna.

"Candide," Joe continued, "would you like to be able to save your parents? Or would you prefer to let them suffer for eternity?"

Candide said nothing, watching the demon intently with bated breath.

"It's probably the least they deserve. If they hadn't left you that night, it never would have happened. Or..." His tone became soft and compassionate, "If they had just taken you with them, like you wanted, you would never have had to be alone."

Candide's face crumpled. A short sob broke from her and Anna felt Eve's grip tense as he watched her, felt the way he fought to stay where he was, silent and still, while everything inside him told him to rush to Candide's side.

"I can stop their pain," Joe said. "I can take away all the sadness they gave you. I can give you all the control you never had." He whispered: "Submit."

With that single word, it was as though a spell were broken. Candide regained her composure instantly. "Never."

"It hasn't been easy, has it? No matter what you do, no matter how hard you work, you will never have all the nice things he has." He motioned towards Eve. "It's so easy for him, isn't it? But life has never once been fair to you. Now we can change this. Align yourself with me and I will give you everything you want."

"In exchange for the book?"

"Just a little more than the book."

"Typical fucking man." Candide put her hand into the bag and pulled out the *Necronomicon* with one of the crosses they had stolen from the church on top of it. She stood and held the cross up to him, leaving the book on the lounge.

He advanced towards her quickly as she retreated. "You know, when I shared your body, I thought to myself, now here's a woman who is pretty smart. For a human. I thought to myself, this woman, maybe she can do some great things by my side. But now I see. You are just as stupid as the rest of them. That cross you have there. Give it to me."

"I won't!"

"Give it to me!" He snatched the cross. "You see? I hold it. It does nothing. I lick it." He ran his tongue along the cross. "Did you think it would burn me? Did you think it would 'compel' me?" he sniggered. "I am older than all these things. I helped create these things. How many of the evils of the world have been done in the name of this cross? And why do you think that is?"

All three, staunch atheists up until that time, silently considered the demon had made a good point.

"You should know better, stupid girl. This cross will never help you. All the women of the last two-thousand years have been burdened by this cross. Why did you think it would suddenly help you today? No. All the real power in this world is in the Book of the Dead. Candide, you will not grow, you will not overcome, you will not help those like you until you learn to do as I say. You still have a chance. But now, because you have wasted my time, this lovely boy dies."

As the demon turned, Anna plunged the stake deep into his chest, missing his heart by millimetres. He barely flinched. He swept an arm across, sending Anna into a wall.

Candide used the distraction to put as much distance as possible between herself and the demon as she started to recite: "Exorcizamus hanc bestiam in Nomine Patris, et Filii, et Spiritus Sancti. Quaesumus, Sancte, corpus hoc ab…"

Joe and Eve put their hands to the stake simultaneously. "You are not strong enough," Joe said. He easily twisted Eve's arms around behind his back and pushed him to the floor. He held Eve down with one hand as he pulled the stake from his own chest with the other. Anna and Candide watched in horror as an acrid-smelling smoke started to rise from Joe's hands and Eve's back and arms. Joe's skin was burning on contact with Eve's.

"Insidiis… uh… insidiis…" Candide stammered.

"Insidiis diaboli defende," said Anna.

Candide continued: "Insidiis diaboli defende. Protege adversus spiritus nequitiam et tyrannidem diaboli—"

"Now you! Stop talking. You see what I'm doing?" The demon put the sharp wood behind Eve's ear and started to push. Eve cried out in pain. "It will take me one second to push this through his brain."

Candide did not speak. She did not move.

"They said to me," Joe growled under his breath, "don't kill that boy. He is off-limits, they said. But you know what? I think I might kill him anyway, just to hear your screams. Not one more word…"

Candide's horrified eyes went from Anna to Eve and back again. Quiet tears ran down her cheeks.

"Last chance." Joe's hands trembled as the flesh peeled from them. His whole frame shook violently. They could see the incantation was beginning to work, that he was losing strength.

Candide let out a sob, then said, "Vade Satana, infernales invasores…"

Joe was thrown violently across the room. Anna charged forward again and brought the *Necronomicon* down upon his convulsing body with great force a second time.

"Putrescentiae mentis et omnes legiones diabolicae. His verbis Satanam sub pedibus nostris opprimimus, ligamus et proicimus in foveam profundam…"

Using every ounce of strength she had left, Anna lifted the *Necronomicon* high over her head. She saw the smirk on Joe's face for only a fraction of a second before he hurled himself through the locked hanging door, knocking it off its hinges.

Candide let out a cry at the sickly thud as Joe's body hit the ground below.

"Keep going!" said Anna. "Louder!"

Candide ran to the doorway and raised her voice. "Expellimus te a nobis immundum spiritum! Pessima bestia, te ad Infernus projicio!"

They stood, looking down at the pavement. Joe had disappeared, leaving only a red slick leading off into the woods. All three collapsed to the floor, huddled in the doorway, catching their breath.

"Eve, your hand…" said Candide. "Anna…" She looked at her bleeding shoulder.

"Let's seal it up," said Anna.

CHAPTER 27

AN ACTUAL PLAN

S lumped on the floor next to the *Necronomicon*, Candide
searched through for the appropriate page.

"It's this one here." She ran her finger down the page. "We
need it on all entry points. The doors first, windows, walls, ceiling
and floor."

They each took a vial of warding fluid and used their fingers to seal
the apartment. When they were done, they sank back down onto the
floor by the book and sat quietly.

"We really need to do something about your wounds," said
Candide.

"Do him," said Anna. "I'll be fine. How do we kill this thing?"

"I don't know."

"Doesn't it say?"

"It's ancient Greek, Anna. I'm still trying to figure it all out."

"Is that very different from modern Greek?"

"I don't know. I can't speak modern Greek either."

"Oh. Sorry." Anna lay down on the floor, her head on the hard wood. Eve and Candide exchanged worried looks and Candide went into the bedroom.

"Anna?" said Eve.

"Mmm?"

"I think you need a rest."

She sat up. "We can't rest. It will be back for us." They heard Candide ripping her bedding.

"I'm going to help you into your bed."

"No, Eve, no. I want to stay here."

"Anna…"

Candide came back with makeshift bandages and wound one around Eve's hand. "Anna, can I take a look?"

Anna, pale with sunken eyes, made no response. Her eyes were glazed and distant and she did not appear to have heard Candide.

"Anna?" Candide went around behind her and lifted her shirt. Anna flinched and cried out. "Okay, um, Eve, just rip it."

Anna was increasingly despondent. Eve gently gripped the shirt above her shoulder and tore it open.

"Oh, God," said Candide. "Oh, um, let's wrap this up." She wound the bandages around Anna's shoulder and arm as tightly as she could while Anna cried softly, leaning against Eve's wounded chest. He picked her up and carried her through to her bed. As he pulled the covers up, she used her last ounce of strength to grip his hand weakly before passing out.

Anna awoke some time later, pressed tight to Eve's chest, his arm firmly around her. He slept next to her, his breath soft and rhythmic, her own body moving in time with the rise and fall of his. Candide lay on the bed opposite her, also asleep, one hand on the *Necronomicon*. Anna drank the water they had left within her reach, then she closed her eyes, snuggled back into Evelyn, and slept again.

The next time Anna woke, she could hear Candide and Eve whispering. She felt she was still warm and safe pressed against him, but it was the anger in their voices, the tension in the air, that had awoken her.

"She can take care of herself, Eve. She has a right to know."

"You know as well as I do, it's just a matter of time until one of us ends up dead."

"You don't know that any of this is related."

"How could it not be? You heard what it said!"

"Eve—"

"No. I'm just going to pretend none of this ever happened."

"That's an awful thing to do! You're a terrible person."

"It's the only way to keep her safe. And you have to ask her to move out."

"I won't!"

"You have to!"

"Quiet! You'll wake her."

Silence.

The next time Anna woke, the midday sun was streaming through the windows and Eve was not there. She looked for Candide in the opposite bed, but she was not there either. Quietly, she made her way into the living room to see Eve and Candide at the table eating.

"Oh! She's awake!" said Candide.

Anna wandered slowly over to the table and sat down.

"How are you feeling?" asked Eve.

"Awful," replied Anna. "But better. What time is it?"

"It's about two," said Candide.

"But that's… Did I sleep all night?"

"You did."

"Oh. Candi, are those vegetables?"

"They are! Let me get you something."

Candide disappeared to the kitchen. Although Anna was in a good deal of pain, her mind felt refreshed from the rest. She could see Eve had no such recovery. His eyes were puffy and heavy, his face pallid and marked with worry. "I wanted to be there when you woke up," he said.

"That's okay. You were there while I slept."

"You noticed that?" There was a gentle, tired smile about his lips, but that was all. Unnumbered hours he had lain with her, kept her safe, watched over her, and still he was unwilling.

"A couple of times. I mostly just slept straight through."

"You needed it. You lost a lot of blood."

"I suppose so. I feel weak, but so much better than I did."

He stared at his teacup on the table, fiddling with the tag of a tea bag still in the cup. He looked as though he were going to say something, then thought better of it.

"You don't have to worry about me, you know," she said, watching him carefully.

"I think I do," he replied, still not looking up.

"Leave her alone." Candide returned from the kitchen with a plate of food for Anna, who set to eating immediately, not having realised how ravenous she had been. "I told you, she can take care of herself. Did you see her whack that demon?"

"You know, just for a second it was nice to not be thinking about that," said Anna.

"Yeah, sorry. Maybe after breakfast. Still, it was a brilliant idea to take him out with the book itself. Why didn't I think of that?"

"I also assumed a cross would work."

"Right? Don't put your faith in that shit."

"Lesson learned. It's nice to know we have one weapon."

"The Book of the Dead."

"The Book of the Dead! How did you go with the translation? Have we found a way to kill it?"

"No. That's the bad news. We can't kill it."

Anna stopped eating. "So, what do we do? Do we just have to live with it?"

"Not at all. We can do a few things. We can trap it, which I don't recommend because, well, whoever it's inside has to be trapped too. For as long as we can trap them. And there's a limit on that obviously, busy campus and all. But it's one option.

"The other option is to exorcise it and then banish it back to wherever it came from. Out of this realm, anyway. Now, that can't stop it coming back forever, but we can certainly do some things to try to keep it out. Regular banishing spells, spells to hide us."

"If it's the book he wants," Anna said, "he will keep coming for it. What are we going to do about that?"

"I think we have to protect the book," Candide replied.

"Not 'we'," said Eve.

"I think that's Anna's choice, Eve," said Candide.

"I don't know that we need to be making choices like that right now, Candide."

"Eve wants to send you away and lock you up safe."

"Lock her up, Candide? Really?"

"Same thing. Why does 'protecting' a woman always equate to taking away her choices?"

"Candide, have you forgotten who you're talking to?"

"Never. But I've never seen you so controlling, either."

"I'm not controlling!"

"He's not controlling," said Anna. "You're both honestly the loveliest people I have ever met. No one ever cared about me this much before." Anna didn't look sad as she said it, nor did she betray a note of sadness in her voice. Even so, Eve moved his leg over to rest against hers and Candide leaned in closer.

"And I thought we had it bad," said Candide.

"You did, by the sounds of it. Maybe we all did. But it feels better to me to stick with you two." She glanced quickly at Eve and away again. "At least for now."

"Told you," Candide said to Eve, who just furrowed his brow and took a sip of tea.

"So we can't kill it," Anna continued. "We can trap it in a human body or we can banish just the demon. That seems better than putting a person through all that suffering."

"For sure. Especially when it would come for us as soon as the person were set free."

"And we don't really have anywhere to keep someone captive."

"That too."

"No other options?"

"Well, one, but it's kind of pointless."

"What is it?"

"Okay, so, you can kill it."

"What? How?"

"But not in this realm."

"Huh. Okay."

"So you would need to go into the spiritual realm somehow and kill it yourself."

"And we are not doing that," said Eve.

"Why not?" said Anna. "How do we do it?"

"I haven't figured that out yet. It's incredibly difficult to get a human soul through and then bring it back again, intact, and put it back in the correct body."

"Yeah, that does sound really hard. Really risky. But if we can't banish it permanently, and it's going to keep coming for the book, that means we never stop dealing with it unless we kill it?"

"Sounds grim. I think we have to find a way to put the book somewhere safe that's far away from us. Find a way to protect it without actually being near it."

"Hide it from demons."

"Yes. Permanently."

"How did it even get here?"

"And that's the big mystery. Why here? And why now? When Eve lived in this apartment, it wasn't here."

"That's right," he said. "There were other people living here for the year after I moved out, but the guy I met just seemed like a normal student. He would have been living here now, but he took a tumble on the stairs. Quite conveniently for all of this in hindsight... He had a roommate who I never saw, but he moved out when all that happened. I guess we should try to track him down and see if he left it." He looked out the window and across the field, thinking. "It's an odd thing to forget."

Suddenly, all three exchanged looks as the same idea dawned on them simultaneously.

"Oh shit."

"No way."

"Who would do that?"

"What an arsehole."

"Yes! What an arsehole! Dumping their demon on us!"

"That's a real shit move."

"For sure."

"Oh, well that's it then," said Anna. "We banish this fucker, then we go find that jerk and give them their goddamn book back."

"That's a plan."

"We've got an actual plan now!"

"Okay, great, so... What do we do first?"

"Do you think Joe is still alive?" asked Eve.

"I don't know," said Anna. "I don't really see how he can be. There was so much blood. And it's been days. It didn't sound like he was going to be feeding him."

"It did say it wanted to keep him alive though," said Candide. "To torment him."

"That is seriously messed up," said Anna.

"Demon stuff."

"Demon stuff."

"I could swear you two were separated at birth," Eve mumbled. "It's weird."

"It's nice," said Candide.

"It really is," smiled Anna.

"So, do we need to find Joe, or if we summon the demon, will he come here as a spirit or in, er, Joe-form?" asked Eve.

"According to the book, if he is still in Joe, or whoever he's in, if we summon him, he will come. We don't know when. The book says he will be 'compelled to walk'. We might have to wait a while, depending how far he's gone. If he's not in a person, and just hanging around in spirit form, he would be here almost immediately."

"Okay, then what do we do to trap him, or hold him, until we can exorcise him?" Anna asked.

"The summoning spell should hold him to a spot, one location we choose, until we close the spell. That means it could, in theory, go on for days if he's far away. If we break it, we lose control over him."

"You need some sleep before we do this, Eve," said Anna.

"I'm fine."

"You're totally not," said Candide.

"He's totally not," said Anna.

"Really weird," said Eve, eyeing the pair of them. "Just, let's finish this plan first."

"We get him here, we exorcise him, we banish him."

"This sounds suspiciously easy."

"It does. But that's what the book says."

"There has to be a catch. Supplies?"

"That's the catch. We need supplies."

"Always a catch. What supplies?"

"That's the good thing. Nothing we can't find on campus. We still have enough warding fluid, I think, we have holy water. We just need so much salt. So much."

"Chem. lab.?" asked Anna.

"Yep."

"So that's going to be the most dangerous part, getting over there and back," said Eve.

"Yes. And neither of you are going," Candide replied.

"Candide, you must be joking," said Anna.

"Have you seen yourselves?"

Eve and Anna looked warily at one another and consequently became more aware of themselves. Eve pulled the blanket more over his naked chest, much to Anna's dismay, and sat up a little taller in his chair. She noticed that the bandage on his hand had been changed but had bled through again. Seeing where her eyes went, Eve moved his hand under the table and rested it on his thigh.

For her part, Candide had made such a thorough job with Anna's wrapping that she had no need to worry about wearing only a bra underneath. Still, she was aware her bandages were makeshift, dirty and increasingly unsanitary.

"I feel like I need a shower," she said. "And new bandages."

"That's gonna hurt."

Anna thought for a moment. "Candide?"

"Mmm?"

"Is the med. lab. storage near the chem. lab. storage?"

"It is, but it's much harder to get into. We would probably be better just cooking something up from the chem. lab."

"Candide, did you say, 'just cooking something up from the chem. lab.'?" said Eve.

"What? I'm being realistic."

"Anna is not taking something you 'cooked up from the chem. lab.'."

"You know, if you don't have any solutions, then maybe don't try to think up problems."

"Candide, when are you going to grow up?"

"Grow up? What the hell! I'm the one coming up with all the ideas, spending hours translating this book, and you're just sitting there complaining about everything."

"You have always been like this! You never think anything through and you just run with it."

"I get things done."

"I clean up your mess."

"Then don't!"

"I wish I didn't have to!"

"You don't! Stop being such a martyr. Like you're so perfect."

"I never said I'm perfect!"

"I should hope not!" They were both quiet for a moment. Then Candide continued more calmly, "Because you're a jerk."

"You're a jerk," he said.

"You are."

"Okay, so where can I get some drugs?" said Anna.

"We'll all go," said Eve. "To the med. lab. I'll figure something out."

"You can pick a lock, too?" There was a distinct sparkle in Anna's eye.

"What? Why do you assume that?" Eve replied, attempting to appear shocked but clearly flattered by her idea of him.

"You can hot-wire a car. Eve, why *can* you hot-wire a car?"

"Only old ones. We just got lucky."

"That doesn't explain—"

"Come on," he said. "We should go get these things."

"No, not until you've had a sleep," said Candide. "You're grumpy. And stinky."

"I need a shower."

"No showers until we banish the demon."

"Are you for real?" said Eve.

"Seriously?" said Anna.

The impossibly fresh and beautiful Candide threw back her perfect hair. "It wouldn't be safe. The sooner we banish the demon, the sooner you can both smell nice again. Now go to bed, Eve."

"You can take mine," said Anna.

Eve looked as though he were about to protest, but it was clear the offer of a cosy bed and a few hours of peace was too much for him to fight. "All right. Thanks, Anna." He paused for a moment before saying, "And you two are just going to stay here and memorise incantations or something, right?"

"Of course," said Candide. "We have lots of work to get through. So go away now."

He ruffled his hand through Anna's hair in a mortifyingly brotherly way as he made his way into the bedroom with no further protest.

Anna flipped her hair back into place and leaned in towards Candide. "We're totally going to sneak out, aren't we?"

"We totally are."

CHAPTER 28
AN "I LOVE YOU"

Candide spread out various papers that were piled up on the corner of the table. "There's the summoning spell, which we need to know by heart to be able to concentrate our energy on getting him here. This one is the exorcism, which we're pretty good with, I think, but it wouldn't hurt to go over it again. This one is the banishment. He's going to get pretty angry by then, and we need to be able to say this like clockwork."

"So, this is the most important one?"

"I suppose so, but they're all important."

"Do we have coffee?"

"Of course."

"Do you think…"

"We could get some real coffee from the cafe on our way back? It's not that much of a diversion."

"I guess we're in a hurry, though. Is Eve going to have time to learn it?"

Candide rolled her eyes. "Photographic memory."

"Are you still annoyed with him?"

"I'm fine. We're always fine. Eventually. And he's not really a jerk. Someone needs to tell him he is sometimes, though. Stupid, impossibly perfect Eve."

"Candide—" Anna caught herself. "Sorry, I mean Candi."

"No, it's fine. It is Candide. Probably time I gave the Candi thing a rest. I don't even like it. It's just different. I'm not going back to frumpy Candide though, even if he thinks that's who I really am. And I'm keeping the blonde."

"And so you should. It's beautiful."

"Eve doesn't understand it."

"Men never do."

"Don't tell Eve that. He's been a card-carrying feminist since birth. You'll break his little heart."

"I never would. The world needs good men."

"And he is one. For sure. He's kind of ruined men for me, though. I rarely meet any who can live up to the example he sets."

"That just leaves women, then."

"It does, actually." They smiled at each other in recognition and then were quiet for a few moments until Candide said, "Anna, I want to tell you something. The person I was seeing last year—"

"Gothic in Art!"

"How did you know?"

"Because you and Eve are about as subtle as a brick," Anna laughed.

"I told him to stop shushing me all the time!"

"You're just as bad as he is."

"That can't be true!"

"It's totally true! But it doesn't matter. I wouldn't tell anyone, anyway. And she's very beautiful as it goes. I can see how that would happen."

"Beautiful on the outside only."

"The age gap is something."

"Right? What was I thinking? But also, what the hell?"

"Yes! Especially that."

"But it's all over now. Thankfully."

"Candide, I just have to ask something... When you were mad at me, at the cafe, was it... It wasn't because you were, uh, how do I say it..."

"Interested in you?"

"Maybe..."

"Anna, you're not my type."

"What?" Anna looked at her in faux-shock. "You don't like short, cute and busty?"

"My roommate isn't my type. Ever. Especially when she's in love—I mean—especially when she may have interests elsewhere. I did think at the time maybe you were implying something when you said that... Implying something about how you felt about me. Which was upsetting, the way you said it. That or you were telling me my closest friend in the world was beneath you."

"That was a pretty awful thing to say in hindsight. I'm sorry. I just didn't want you to think I was interested in your boyfriend."

"But you totally were!"

"I felt awful, if it helps."

"It helps a little. It's nice to know we're unlikely to be rivals in the future."

"That's *very* reassuring from my perspective. Is there anyone now?"

"There is. Kind of. But she's being weird. She keeps saying she'll come over, then she doesn't turn up. She's supposed to be going away soon, and I was hoping to see her. But then we're never here lately... I don't know. Maybe she's just not that interested."

"I find that very hard to believe."

Candide smiled and left the conversation there. Anna picked up some papers and started looking over them, subtly studying Candide as best she could while trying not to draw attention. She was undoubtedly gorgeous. There wasn't a person alive who would not instantly note the high-set cheekbones, the wide pink lips, the green eyes behind long lashes and the light smattering of freckles that only drew more attention to those eyes. Yet even as Anna loved being in her presence, loved to look at her, to study every feature, she no longer felt the sexual attraction she had days earlier, nor had she, she knew, since the night of the séance. She would have much preferred to find herself still interested in Candide. As it was, she felt an uneasy sickness in the pit of her stomach as she tried to push the possibility out of her mind that it had never been Candide she wanted that night. The repellant curiosity still lingered, and it made the imminent meeting with the demon that much more terrifying to Anna.

"You're completely smitten, aren't you?" said Candide.

Anna blanched, forcing her eyes to the papers in front of her. She was silent for a moment, trying to bring her thoughts back to the moment. Back to Evelyn. "Pretty hopelessly, I think. Not that it matters. But let's concentrate on this. We have one hour to study all this, then we leave. I really want to be back before dark. And before he wakes up."

"All right. Remember, you can't say anything out loud while we're studying. As soon as you say it, the spell begins."

"Got it. Can I copy it?"

"Of course."

They worked for some time, Anna studiously copying down Candide's words several times over in silence, drinking coffee, happy to be together regardless of the task ahead. Eventually, Anna suggested it was time to get ready to leave. She went straight to the dresser in her bedroom and pulled the drawer slowly open. It made a soft scraping sound and Eve's hand, hanging over the edge of the bed, flinched slightly. She paused for a second and waited to hear his even breathing. When she was satisfied, she removed her clothes and pushed the drawer back without a sound. Turning to leave, she paused to look at Eve. Even in his sleep, his brow was furrowed. She wanted to reach out and smooth it down, though she daren't.

She sat down on the floor by the bed just to be close to him again, if only for one short moment. He was lying on his side, his head on her pillow, facing towards her. She touched her face slightly to his injured hand hanging over the bed and remembered the feeling of his soft fingertips tracing across her skin. Her head on its side to mirror his, she studied his face, noted the pinkness and shape of his lips, the length and shade of his brown eyelashes, the light freckles she had never noticed before. His chin, she saw, had a soft cleft and his neck was elegant and smooth. All she wanted in that moment was to crawl in close to him, bury her head in the nook of his arm, to lie with him and forget the world existed. In Eve, she saw only happiness in any quiet moment she could be completely alone with him. He seemed to her to promise every freedom, every happiness, every hope and dream and desire she had ever had in his very presence.

Yet, as she reflected on these lovely ideas, she felt a selfish jealousy slowly wind its way around her heart, and just for that moment, she wished he would stay asleep forever, immortal, always young and beautiful and always hers, only hers, to visit and keep and love.

She knew he needed someone better than her. Someone strong enough to overpower his need to protect and control his world. Someone he would have instinctively let in, in just the same way he locked Anna out. He needed someone unselfish, giving, someone calm and level-headed and self-aware. She could never be any of those things for him. She couldn't even be those things for herself. But she didn't want to let him go, and she hated herself for it. Eve was the most perfect thing Anna had ever seen. Why should he be for anyone else? And why shouldn't she give him all her own crushing, desperate adoration?

Because Eve was too good for her. She believed this in the very fibre of her being.

He might fall hard for her if she let him, because he was sweet and caring and beautiful inside and she would happily give every piece of herself to him, recklessly meshing their souls together for eternity in a heartbeat. And she would ruin his life one way or the other if he stayed with her, because she had nothing but darkness and emptiness inside and she wanted, selfishly, desperately, to fill herself up with all the light and beauty that Evelyn Worthing was to her. And what would be left for Evelyn? Nothing. She could give him nothing in return except her selfish, destructive, obsessive love. She felt her eyes welling up and touched her face on his unfeeling fingers again as she stood up. She pulled the covers over his shoulder and tore herself away.

Candide noticed the change in her immediately. "Are you okay?"

"Yeah. I just… I don't know how I'm going to get my shirt on. I can't reach to do the buttons."

"I'll help." Candide guided the black linen shirt up Anna's arm and over her wound. She held it open as Anna slipped her other arm in, then she came around the front to button it. "Are you going to be okay tonight?"

"I am. I promise. I think I have this all down now, anyway. Do you?"

"I think so."

"Should we go soon?"

"We should. He probably has a few more hours before he wakes. Was he sound when you went in?"

Anna looked away. "Mmm. I think so."

Candide finished her buttons and sat back down. "He barely slept at all, you know. That whole time. He was so worried about you."

Anna still did not look back up. "I'm sure he has plenty of women to choose from."

"He does. You don't know the half of it. And that won't ever stop."

Anna didn't say anything.

"It's just that… if you were together… it can be hard to get used to that."

"We're not going to be together. Eve was quite clear about that."

"Eve says a lot of things. Do you believe him?"

"I don't know. Shouldn't I?"

"Not from what I've seen."

"We're in a weird situation."

"We are. But… don't listen to what I said earlier. He's not a jerk. I'm just jealous."

"Of Eve? I can imagine. It must be hard growing up in the shadow of a prodigy."

"It is. Or was. He always gets everything. Everyone. That doesn't make him a bad person though, and… Anna, I can see how he feels about you. And how you feel about him…"

"I think it's obvious how I feel, but… he doesn't want me. And we're not right for each other. So after we banish this demon, I'm moving on with my life. Without Eve."

Candide looked at her in alarm. "Anna, you must know things are complicated—"

"Excruciatingly complicated. And I know you're not allowed to tell me what the big secret is—"

"I can't—"

"And I honestly don't care."

"Anna, I think you would be making a terrible mistake to throw away what you have."

"Don't say that to me, Candide."

Candide was silent for a moment, thinking, then in a low, quiet voice, "Anna, Eve has a really bad habit of thinking people judge him by his intentions instead of his actions. He kind of assumes that people understand where he's coming from, when they don't. It's caused a lot of trouble for him in the past."

Anna was stalled in her act of carefree bravado. "That's really weird. I feel like I'm exactly the same way. But no one ever put that into words for me before."

"Anna," a pause and a deep breath, "did you ever think maybe—"

"No. Stop talking about him. I'm serious. I want you to stop."

"Sorry. I'm sorry. Weird situation. I just… I felt like I should say something. And maybe I feel like we're closer than we are. Because of everything."

"No, we're close, we are. Candide, I hope it's not weird to say, but you're my best friend and I love you so much."

"I love you too, Anna."

"I don't want what's going on with Eve to ruin what we have. To tell the truth, I'm really not okay with everything and I just can't talk about this."

"No, you're right. I won't bring it up again. Unless you do. Finish getting dressed. I'll double check the list and we'll go."

"And you think he's fine here?"

"He's safer here than he would be with us."

Anna changed into a fresh pair of trousers with much difficulty while Candide organised a range of bags for the planned heist. "You're not going to be able to carry much, are you? Oh well, we'll make do."

"Remind me again why we can't take Eve?"

Candide walked back over to Anna. "Just between you and me, I don't think he's coping as well as he says he is. I think he really needs to sleep and if we want to be back before dark, we really have to go now."

"And you're sure this isn't some getting back at him thing?"

"No. Nothing like that. We're fine. I promise."

"If you say so. Let's leave him a key."

"All right. A key and a note. But it's four and it will be dark really soon. We have to go."

Candide waited impatiently by the door while Anna ripped a page from her nicest notebook and quickly wrote a message. She looked around. "We have no coffee table. Where will he see it?"

"Come on, Anna, we need to go. We'll be back before he even knows we're gone if we hurry."

"I would want to know if I were him. Hang on."

She took the note and the key into the bedroom and quietly removed a long length of tape from the reel. She folded the note four times, placed the key on top, and gently taped the package to Eve's wrist, still extending out of the bed. She paused before leaving to take a final look at him. It was with a heavy heart she resolved that she would not attempt to convince him that they should be together. If he wasn't sure now, then he never would be. For her part, she did not wish to destroy any of the untarnished beauty she saw before her. She recognised that she would only be a dark blot on his charmed life—something she refused to be. She stiffened, raised her head high, and left the apartment.

CHAPTER 29

A PERILOUS JOURNEY

The chem. lab. was located next to the med. lab. To get there they had to leave their apartment building, walk halfway across the courtyard and cut through the sandstone building, and into the shiny and modern surrounds that chemistry and medical degrees pay for.

Even though the sun was just beginning to dip below the buildings, the evening was cold and the central courtyard was deserted. Deep red, brown and yellow autumn leaves blew through from their own courtyard to rest against the bases of well-maintained tables and chairs, giving them an air of the gothic which would have been totally absent any other day. Candide and Anna pulled right and into another, shiny, clean, modern, but still sandstone building.

"So this is how the other half live," said Anna quietly.

"Just wait until you see the lab."

"How do you know your way around here?"

"Frat boy."

"Frat boy was a chem. major?"

"For sure. And he used to access the building out of hours a lot. Supplies, you know. But we're not out of hours, so keep quiet."

"The place is deserted, though."

"It's Friday. They've probably all taken off for the weekend. Eerie, isn't it?"

"Very. But shiny."

They walked past the first well-lit hallway on their left, and instead turned down the second one, with a row of fluorescent lights down the centre and windowless rooms on either side. Both sides were lined with stainless steel all the way up until it met the crisp, white ceiling. About halfway down the hall, Candide pulled over to a door. She tried the silver handle. It gave easily.

"That's odd. It should be locked," she whispered.

"Is someone in there?"

"Let's see." She peered around the door and swept her eyes over the visible part of the room. There were several rows of tables with various glass bottles and scientific apparatus set out for class. Beyond, there was row upon row of dark storage space. They closed the door behind them.

"Hello?" Softly at first, then more confidently, "Hello?"

They waited. "I think we're good. The salt is over here." Candide moved quickly across to a bench and flipped up the curtain that shut it out from view. "It's empty! They haven't replaced it." Anna and Candide both commenced searching under all the benches. "Nothing!"

"What do we do?"

"There should be some in the storage area. Come on."

Anna's shoulder sent a painful reminder of itself as she moved her arm. "No, listen, I might try next door. It's getting late and I want to get out of here."

"It's bound to be locked. I really think we should try to find every-thing we need here and make something ourselves."

"It's worth a look. Maybe they just forgot to lock up today?"

"Okay, you go look. Come right back if you can't get in, all right?"

"All right."

Candide disappeared down one of the dark aisles, and Anna slipped back into the hall. She tried the door. To her great surprise, it too gave easily, and she advanced into the centre of a cold room. It was composed of a combination of pedantically polished stainless steel and sparkling glass. There was a metal bench running around the edge of the room, above which was an endless array of medication, liquids, solutions, pieces of people and small animals suspended in fluids, all kept safely behind locked glass. There were row upon row of stainless steel medical operation tables and several chairs placed here and there. The only light in the room came from the inces-santly buzzing fluorescent bulbs overhead, giving the place an uncanny, timeless otherworldliness.

Anna made her way methodically around the edge of the room, searching for pain medication. She was some distance from the door when she heard a soft click behind her. She realised even before she turned, it was the sound of the door locking. With wide eyes and heart beating fast, she beheld the figure of Joe Bruno, his back pressed against the door, head upright in a proud, contemptuous manner, watching her, saying nothing.

She met his eye. "I don't have your book."

"I know," he replied. She felt a sickening thrill run through her.

He maintained his watch, seeming to enjoy her growing discomfort, and while she did grow ever more disconcerted, hideously exposed as his eye ran, not unappreciatively, over her curves, she felt instinc-tively secure under his burning gaze.

She noticed at once he did not look the same as he had last time she saw him. Gone were the pallid skin and sunken eyes, replaced by a healthy, beauteous glow. His tan skin was vibrant, with a warm and alluring flush to his cheek. Though still wearing his religious garb, it looked as though he had changed his clothes. He was clean all over, even his hair was fresh and beautiful and played eloquently around his temple. There was no sign of any injury that could have resulted in the enormous amount of blood that still painted the pavement behind her apartment building.

He cut through her thoughts: "Do you like what you see?"

"You're... He's not hurt!"

"No. He would have been dead. I fixed him. Demons are very good at this. We can fix anything. He is very beautiful, isn't he? I thought it would be a waste to destroy this body."

"Is he... is he still... alive?"

"Oh yes. He watches you even now. He watches me. He wonders what I am going to do to you."

On her guard, yet with a disquieting warmth in her neck and her face, she tried to seem as though she were in control of herself. "What are you going to do?"

"What do you want me to do?"

Anna's heart skipped a beat, and she felt her stomach tighten guiltily. She forced her eyes to the floor. "You can't touch me. I have the mark."

"The mark doesn't matter."

"How! How can it not matter? I saw... when you touched him... you were burned!"

"He did not want me to touch him. But you do. And when you submit to me, that mark means nothing."

The thought of it, although she could hardly admit it to herself, made a pleasant, light sweat break out on her palms. "I won't submit to you."

"I know all about you, Anna. You don't need to feel ashamed with me."

"Please, go away."

"You don't mean that."

"Yes, I do." It was barely more than a whisper.

"I can give you everything you want."

She said nothing.

"That delicate boy…" She looked up in alarm. "He can't give you what you want. You know that."

"Leave me alone."

"Would you like me to leave him alive for you?"

"Don't touch him!"

"I can do that for you. But that girl will knock on the door soon. Shall we let her live too?"

"Yes!"

"It's nice to be in control, isn't it?"

"Please leave them alone," she said.

He watched her, quizzically now. "I wonder why you protect them. They lie to you. They use you. You know they're both keeping secrets from you."

"I don't care."

"Of course you care. It is natural for a human to want to be loved. To want to be looked after. Especially after everything you have seen."

He stood tall and removed his coat, carefully folding it and placing it on the bench next to him. He walked towards her. She didn't like the heat that now ran through her entire body and she took a step back towards the wall, trying still to avert her eyes.

"Anna James…"

"I won't give you the book."

"I didn't come here for the book."

"That's not true…"

"You know it's true. I came for you."

She looked up brightly, a challenging flare in her eye. "Then you should know I won't sell my soul."

He laughed. "Anna, I don't want your soul. You're already destined for Hell."

"What?" she gasped.

"Surely, this comes as no surprise to you. Anna, you're a terrible person. Why do you think he doesn't want you? God doesn't want you. Even your own parents never wanted you. Why do you think they threw you away like that? No one here wants you because you're rotten to the core. You were just born… wrong."

There was no use denying anything he said. She knew in her heart it was all true. The idea was so ever-present in her mind that it didn't even draw a tear, just a resurrection of the usual, vague, endless sadness that accompanied her at almost all times before she arrived at Endymion College.

"But, Anna, these things are exactly what I like about you. You're like me. There is a place where you and I belong. When you get there, and you will, don't you want the power I have? Believe me, you don't want to be like the rest of your kind. They suffer at the hands of creatures like me. But you—I can give you my protection, now and in the future. Submit."

She stared at the floor in silence.

"I don't know why you want to protect these people who hate you, but I will spare them. I will spare them and you will have my protection. This is the only time I will make you this offer. I will give you anything you want, but only if you do as I say from now on. Submit, and I promise you... you will love every second of it."

He pulled the white collar from around his neck and let it drop to the floor. He started to unbutton his shirt. She did not move. Then the shirt hit the floor, and she felt a burst of fresh blood run through her as she finally gave in to her desire to feast her eyes on him—his chest gloriously formed, his biceps strong, his face handsome and his eyes intent. He was easily the second most beautiful thing she had ever seen purely in his physical form, but that something else—that strange, indescribable attraction she felt whenever this creature was present. It was undeniable. Almost irresistible. And worse than that, everything he said made sense. Here was a guarantee. A guarantee of safety, of happiness. Not just for today, but for eternity. And he was right about her. She sensed her own darkness, she knew she would never be good enough to deserve all the nice things other people had. That's why Eve didn't want her. That's why no one ever wanted to be near her. And why should she only have horrible things all her life? Why, when she was doing no harm to anyone else if she accepted this offer, if there was nothing else waiting for her, if she was protecting the people she cared about and all she had to do was accept this beautiful man she desperately wanted...

She hated herself even as she whispered it. "Come."

Joe advanced quickly forward and pushed Anna up against the wall. She breathed in sharply as her wounded shoulder hit the cold steel. He leaned in close and she felt his hot breath on her neck. With one hand on his firm chest, she felt his heart beat strong and hard. He put his hand into her hair and tightened it into a fist. She felt the tingle down her neck and back as he pulled it hard and kissed her on the lips. His other hand moved along the top of her aching shoulder, his fingertips tracing down her arm, interlocking with her fingers. In one sudden, sharp movement, he forced her arm up over her head. She screamed out in pain, in ecstasy, and then, hating herself all the while, she pulled him in close and kissed him back. She kissed him desperately, passionately. He reached one arm around her waist and picked her up easily. Her lips still locked against his, she wrapped her legs tight around him and he thrust her hard against the wall. Suddenly she could hear the door, she could hear yelling outside, but it was as though she were lost in a beautiful dream and she did not want it to stop. Then a sickening realisation started to trickle into her dream.

She opened her eyes and looked up at him. "It's not right," she whispered. "You're not Joe. It's his body, but you're not him. I can't do this!"

He paused, his face close to hers, his breath hot on her cheek. "I promise you," he kissed her neck, "he wants you too. His body aches for you. Can't you feel it?" He pressed himself hard against her and her whole body thrilled with delight. He moved his hand up from her waist, over her breast, her legs holding him, and pushed her other arm up above her head to meet the first. She wrenched that arm back down and she tore open his belt. She kissed him again and again and longed to be able to stay here forever, to finish what they had started. She ripped the first button from his pants.

"Anna!"

"Eve?" she whispered, as if awaking from a dream. "Eve!" She pushed the demon away and felt his grip soften and release her as the door crashed open. Too ashamed and shocked at herself to look up, she saw only that Joe's body suddenly fell limp to the floor, the *Necronomicon* landing in a bloody heap next to him.

Anna looked down at him, his eyes closed, a gaping wound in the back of his head caused by the book that had clearly smashed his skull. Eve's arms were around her. "Anna? Are you okay?"

She burst into tears and buried her head in his chest. "Eve. Eve, I'm so sorry, Eve."

"Oh, Anna, no, no. You didn't do anything."

She sobbed hopelessly, repeating his name over and over.

"Oh my love, how could I have let you go? Anna. Anna, look at me."

"No."

"Anna…"

"I can't."

He held her and kissed her hair, gently rocking her while she cried. He looked up at Candide, and spoke softly. "Is he dead?"

"You had to," Candide replied, her voice firm and her face resolved. Eve nodded and buried his face in Anna's hair again.

Suddenly, eyes wild and breathing hard, Anna pushed Eve away, grabbed the *Necronomicon* from Candide's arms and brought it crashing down on Joe, once and again, and again, until Candide pushed her to the floor.

"Anna! Anna, stop! We're not supposed to get blood on the Necronomicon! Also, he's dead already."

"We're not supposed to get blood on it? But it's written in blood!"

"Fresh blood!"

"Well, what happens now?"

"I don't know!"

"How bad is it?"

"I don't know!"

"Why didn't you tell me?"

"I didn't think we were going to kill anyone with it!"

Anna's eyes traced across the floor and over to Joe. It was Joe. She saw his eyes closed, blood running from various places on his once-beautiful face, the face she had kissed only seconds earlier, and now it was cracked and broken and she had done that too. What else had they done to him? What would even be left of him when the thing was finished with him? Somehow she had forgotten entirely who he was, and she felt a deep and all-consuming loathing within herself, disgusted at her actions, amazed and repulsed that she was even capable of such a thing.

"We have to get it out of him."

"What?"

"He's not dead. Not for long. Get it out of him." She stood up. "Candide, get the salt."

Candide moved swiftly to the door and hauled in a huge vat of rock salt.

"Chair," Anna said to Eve. As he retrieved the chair, he watched her, disturbed by the sudden change in her, yet strangely reassured by her evident indifference to him. Faced with the decision to try to control Anna's world and keep her safe or let her do what she needed to do, he made the wisest decision he or any other man could have made in that situation. He said nothing and did exactly as she asked. Anna turned her back to him and started searching the room. She found the bandages she was looking for.

"Put him in the chair," she said.

Anna tied Joe's hands behind his back and to the chair using the bandages. She wound a length around his chest, tying him tight again. She wound them around each ankle, tying him firmly to the legs of the chair, then around one thigh, then the next.

"I don't know if that's going to be strong enough," said Candide.

"Hang on. They'll have cable ties in here somewhere." Eve started searching drawers and cupboards frantically.

"Will electrical cables work?" asked Candide.

"Yeah, yeah they should," said Eve. "I'm good at knots."

Anna felt her heart flutter a little at his innocent comment and hated herself even more. "Just get everything. We'll use everything we have."

Even as they wound the various ties around his every limb, Anna saw the hole in Joe's head healing, growing smaller. As she fixed the last cable to his thigh, she became aware of his presence. "I bet you're enjoying that," he purred. She looked up and saw a teasing smile on his previously handsome face, though even the fresh wounds she had just given him were beginning to heal.

She took a step back. "Salt," she said. Eve and Candide helped her form a thick circle of salt around Joe. "Let's exorcise him." Eve pulled a note from his pocket and started to read. Candide joined him, reciting the words from memory.

Joe kept his eyes locked on Anna. "It won't work," he said. "You have to want me to go."

"I want you to go."

"We both know that's not true."

Anna joined in the Latin incantation. Joe looked over at Eve and raised his voice above them. "You will see. She can't let me go because she knows you cannot satisfy her. No human can. Not like a demon can." Anna looked at Eve uneasily but he continued reading, his eyes fast on the paper, as though the demon had said nothing. Anna started reciting louder. Joe laughed under his breath, then his face turned serious and he leaned his head forward, watching her intently. They reached the end of the incantation and nothing. Nothing happened.

"I told you," he said. "I told you and you know I would never lie to you, Anna. Unlike them. Now stop this. Tell him about us. Tell him you enjoyed what I did to you. What I was going to do. Tell him you enjoyed what you did to this body." Tears of anger and frustration rose to her eyes. She stepped into the salt-circle and slapped him.

"Anna!" Candide gasped. Evelyn watched her, his face expressionless, his eyes dark. He turned them to the floor.

"Evelyn, you see?" the demon yelled. "This is what she likes. She likes to hurt beautiful men, even if they aren't in control of their own body."

Anna slapped him again, furious. "Keep reading!" she shouted. Eve and Candide started the incantation again. She walked to the sink and stood for a moment, catching her breath, thinking. Then calmly she filled a metal tray with hot water. Candide looked over at Eve, but his eyes were again locked on Anna as he spoke the words. She reached into another cabinet and pulled out a scalpel.

"Anna, no," Candide said. "He's tied up. You don't need to do that."

"Keep reading," she said calmly. She picked up the salt vat and upturned it on the surgical table next to Joe. She picked up two handfuls of salt and dumped them in the hot water, stirring to dissolve it with the scalpel.

"Get out of him," she said under her breath. "You go now, or I will make you go."

"I won't. I like it here. I like you."

Anna pulled the scalpel out of the water and let a drop fall from the sharp tip onto Joe's bare shoulder. She saw the smoke, heard the sizzle, smelled the sulphur. He flinched at the pain. Candide's movement forward was arrested by Eve, who, reciting all the while, shook his head and pulled her back.

Anna stirred the scalpel in the water. She sat on Joe's thigh, just the same way she had sat on Eve's thigh, and leaned in close, forgetting entirely that Eve and Candide were watching her. "You will do everything I tell you to, or I am going to torture you. For some time. And I think we both know I'm going to enjoy that."

"I can't go. He wants me in here. He wants you."

"That's not true. I know that's not true."

"Then it must be you keeping me here."

"Get out!" she yelled, stabbing the salty scalpel into his thigh. He screamed in pain. Then he laughed.

"Anna, stop now!" Candide pleaded. "It's Joe's body! You can't torture him."

"I can," she dipped the blade back into the salt water, "and I will." She put the scalpel to his chest and began to carve the symbol she now knew by heart.

Joe cried out in pain and begged her to stop. Real pain—as though it really was Joe—as though the demon had fled.

"Anna, please stop! Eve, do something. She'll listen to you!"

Eve, pale and clearly shaken, turned his back on the scene and kept reciting. "Eve!" Candide yelled.

The demon stopped crying abruptly and whispered to Anna, "Do you want to know why you can't resist me?"

"I can resist you."

"It's because you're broken inside, just like me. It's because you crave the power I have."

Anna felt a creeping uncertainty in the pit of her stomach but pressed on, regardless. "I don't want anything from you."

"You and I both know we're going to end up together at the end of this," Joe said. "You're mine already."

"No," she replied quietly, still moving the blade over his chest in confident strokes. "I belong to no one. And that's why I don't care how much Joe suffers, and I don't care what I did, and I don't care what happens to me after this. But I won't let you have him because he's not like me. He doesn't deserve this. Now…" She sat up tall and straight to admire her finished work. "It's time to go." Her bloody hands reached for the salt. "Get out!"

"Anna—" Candide started.

"Read!"

Eve turned back to face her and said the words louder to drown out Joe's screams as Anna shoved the salt into his wound. Seconds later, Joe started to laugh again, but this time it was a deep, unnatural laugh. No longer was it Joe's voice, but the true voice of the being that possessed him. Anna took a frightened step away from the thing.

For the first time, she started to doubt the spell, the torture, that the combination would work. An overwhelming guilt washed over her as she began to wonder if it was all true—everything the demon had said. Was Joe to be forced to live, who knew how long, watching this demon control his own body, all because she—she who could never understand why she was the way she was—wanted, needed this loathsome creature? And why? Why was she so broken that she couldn't even find it in herself save this perfectly innocent man? This man who had tried to help them. This man she was torturing, perhaps for no reason at all.

As the thing laughed at her, she felt the heat rising off his skin while the salt burned into the newly broken flesh. Her tears started to fall. She looked in horror at Candide as she suddenly remembered where she was, realised what Candide and Evelyn must both think of her, her actions, everything the creature had said.

Candide, crying, looked away from her and started to read the words aloud again in a resigned voice, as though she too knew it was hopeless.

Anna looked at Eve, but he would not look at her. She knew he felt her eyes on him, but he did not look up, he just kept saying the words.

"Eve?"

Finally, he forced his eyes to meet hers, only for a few short seconds. What she saw there she had seen from no other person in her entire life, and she felt it deep within her soul. It was the same way he looked at her in the church when he thought she wouldn't notice him. The same way he looked at her when they enthused about

Keats. The same way he looked at her when she yelled at people in class because she was unable to keep her mouth shut when she sensed a literary injustice. It was the same way he looked at her when they both realised how lost and exhausted they had been their entire lives, and that they had finally found someone else who understood. He almost immediately caught himself and turned away again, but it was enough. She reached for the salt water.

"Last chance," she said.

The demon smiled at her maliciously. "I'll be back for you."

"I'll look forward to it." She grabbed his face, pushed his head back and poured the salt water into his mouth. She stood tall and watched as his entire frame shook, smoke rising from his mouth and his eyes. His body arched and writhed as much as the tight binds would allow, and a low, guttural moan came from deep within him.

"It's working! Read!" And with that, she shoved bloody handfuls of salt into his mouth and held it closed as he tried to scream, tried to spit it out, struggled hopelessly. She stood over him, staring down into his agonised face, and then all at once she saw his eyes change. She saw them clear, she saw for the first time a look of recognition, of clarity, of terror. Immediately she removed her hands and Joe started convulsing, throwing up on himself, on Anna, all over the floor.

"Banishing spell!" she yelled. She led with the words as the other two hesitated to pivot to the new spell. The lights started to flicker, and the three did not deviate once from the correct words as Joe coughed and wretched and screamed and writhed in front of them. And then suddenly, all was still.

Joe's head rolled back, eyes wide open, not breathing, lifeless.

CHAPTER 30
ATTEMPTED RECOVERY

"Oh shit! Oh shit!" Candide grabbed the scalpel and started cutting the ties and bandages from Joe. Eve, having made the snap assessment that Joe needed him more than Anna, helped Candide move Joe onto the floor. They were talking about CPR, arguing about how to do it, but Anna could barely hear them. She stumbled back, her hands shaking, and turned away from the scene. She leaned on the metal counter top for a moment, then looked up. Oxycodone. She became aware of the aching pain in her shoulder, her entire body, her mind. She picked up another metal tray, and with her hand inside, smashed the glass cabinet.

She popped the pills from their packets and swallowed them, one after another, forcing them down her dry throat.

"Anna, stop," said Candide, pushing hard on Joe's chest as Eve breathed air into him. Anna didn't hear. She kept taking the pills, one at a time.

"Anna!" She felt Candide's hand on her arm, taking the packet from her. Candide inspected it quickly. "That's enough. Sit down." She pushed Anna to the floor, where she sat, stupefied, waiting for the drugs to take effect.

Then Joe was rolling on the floor, coughing and convulsing, and a warmth spread right the way through her body, from her feet, up her legs, and through to her fingertips. A soft, ecstatic tingle covered her frame, and she stood up to leave.

"No, no," said Candide. "You wait for us." Candide guided her to a chair and she sat down obediently. Everything went on like a play in front of her. She saw Candide give Joe some pills, help him drink water so he could swallow them. She saw Eve and Candide whispering. "They're not that strong. She'll be fine," said Candide. She watched them pack their bags up, tidy up the room halfheartedly as they waited for Joe's medication to take effect. They stood up, all of them, Eve supporting Joe, and Candide held her hand out for Anna.

It was dark as they walked back, Eve occasionally throwing concerned looks behind him to Anna, yet saying nothing as they crossed the courtyard, climbed the stairs, and laid Joe down in Candide's bed while Anna sat on an armchair watching them. She saw them whispering in the bedroom, Eve objecting, then reluctantly agreeing to something.

Candide was suddenly close by. "Anna? How are you doing?"

Anna smiled and reached for Candide's hand. "I'm good. How are you?" She curled into a ball and held Candide's hand tight in her sweaty palms.

"Anna, I need to change your bandage. Can I do it now? I think we should do it before you go to sleep."

Anna thought for a minute. "Okay, if we have to."

"We really do."

"Okay."

"Let's take a look."

The drugs allowed Anna the movement necessary to undo her own buttons. Candide helped her out of her shirt while Eve busied himself around the apartment, pulling the sheets from her bed, rather unnecessarily Anna thought.

"Eve," Candide called. "I'm going to need your help." She looked back at Anna. "Anna, it's stuck on. The blood is all dry, so I'm going to put you in the shower, okay?"

"I don't want to go there," she said, panic rising inside. "Please, will you stay with me? I don't want to go there alone."

"No, no, I'll come. I'll stay with you. Is that okay?"

Anna nodded. Candide gathered supplies while Eve disappeared into the kitchen. Anna lost track of time for a short while, then it was time to go, and she felt Eve's hand take hers, helping her to stand, and finally he wrapped his arms around her and pulled her in tight and she melted into him. She rested her head on his chest and lost herself in his heartbeat and the warmth of his arms and the steady rise and fall of his breath and the comfort of his cheek against her hair. They both would have remained exactly like that for as long as either of them could remain upright had Candide not been insistent they change Anna's bandages and get her to bed immediately. They left the apartment and walked slowly down the long hall with Anna's head on Eve's shoulder and his arm around her.

Eve turned the shower on, then turned to say something to Anna, but as Candide and Anna had already started to remove her clothes with no regard for his presence, he blushed and left the bathroom without another word or glance at either of them. Candide helped Anna into the shower where she sat on the floor, resting her head against the wall, exhausted. She felt Candide clean her face, wash her hair. She barely noticed the bandages coming off, and it wasn't until the shower turned off and she was fresh with a clean towel wrapped around her that some semblance of reality began to come back to her.

"I feel so much better," she said.

"You're very, very high," laughed Candide.

"Yes, but I do feel better." Candide dressed the wound properly with supplies Anna had not noticed her taking from the med. lab.

"I think you're going to be okay," said Candide.

"Thank you. Thank you for taking care of me. I'm a bit useless right now."

"No, Anna. Not useless at all. Not ever."

Candide dried her hair, helped her dress again, then they left the bathroom and made their way back to the apartment. Eve was waiting there for them. She smiled an embarrassed smile. He smiled his lovely, glorious, sweet smile back.

"Better?"

"Better."

She found her sheets were fresh, and she was very thankful to Eve for that after all, and she lay down in her bed, a glass of water set on the desk by Candide, who pulled her covers up and sat protectively by her, exactly where Evelyn had been the night before, stroking her hair to help her fall asleep. Straight ahead in her line of sight, Eve had taken up position in an armchair with a book, and he smiled over it at her, then she smiled back at him and rolled over to sleep. The last thing she saw, in her confused, exhausted state, was Joe, sleeping fitfully in the bed opposite her, his face still cracked, swollen and bruised. She thought for a moment she saw him watching her, but she later considered maybe she dreamed it after all.

When she woke, the bed opposite was empty. The day was dark and gloomy and a harsh wind whipped the branches of the ash tree against her window. She sat up. "Candide?"

"I'm in here."

Anna wrapped her blanket around herself and found Candide on the couch, drinking tea, reading a book with soft lamps and candles aglow. Anna sat down on the couch next to her.

"Want some tea?"

"Maybe in a minute."

"Okay."

They sat quietly. "It's so nice in here," Anna said. She realised the broken coffee table and all the shards were gone, the surfaces were clean, there was no salt on the floor. The warding symbols and a small hole in the wall, still with a smattering of Evelyn's blood on the splinters, were the only reminders of what had happened there.

"I wanted it to be nice for you. We can start our life now." The two had been thrown together relentlessly over the last week and there was a slight bashfulness, a vulnerability in the way Candide delivered the words. It went at once to Anna's heart.

"Thank you, Candide."

"Thank you."

The heating was turned up high and Anna found she no longer needed her blanket. She took two pills Candide gave her, the latter carefully stowing the rest, and was soon moving around her own beautiful apartment in relative comfort. All day they sat together, talked, shared meals, read books, and they did not mention what had happened until evening.

"Is he going to be okay, Candide?"

"Joe is okay. He's a bit of a mess, but he's surprisingly okay. We had a really long talk, and you slept through the whole thing, of course, but he's so nice. I think it's going to take a lot of therapy to deal with everything. At least the demon mostly healed his body. Oh, and he's going to talk to the church for us so we don't get in trouble for that mess we made."

"That feels like so long ago."

"Doesn't it? This has been a really long week."

"Only a week."

"We met one week ago today."

"It's Sunday?"

"It is."

"I have my lecture tomorrow."

"You do."

Anna played with the edges of her book. "Is Eve... coming back?"

"No."

"Oh." Anna's face revealed in no uncertain way her disappointment, though she turned away quickly in an attempt to hide it.

"We thought... I told him, and he agreed, that it might be better if you had some space."

"I bet he did."

"I feel like you don't want to talk about what happened—"

"No."

"But it was a lot. Maybe you should just take some time—"

"I have to see him tomorrow."

"You don't have to. If you don't want to. I can get the notes to you easily enough."

Anna watched the candle flames flicker in the dying light of the dark day.

"You know, you can go see him if you want to." Anna looked up at Candide. "I wanted you to have the choice. I think he would have stayed, but he had to take Joe home. And he was stinky."

Anna laughed, then returned her mind to the calm and warmth of the apartment. "You took really good care of me. I do remember everything."

"I know you would do the same for me."

"I would. You probably wouldn't get yourself into that sort of state, though."

"It took me years of expensive therapy to get here, Anna." Her comment was short and sharp and went straight to the heart of the matter. "I understand."

"I know you do. But thank you."

"Stop saying thank you."

Anna smiled and attempted to keep reading *The Necessity of Atheism* by Percy Bysshe Shelley, but she found it hard to concentrate.

"It's getting late," said Candide after dinner.

"I suppose so," said Anna.

"If you were going to go out tonight…"

Anna's stomach tightened into a knot and she unconsciously tapped her foot in fast repetition. "I might…"

"Mmhmm…"

She sighed and stood up. She slipped her key into her pocket. "Candide, will you be okay alone for a while? I'm sure I won't be long."

"I'm fine. I've seen Joe. I know everything is all right now."

"But the ghost. We never really figured that out."

"What?"

"We never, really… I don't know, I haven't seen him."

"Anna, are you okay?"

"Yeah, I'm fine. Why?"

"Nothing." Candide didn't look sure. "You want me to take you over to see Eve?"

"No, no, I should go alone."

"Okay, if you're sure. Oh, but I actually left my key with Eve, in case I needed to go out. Could I borrow yours and maybe you can get mine back?"

"Sure." Anna passed the skeleton key to Candide.

"Anyway, the place is warded for ghosts."

"Huh? Ghosts?" said Anna.

"Yeah, it's all warded. No ghosts can get in."

"You mean demons? Yeah, for sure. I know you're safe. Just come get me if you need anything."

"I'm fine."

"Okay, I'll see you later."

"Okay. Oh and Anna?"

"Yep?"

"Don't let him bullshit you, okay?"

"Okay," Anna laughed as she closed the door behind her and stepped out into the dark hall.

CHAPTER 31
THE ASTOUNDING FINAL CHAPTER

E ve's door was, as always, open. Even from her own door, Anna could see the soft yellow light escaping into the hall. She approached as quietly as she could, not allowing herself to second-guess her decision to go see him.

She saw him before he noticed her. He sat on his lounge in a grey, cable-knit sweater. She knew without touching it, it would be cashmere. His legs, clad in brown corduroy, were stretched out on his coffee table next to a glass of whiskey. He wore his glasses, as he had been reading or, she conjectured from his pose, attempting to do so. His arm was outstretched, and his book had fallen face up, held vaguely by an absent hand, as he stared straight forward. He twisted a pencil around in his other hand, his attempt to make notes fallen by the wayside.

"Eve?" she said softly.

"Anna!" He stood up. "I was hoping you would come." He looked perfectly happy and his eyes danced in the light. He looked, for the first time in a long time, sweet and boyish, unsure where to hold his hands, and she felt her heart buoyed by the welcoming reaction.

"You were?" she said, and she came into his room lightly, her stomach now a flutter of hopeful excitement.

"I was," he replied. But the words came out slowly. She noticed a subtle change in his demeanour, the smile disappeared from his lips and his voice hardened slightly, though it was, as always, still soft and gentle. "I wanted to talk to you. Can I get you a drink?" He tossed his book and pencil down on the lounge carelessly and turned his back to her.

"Okay," she said.

He moved nervously around his own kitchen, as though he were only just figuring out where he kept his ice, his glasses, his whiskey. She opted for the armchair by the door rather than share the couch with him, suddenly conscious of intruding on his space. She looked away from him and around the apartment, aware her gaze was probably making him more anxious. He eventually passed her the drink and then took his place on the edge of the couch, closer to her.

"How are you?"

It was such a simple question, but asked point blank with no diversion available, she felt panic inside. Her face tensed as she tried not to show any emotion.

"Maybe I shouldn't ask," he said.

"It's okay. I'll be okay." She wiped away a rogue tear with frustration at her body's betrayal. He sat quietly for a moment, unsure of what to do. She wondered why he didn't at least reach a hand out for her, give her some sign of warmth, some sign that everything they went through had affected him the way it had affected her.

"Maybe I shouldn't have come," she said.

"No, it's good you're here. We should clear the air. If you're ready."

"Clear the air?" He was speaking like a teacher again. He was preparing her. Imparting the distance necessary to get them through the coming months or years professionally, cleanly, until he could finally be rid of her. He did not meet her waiting eye. He was embarrassed of her, she knew. Ashamed. Disgusted probably. She moved her gaze down into the untasted whiskey in the glass, watching it sparkle, hearing the ice clink, imagining if she could just get lost in those sensations, she could dip out of reality completely and avoid what was to come.

"Anna—"

"Eve, I like you. I like you and I want to be with you. And now I have told you that… Now I won't have to wonder what might have been, if I never told you that."

"Anna—"

"I had to do that. For me. I'm sorry if that makes things harder for you now, and for the future, because I already know what you're going to say."

His face didn't soften. He didn't smile as she hoped he might. He didn't jump in to correct her, to tell her she had it all wrong. His eyes looked sadder and his face older, tired.

"I'm just going to go now, okay, so we'll pretend this never happened. And… God, I wish I hadn't come at all. I'm sorry." She stood to leave.

"Anna, don't go, not like this. I…" he caught her hand and guided her back to her seat. "I don't want to leave things like this."

"Eve, I can't. I'm so tired. And I already know. I'm younger than you, you feel responsible, it's not professional, whatever your big secret is—I just can't hear it again. I just thought maybe something had changed." Another tear fell, traitorously, and she brushed it away angrily too.

"No, it's not that. It's not." He took her hand in his. "Anna, I was sitting here a moment ago, daydreaming that you would come in here and say those words. Say that you didn't care about all those other things and that it would be okay. And, I thought, I would grab you and kiss you and forget it all and never let you go."

Her hand trembled slightly in his and she looked up at his face, but it was still serious and stern and he still would not meet her eye.

"You are so smart, and so strong and I was already falling for you... and then yesterday happened. And... And I realised something." He paused, trying to get his words right. "I don't think I would be good for you."

She withdrew her hand and looked at him, shocked, but also irritated. He kept his in place, as if savouring the feeling that had been there only seconds before.

"Are you doing this?"

"Anna, I'm sorry——"

"You're giving me, it's not you, it's me? I just told you I can't hear this and then you say that about kissing me and then——"

"I'm trying to be honest."

"Enough with your goddamn honesty, Eve! You're just hurting me. Why? To make yourself feel better?"

"No, Anna, it's not like that. I just——I want you to understand. I have never seen anything like that. Never experienced anything like that. And you, what you did, what he did to you. I don't even know what he did to you——"

"Nothing! He didn't do anything!"

"You must have been so scared, and so alone, and so angry and... you just did all those things."

"I had to."

"I know you did. And I watched you. I watched you do all of them and... I am... I am... I think 'ashamed' is the right word..."

Anna's breath caught in her throat. "You're... You're ashamed?" Her tears fell fast and hot on her cheeks. He reached out a hand for hers, but she slapped it away and stood to leave. Then she turned. "Eve, how can you be so cruel?"

"No, no, I don't mean that. No! Wait!" He grabbed hold of her again as she moved for the door. "Not you. You were amazing. You were incredible. I am just... so ashamed of myself... because..." He rubbed a hand over his temple as she waited, exhausted, impatient, shaking her head in disbelief. "Anna, when I came in and you were crying and... I just wanted to pick you up and protect you and I felt so horrible seeing you like that. And then... it's like you were different. And all those things you did to him..."

"Eve, I—"

"I liked it." His voice was quiet, barely above a whisper, and he looked at her with burning eyes, then cast his gaze to the floor. "I liked watching you. And that is bad, and that is weird and, Anna... I probably would have let you kill him a second time. If you hadn't stopped when you did... I wouldn't have stopped you. Isn't that messed up? You were angry and upset and just trying to get a job done, but you were so powerful and... capable and... in control and... and I was thinking about you in a way I shouldn't have been... at that time... I keep thinking it over and I am... deeply ashamed of this, I don't know, part of me, that I just discovered. And because of that, I wasn't there when you needed me, the way you needed me to be and I'm not proud of myself, or the person I apparently am, and that is why—"

Anna felt like she had been punched in the stomach. In a good way. She cut him off. "You liked that?"

"I'm so sorry. I'm sorry. It's weird and I really shouldn't have told you. God, you have to live with me now. I promise, I won't be weird about it. And if you want, I'll just drop the class. And you can keep going and I will try to get someone else to take over. After tomorrow, if that's okay. It's Percy Shelley, and he was a jerk and I just want everyone to know that he—"

"And you didn't believe any of those things he said about me?"

"The demon? No! Demons lie. That's their whole thing, right?"

"I thought you wouldn't like me anymore."

"No, I like you. So much. And, that's why, I just, I had to tell you because I didn't want you to get the wrong idea. Which you had. And now I've said too much, because I'm rambling—"

"And this isn't another weird breakup?"

"Maybe? I don't know. It probably should be, but you said you might want to do this, before I messed everything up, again, and so in case you would even consider that now, I need to tell you that I am a deeply traumatised individual and trouble seems to follow me wherever I go and I always, always say the wrong thing and... and I think you're wonderful, Anna." He sighed and put his hand on her cheek, that new but familiar sensation she didn't realise how much she had been longing for. "And I don't want you to go. And I adore you and I am weirdly obsessed with you and I think you should know how much... I love you." And he kissed her.

"Eve..."

"And now you can go." He stood tall again and looked her in the eye, calmly, respectfully, hopeful and melancholy. "I think you probably should go because I don't think I would be a very good boyfriend. But I won't ask you again because... I can't. I don't want you to go. I just wanted to tell you..."

"Eve?"

"Yes?"

"I love you, too."

At once his face was lit with a beautiful smile, and he moved closer to her, and kissed her again. She ran her hand through his hair, over his shoulder, his lovely arm, down his back, over his hip. She felt his warm breath tingle down her neck as he kissed her, over and over, as she luxuriated in the feeling of his body, finally pressed against hers.

She paused.

She whispered…

"Evelyn?"

"Yes, Anna?"

"Close the door."

Eve stepped one beautiful, glorious, perfectly formed foot back, and slammed the door shut.

THE END

WHICH BEGS THE QUESTIONS...

Who is that ghost child?

Why does Anna have that key?

What secrets are Evelyn and Candide keeping?

Where did the *Necronomicon* come from?

Why is Anna even like that anyway?

Find the exciting answers to these questions and more in *Endymion College 2: A Study in Survival.*

IF YOU ENJOYED THIS NOVEL...

Please leave a review. This is the best way to help the series thrive.

Sign up for the newsletter at www.whlockwood.com for special content, new release news, and to keep up to date.

Please join us in the Endymion College Book Club on Facebook to discuss the trilogy and all related topics.

ACKNOWLEDGMENTS

A huge thank you to everyone who supported me, offered advice and helped me shape this novel into what it is today.

Specifically, a huge thank you to Letizia for the monumental amount of work you put into this, and for forgiving me when I made you cry. You have forgiven me, right? If not, I have a bottle of wine with your name on it. Kisses.

Krystel, Joe (the other one) and Daphanie. Thanks so much for all the back and forth and listening to me. Seriously, Krystel, this never would have gotten off the ground without you. You three know how much I love you.

Emma, Mycroft and Hannah for being the best book club in town who put up with me talking about my own books for months, and especially to Emma for all the time you put into my books, even if you are the fastest reader I ever met. Thank you!!

Tiffany, Alyssa, Natalie, Annie, Katie, Kim and Bethany. Thank you for the hours you spent on these books. I will always appreciate all your help and advice.

Last but not least, Matthew. This could never have happened without you. To the most romantic romantic lead in all romances: thank you. To you, to Alex, Ada and Mary, too. I love you all so much!

ABOUT THE AUTHOR

W.H. Lockwood writes feminist gothic and historical fiction, dark academia and cosy horror, all with a romantic twist.

Raised on a diet of Point books and Pepsi, only willing to leave her den to attend chess club at public school, W.H. Lockwood started writing at a young age and has kept this passion throughout her life.

Always a voracious reader, she obtained an undergraduate degree in literary studies from a gorgeous sandstone university, following that with a master's degree in publishing and editing, then another master's degree in astronomy, thus uniting her two great loves of the arts and science, leaving her utterly unqualified to cope with the real world.

These days W.H. Lockwood works as a professional editor and can often be found aimlessly wandering through the coffee shops and bookstores of the beautiful city she calls home.

instagram.com/w.h.lockwood.books

ALSO BY W. H. LOCKWOOD

Endymion College 2: A Study in Survival

Endymion College 3: An Education in Evil

And…

Cosy horror? Historical romance? With Monsters?

Monsters of Manchester

coming soon…

Made in the USA
Columbia, SC
27 September 2022

68031413R00176